the further adventures of

SHERLOCK HOLMES

THE CRUSADER'S CURSE

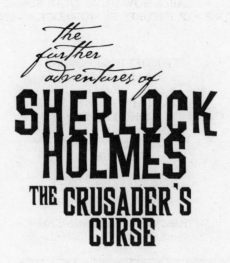

the further adventures of

SHERLOCK HOLMES

THE CRUSADER'S CURSE

STUART DOUGLAS

TITAN BOOKS

THE FURTHER ADVENTURES OF SHERLOCK HOLMES:
THE CRUSADER'S CURSE
Print edition ISBN: 9781789091588
E-book edition ISBN: 9781789091595

Published by Titan Books
A division of Titan Publishing Group Ltd
144 Southwark Street, London SE1 0UP

First Titan edition: December 2020
10 9 8 7 6 5 4 3 2 1

Names, places and incidents are either products of the author's imagination or used fictitiously. Any resemblance to actual persons, living or dead (except for satirical purposes), is entirely coincidental.

A CIP catalogue record for this title is available from the British Library.

Printed and bound by CPI Group (UK) Ltd,
Croydon, CR0 4YY.

What did you think of this book? We love to hear from our readers. Please email us at: readerfeedback@titanemail.com, or write to Reader Feedback at the above address.

To receive advance information, news, competitions, and exclusive offers online, please sign up for the Titan newsletter on our website: **www.titanbooks.com**

For Alex, Cameron and Matthew, love you all

Chapter One

A Ghostly Crusader

"A ghostly Crusader! Preposterous!"

The scorn in Holmes's voice was enough to cause me to look up from my newspaper with an enquiring look.

"What was that, Holmes? Have you grown so bored that you've taken to reading Le Fanu to pass the time?"

My question was deliberately light-hearted in tone, but in truth I would have been happy to find my friend absorbed in a volume of Mr le Fanu's ghost stories. Baker Street had been quiet of late, with little passing through our doors to interest Holmes. In consequence he had retreated into the dark mood that I knew from past experience often led to the needle and his preferred seven per cent solution of cocaine. Any distraction that kept him from that infernal vice was, in my opinion, to be encouraged.

It seemed, however, that this was not the case. With an exasperated grunt, Holmes crumpled the letter he held into a ball and threw it across to me.

"Hardly, Watson," he growled. "Though at least that gentleman has the good sense to admit that his work is simple fiction. No, this is altogether more foolish."

While he spoke, I smoothed the paper out on my knee, revealing it to have come from the peculiarly named Faraday Thompson. The letter was somewhat verbose but, in light of what was to follow, it is worth quoting in full.

Dear Mr Holmes,

Please forgive me for not consulting you in person, but recent events make it impossible for me to travel to London, and the task for which I wish to engage your services is one regarding which time is of the essence.

My name is Faraday Thompson and I have for the past three decades had the honour to act as solicitor to Lord Thorpe of Thorpe Manor in Yorkshire. Sadly, his Lordship passed away two months ago and it has fallen to me to handle the execution of his estate. In general, this is a relatively straightforward matter; his Lordship had no children and had named as sole heir a distant American cousin. This cousin, Mr Nathaniel Purser of Boston, Mass., has no desire to live in England and has instructed me to sell off both the manor house and grounds, and its contents.

As directed I have, therefore, arranged for the sale of his Lordship's art collection, and invited sundry parties interested in purchasing the estate itself to stay at the manor this weekend. It is where these two areas overlap that I – or rather Mr Purser – wish to make use of your services, if you are agreeable.

First, the extent of the Thorpe art collection, for centuries renowned for its range and quality, is not at all as expected. When last catalogued by the sixth Lord Thorpe in 1784, it contained a myriad of paintings and sculptures, by some of the great masters, and was valued, in today's terms, in the region of £10,000. Inexplicably, when my firm sent appraisers to the manor last month, only a handful of family portraits could be found. The whereabouts of the remainder is a mystery, which we hope you might be able to solve.

Secondly, I do not know if you have heard of the Thorpe Ruby? Local legend has it that the third Baron de Trop brought back a fabulous blood-red stone encased in an intricate golden setting from the Crusades. Unfortunately, it was lost soon after arrival, along with the Baron himself, who was found dead in the main hall, horribly mutilated. Allegedly, someone – or something – followed the Baron back from the Holy Land and tormented him, seeking the location of the ruby in order to return it to the heathen temple from which it was looted. They failed, but killed the Baron for his defiance and his ghost now roams the grounds, cursed to protect for ever the secret that killed him.

At least, so the legend goes.

Mr Purser informs me by telegraph that he has no truck with ghosts or legends, but if there is potentially a precious stone secreted somewhere on the estate, he feels it would be remiss not to make some attempt to locate it, before the manor and all it contains is sold to the highest bidder next week.

With that in mind, he would like to engage you for a few days, Mr Holmes. Perhaps your famous talents might be turned to the detection of lost paintings and a legendary gem, rather than a desperate criminal!

The letter concluded with directions to Thorpe-by-the-Marsh railway station and the hope that Holmes – "and your ever-present colleague, Dr Watson, of course" – would see fit to present themselves at Thorpe Manor the following day. A postscript requested that nobody should know the reason for our presence, and added the name of a gentleman who would meet us at the manor, Lawrence Buxton.

Given a choice, I should have preferred something along more criminal lines, but beggars cannot often be choosers and this was the first potential case in weeks that had raised any reaction from Holmes. It was true that the reaction had been a negative one, but still, I was determined to encourage him to become involved.

"You are too harsh, Holmes," I said with a smile. "I think it a fascinating tale, at least. A murdered knight, missing paintings, a cursed gem and a haunted house. Mr le Fanu can scarcely have conjured up a story with more intriguing elements."

In reply, Homes snorted in derision. "I have said it before, Watson, but your scribblings have sadly served to abrade your critical faculties."

I allowed the insult to pass, though inwardly bridling at his use of "scribblings". "Be that as it may, it would be good to get out of London for a while. This spell of inclement weather shows no sign of abating, and some fresh country air would be a tonic for both of us."

To this, Holmes gave a small, almost imperceptible nod. There was no denying the foulness of the London air in recent days. Even now, I could see a thin rain streaking the window and, beyond that, a thick dirty fog which obscured all but the nearest buildings.

"It is true that I find the present climate dispiriting but that is hardly cause to abandon the city in pursuit of what will no doubt prove to be a combination of overly febrile imagination and a credulous local population. Although there is always the chance of a genuine case while we are on this wild goose chase. However slight that chance may be," he concluded with a resigned sigh.

I am not proud of what I did next, but I was worried enough about Holmes's state of mind that I assured myself that the small deception was for the greater good.

"Actually, Holmes, I was hoping that you would be willing to leave London for reasons of my own. My leg has been troubling me a great deal recently, and I believe that a period of relaxation away from the hustle of the city would be by far the best curative possible."

I rubbed my old wound and grimaced just a little for effect. "I could go alone, of course, but I fear boredom would soon have me back in Baker Street. A short spell in the country, with good company and a small mystery to occupy the mind, would be far preferable."

Holmes is, of course, no fool, and he looked hard at me for a moment, cocking an eyebrow at my amateur theatrics, before allowing a smile to play upon his lips.

"If it is a matter of your health, Watson... Old wounds can flare up most suddenly, I believe, and at the most unexpected moment. Your courage in never once mentioning this to me before now is to be commended, but is exactly what I would expect of an old soldier like yourself."

Again I let the implied doubt stand uncorrected (how could I not when he had every right to question my veracity?) and, before he could change his mind, I struggled theatrically to my feet and located Bradshaw's Guide on the shelf.

"Splendid!" I said with a smile of my own. "Perhaps you

could arrange for a telegram to be sent to Mr Thompson, while I ascertain a suitable train time? Tomorrow morning would be best, I think, as for once we are in no great hurry."

Taking Bradshaw's and a slice of toast with me, I repaired to my room to dress, delighted at the turn of events and looking forward to a few relaxing days in the country. A change of scenery would do us both the world of good, I was sure.

As events transpired, I could not have been more wrong.

Chapter Two

A Trip to Thorpe Manor

As it happened there was no direct train on a Saturday to Thorpe-by-the-Marsh. Still, the weather improved a little as the London line made its way deeper into the countryside, and it was a relief after a few hours travel to stroll across a country platform and board the small rural train which would take us to our final destination.

The line to Thorpe-by-the-Marsh was clearly not a busy one, for the train required but a single carriage and we had that almost to ourselves, our only travelling companion an elderly man, dressed in a suit of old-fashioned cut. He sat by the window, watching the station fall away behind us, his legs crossed, and his hands resting carefully on a tall felt hat, also of forgotten vintage. As we took our seats opposite him, I noticed that he wore working men's boots, polished but pitted with the marks of a life spent outdoors.

Perhaps he felt my eyes upon him, or saw me reflected in the window, for he turned his face towards us and, without further introduction, announced that he was returning to Thorpe-by-the-

Marsh after a trip to London for a funeral. It was the first time he had left the village in his life, he said, and, having now seen London, he would be glad to be back home.

"The city is all very well for those who care only for dirt and smoke," he told us without invitation, "but for those who prefer sunlight and green things, it's a mite dark and unwelcoming."

He lit what was the most pungent pipe I had ever encountered and settled back in his seat, eyeing us curiously through the thick white smoke.

Holmes returned his gaze from beneath hooded eyes, but said nothing. Feeling that someone should reply to the man, I explained that we were headed in the same direction and would be staying at Thorpe Manor for a few days.

He sniffed loudly at that, as though the fumes of his pipe were not the most noxious stench in the carriage. "You're braver men than I then, that's all I'll say. I wouldn't spend a night in the manor house for any reason, for I'm attached to my soul, I am. And my life, too, for men have died up there, in the night, struck down by the curse."

"You believe the legend, then?" asked Holmes, making no effort to hide the amusement in his voice. "That the host of the Baron de Trop stalks the halls like Hamlet's father?"

"Hamlet's father?" the man replied with a frown. "I don't know the man but I wouldn't be surprised at anything that goes on in London. But even if this foolish fellow would, I, Simeon Forward would not. For only a simpleton does not believe what his own eyes have seen."

He leaned forward in his seat as he spoke, challenging us to doubt him.

"You have seen the ghost then, Mr Forward?" Holmes replied, unabashed.

"I did. He walked in front of me, he did, pale as a summer moon, and turned and looked me in the face. Chilled me to the bone, it did, though it were a warm night. And his eyes! Narrow, they was, but cold and filled with hatred. Hatred for everything that lives."

"And did he say anything, this spectral visitor?"

The man shook his head and gave a sour laugh. "Say anything? How could he do such a thing, when everyone knows the old knight never utters a sound?"

He continued to chuckle to himself as he unwrapped a parcel of sandwiches he had drawn from his pocket, but said nothing more for the remainder of the journey. Holmes cast a look of amused resignation in my direction, then closed his eyes, leaving me to pass the rest of the trip watching the fields and streams, as the train slowly made its way towards Thorpe-by-the-Marsh.

The station at which we arrived some time later was small and quiet, barely more than a platform and a ticket hut, but attractive enough in the fading early evening light.

Our travelling companion having scuttled off without a word as soon as the train pulled to a stop, the sole railway employee in attendance gave us directions to the manor, but warned us that as we had just missed the cart taking the weekend's supplies to the house, we would have to walk the half-mile distance. The weather had turned colder again but fortunately not to an unpleasant degree, and though there was little to look at in the surrounding fields, it was no hardship to stroll along a succession of short well-beaten lanes, each of us carrying a single bag packed with the essentials for a day or two in the country.

At first, we walked in companionable silence, but after a few minutes, Holmes gave a laugh and turned to me with a smile.

"As pale as a summer moon, Watson, and terrifying enough to chill our man to the bone. Clearly we are about to embark on our most dangerous case yet!"

I was pleased to see the change wrought in Holmes, no matter the cause, and joined in his laughter. Though the man had been the very epitome of the superstitious yokel, I was grateful to him for lightening my friend's mood.

"We must be sure to remain attached to our souls, Holmes," I replied in mock seriousness. "Otherwise the ghostly knight will be away with them and perhaps we too shall be cursed to haunt Thorpe Manor."

Just then, the lane made a sharp turn and, as we emerged from behind the tall hedges that lined it, we had our first sight of our residence for the next few days.

Thorpe Manor was a squat, wide affair, comprised of a main building, two storeys high, with a long wing to the east, composed entirely of the local brick. A carriage stood in the drive, and a cart was just disappearing round the far corner of the building as we approached. Otherwise, everything was quiet and still.

Even to one so ignorant of architectural history as I, it was obvious that little of the crusader's former home remained. I had half expected battlements and arrow slits, but instead it presented a plain, rather flattened aspect, with a tiled roof and sash windows of the type popular in the last century. Only as we drew nearer was it possible to make out a set of unsettling carvings surrounding the doorway – not gargoyles exactly, but something reminiscent of the demons that are often found displayed on the exterior of continental churches. Their presence was unexpected and seemed out of place, a remnant of an era long gone, and I wondered if perhaps they were all that survived of the original building.

Holmes too had noticed the carvings. He stopped before them and examined them for a minute, reaching up to run his long fingers across the distorted face of the nearest.

"Unusual," he said, rubbing the stone dust from his hands. "But let us get inside before the sunlight disappears altogether."

I nodded in agreement and rapped firmly on the door. There was no response at first, then footsteps could be heard approaching the door from the other side. It opened silently, revealing a short, elderly man with heavy side whiskers and small round glasses, framed by the gaslight which shone in the hallway behind him.

"Mr Holmes, Dr Watson," he said. "Delighted to meet you. Lawrence Buxton, at your service." He smiled shyly. "You wonder that I know your names already? That is simply explained. Knowing that I have been working on a history of the family and the manor house, Mr Thompson asked me to be here to greet you and the other visitors in his stead." He held out an arm, inviting us inside. "I trust you had no difficulty finding the house?"

"The station guard provided us with directions," I confirmed as we stepped inside. "I rather enjoyed the walk, in fact. Even though it is not overly warm, these country lanes make a pleasant change from traipsing around rainy London streets, and the house is quite striking."

Buxton smiled with pleasure. "I'm so glad you like it. It has, of course, been extensively renovated over the years and in the process lost some of its charm, but one can yet make out some of the more interesting original features."

"The carvings over the doorway, for example?"

We had by now passed through the main hallway, and into a large reception room, but Buxton stopped to consider Holmes's remark.

"Actually no, those date to the fourteenth century, and the core of the house is much older than that. Built to the specifications of the fifth baron, they represent spirits and demons from the pantheon of certain Far East religions, and are echoed by exact duplicates in the grounds' mausoleum to the north of the house. Their identities have been lost to us, but I am currently working on a short monograph in which I suggest potential sources. I would be happy to send you a copy once it is complete."

Buxton was an academic to his fingertips, obviously willing to provide a short lecture on anything touching his area of expertise, no matter how abstruse it might be. I was polite, however, and said I would be honoured to read his paper, which seemed to please him.

"Then I shall be sure to send you a copy in due course. But I am being remiss in my duties. All but one of the other guests have already arrived and are upstairs, settling in. Captain Hopkirk has been in touch to say that he has been delayed, however, and will not be here before eight.

"But perhaps I can show you to your rooms, and you can refresh yourselves before dinner? Or would you prefer a more liquid form of refreshment?" He smiled at his own small joke, and gestured towards a nearby doorway, through which I could see a long room stretching to a magnificent fireplace. "The main hall is much admired by visitors," he concluded, "and offers rather a splendid view of the grounds."

The walk from the station had not been taxing, but it had been warm and suddenly the idea of a refreshing drink seemed a capital notion. I said as much to Buxton and he, with a tiny bow, gestured that we should precede him through the doorway.

The main hall was sparsely furnished and, while grand in size, obviously little used. The only decorations were a map of the estate on one wall and a large painting hung above the imposing fireplace. It showed what I assumed was the Thorpe family, or a previous generation of them at least, for the style of dress they wore was that of the previous century.

Buxton noticed me looking. "Painted by George Hayter," he said, then added conspiratorially, "It is the last truly valuable painting in the collection. Or at least the last which can still be accounted for."

There was no fire lit, but the unseasonal warmth of the day had heated the room to a comfortable temperature, and as Holmes and I relaxed into the two armchairs in front of the hearth, I was pleased once more by the thought of a few days in pleasant surroundings.

Our host brought us each a drink and took a seat between us, facing the fireplace. I pulled my pipe and tobacco from my pocket and began to fill the bowl, content to listen as Holmes and Buxton talked.

"I assume that Mr Thompson informed you why we have come to Thorpe Manor?" Holmes began as soon as he had lit one of his own gaspers.

"Only in the most general terms. You are not one of the bidders for the estate, I know, but are...'interested parties' was the term Mr Thompson employed. Beyond that, however..."

He fell silent, waiting for one of us to provide an answer to his unspoken question. Holmes, however, replied with a question of his own.

"You are an expert on the manor, I believe, Mr Buxton?"

"I flatter myself that I know as much about the house as any man. In part – specifically, this central section of the dining room, the library, the main hall and the rooms directly upstairs – it is an ancient building, however, with a great deal of history attached to it, and it would take longer than the few years I have spent here to claim genuine expertise." He gave a small, self-deprecating smile.

"What of the legends which surround it?" Holmes asked.

The look of dismay that crossed Buxton's face was unmistakable. "I know a little of those, too. I wish that it were not so; the house has enough legitimate history in its bricks that it has no need of the cheap showmanship of the haunted house."

He gave the last words such a weight of loathing that there could be no doubt as to his own views on the subject. Even so, it was best to be certain.

"You do not give the story of the ghost any credence, Mr Buxton?" I asked, in what I hoped was a neutral tone. "We met a fellow on the train who was quite convinced of the truth of the matter."

"On the train, you say? That would be Simeon Forward, I imagine. There are no other villagers away that I know of. Like all of them, he is a slave to superstition. I, however, am not. The historical record concerning the late Edouard de Trop is remarkably complete, and full of both fascination and horror. There is no need for foolish embellishment of the sort propagated by credulous villagers and circulation-hungry reporters. The former at least have the lack of education as an excuse, but the latter..." He tailed off with a sniff of disdain.

"Quite so," Holmes murmured with obvious approval. "Though my question pertained to the legend of the lost Thorpe Ruby rather than to the ghostly presence which is rumoured to guard it. And I believe," he concluded, "that we have found exactly the sort of person to help us achieve that end."

Buxton had grimaced throughout his description of the supernatural but he brightened at Holmes's closing words, and after that could not have been more affable. He insisted on replenishing our drinks then resumed his seat and busied himself with lighting a pipe. Only after we were all comfortably smoking did he proceed to explain further his own opinion on the subject of the de Trop ghost.

"You must understand, Mr Holmes, that I have carried out considerable – and though I say it myself, quite important – work on the history of the local area in the past two years. My forthcoming essay on the practices of worship in rural Yorkshire in the eleventh century, will, I am confident, prove revolutionary once published. And yet, the only thing that seems to be of any interest to the wider world is the, in my opinion, distinctly unchristian local belief in ghosts and ghouls.

"Twice I have had to refuse an interview to reporters from the yellow press, you know, after discovering they had no intention of printing my views on the increased use of candles in the latter Middle Ages, but wished only to know if I had ever seen the ghost!"

Buxton had become rather red in the face as he spoke but now he stopped, and apologised if he had seemed to be hectoring us. With a contrite smile he invited Holmes to ask any question, and he would do his very best to give a satisfactory reply.

"If you could tell us exactly what happened to the unfortunate Edouard de Trop, that would be of great assistance. We have, of course, been given the rough outline of the story, but the devil is in the detail, I'm sure you would agree."

Buxton gave a short barking laugh. "Literally, if the villagers are to be believed, Mr Holmes. But I would be more than happy to provide the verifiable historical facts. They will serve, I hope, as a counterweight to the... more superstitious accounts you will undoubtedly hear in the village."

He puffed on his pipe for a second, considering where to begin.

"You are aware, I assume, that de Trop was accused of stealing a valuable native gem and returning with it to England? That he was accused is certainly true; it is mentioned in two distinct contemporary documents. The gem – interestingly, it has no fanciful nickname – is also potentially mentioned in the writings of a Saracen philosopher of the time, who notes that its loss to an enemy knight was a grave insult, which must be avenged at all costs. However, he appears to be referring to a wholly corporeal form of vengeance, rather than by means of a curse. There is, I must admit, some controversy among scholars over this point, with particular weight placed upon a possible mistranslation of certain key phrases in the account. In any case, what is generally agreed is that, whether a supernatural influence is intended or not, Saladin, the ruler of the Saracen, also ordered a group of his fabled assassins to follow the knight to England, in order to kill the thief and retrieve the gem."

He paused and gestured expansively with his pipe. "It is at this point that events lose some of their historical certainty. We know that de Trop arrived back at what is now Thorpe Manor in the winter of 1188, and there is a single reference by a local chronicler to 'a jewel of great beauty, gripped in talons of gold', which was in his possession. But beyond that we have no definitive means of proving that de Trop acquired this jewel by underhand means, or indeed that the jewel in question is the self-same gem mentioned by the Arabic scholar. What we do know is that the knight was to die in quite horrific circumstances before the year was out, and that 'dark-skinned men' were involved in his death."

"Dark-skinned men?"

"That is the phrase used. Let me see, the exact line is…yes, 'And at the feast of St Lucius was seen the Lord Edouard to return and great was the rejoicing, though all was turned to ash by the dark-skinned men who followed him like dogs to the hare, and slew him in silence and in blood.'"

Buxton had a fine speaking voice and the ancient words rolled from his tongue with a pleasing richness. But I felt a shiver run along my back, and though it was by no means dark outside yet, the sunlight was beginning to fade and shadows in the hall seemed to encroach upon our little group as he completed his recital. I was suddenly terribly tired and in need of sleep.

Holmes's interest had been kindled, however, and I knew that he would be content to stay up all night, teasing out everything he could from the elderly historian.

"Fascinating," he said, leaning forward in his chair, pipe and whisky forgotten. "'In silence and in blood'? An odd way of phrasing it. But then, I have never had an ear for poetry."

"Poetry, perhaps, but entirely explicable, I assure you, Mr Holmes. The story has it that de Trop, as a staunch and hardy Englishman, was horribly tortured, with both his arms and his legs broken, to force him to reveal where he had hidden the gem. In the end, so determined was he to say nothing to his savage captors that he bit through his own tongue, rendering him unable to speak."

I grimaced, but Holmes, as ever, was uninterested in what he would no doubt have described as "local colour". "And the gem was never found?"

"No, Mr Holmes. The gem, if it ever actually existed – and I for one am not convinced of that – disappeared on the night of de Trop's alleged murder."

"Much as the Thorpe art collection has now disappeared?"

Buxton gave Holmes a curious look. "Indeed, Mr Holmes, though there has long been gossip in the village that Lord Thorpe must be funding himself somehow, for he has not made a penny from his land in forty years."

"Have you noticed paintings going missing in the time you have been visiting the manor house?" Holmes pressed.

Buxton shook his head. "I have not, but I would not be likely to. The entirety of my access to the house before this week was to pass from the front door to the library and back again, and the majority of the Thorpe Collection was, allegedly, kept under lock and key in a storage room upstairs. Whenever I visited, the doors to the other rooms were always closed and I was not encouraged to open them."

"That is a shame, Mr Buxton," replied Holmes. "It would have been interesting to be able to establish a timetable of some sort. But I must admit that the walk from the station has left me both hungrier and a little more tired than I thought, and it would be good to freshen up before dinner."

"Forgive me, gentlemen," replied our host, jumping to his feet. "I have been remiss in my manners. As I said, few visitors come to Thorpe Manor and none with so sympathetic an ear. I fear I have kept you from your rest in my enthusiasm. Please, do follow me, and I will show you up to your rooms."

With that, he led the way out of the hall and up the staircase, indicating the various rooms as he did so. The main hall from which we had just departed was positioned to the right of the stairs and behind it was a small library ("now poorly stocked", according to our guide). Beyond that, behind the stairs lay the servants' area ("largely abandoned", Buxton explained) and a doorway which led down to an extensive storage cellar. On the left-hand side of the main stairs lay the dining room, to which we would repair for dinner later. Upstairs, Buxton continued, were the guest rooms and the entry to the east wing ("shuttered and closed for thirty years and more", our host confided). Apart from that, he concluded, everything of interest on the estate lay in the grounds. Exactly what he meant he did not say, but in any case I felt a headache coming on, and decided an explanation could wait.

Rather than speak further, therefore, I was happy to take my leave and open the window of my room, allowing the cool early evening air to circulate. We had been travelling for most of the day and I had taken two large whiskies on a largely empty stomach. A wash, a change of clothes and, most importantly, a good meal and all would be well, I was sure.

* * *

An hour later, the sound of a gong announced dinner, and Holmes and I met on the landing outside our rooms. He appeared in good spirits, the best indeed that I had seen him in since he had revealed the identity of the real Duke of Forgill several months before.

"I think this may well turn out to be a diverting break, after all, Watson," he announced as I closed the door to my room behind me. "Mr Buxton is, in his own way, as much a fantasist as the ghost-fearing Simeon Forward, but some of his conversation is not without interest, and I fancy the next day or so may prove of more consequence than the same period spent in Baker Street. And clearly the country air has already done wonders for your leg, for I saw no sign of a limp as you positively strode along the path from the station."

I smiled ruefully. "A change in scenery can be beneficial for all manner of ailments, Holmes."

We both laughed at that, and still laughing, we made our way downstairs.

Chapter Three

Dinner for Seven

I had thought we would be given an opportunity to meet our fellow guests over a drink before going into dinner, but Buxton met us at the bottom of the stairs with an apology, explaining that, due to a lack of staff, it had been thought prudent to go directly through to the dining room, where introductions might be made while we ate. Holmes, never one to stand on ceremony, was quick to reassure him that no apology was needed.

I must admit that I too was not displeased to have a chance to observe the others before learning anything about them. Holmes routinely surprised and impressed strangers by deducing their professions and way of life apparently from thin air, and the thought occurred that it might be interesting to see how accurate I could be in the same position.

We therefore followed the little historian through, the final guests to arrive.

* * *

The dining room, like the main hall, gave the impression of a once great room now much reduced in stature. The two magnificent chandeliers suspended above the long oak dining table must once have illuminated every corner with a shimmering light, but now hung dusty and unlit, replaced by a series of elegant but unpolished silver candelabra. The wallpaper, which showed in deep maroon rectangles at regular intervals where paintings had once hung, was faded and frayed at the edges and even in the uncertain light of a candle flame, the chips and marks on the paintwork of the wainscot were plain to see.

At least the view through the large window which took up most of the farthest wall was undiminished; through it I could just make out some low-lying hills in the distance and, closer at hand, a wide expanse of garden, dotted by strange shadows of irregular shape and size and small groves of trees.

"If you would care to sit over there, Dr Watson?"

Buxton indicated a seat on the far side of the table, between a young woman of around twenty-five, with light auburn hair and large, round brown eyes, and an older gentleman, who stood politely and gave a small nod of greeting as I approached.

"How do you do?" he said as I took my seat. "Stephen Reilly, at your service."

He held out his hand and I shook it. From his deeply lined and heavily tanned face, and a very slight accent to his speech, I would have hazarded a guess that he was in his mid-sixties and, though English by birth, had spent much of his life abroad. His grip was firm and he exuded the unmistakable confidence of one used to command. A colonial administrator, perhaps, or a highly placed businessman with property somewhere in the further reaches of the Empire. No doubt he was looking to buy an estate back home in the English countryside, one to which he might retire in the twilight of his life.

Whatever the truth of the matter, there was no denying his manners. Before sitting, he indicated the young lady to my left. "May I introduce…"

"Julieanne Schell," she interrupted, in a soft voice, holding out a pale, slim hand. Her accent was American, but cultured: New England, I thought. Her skin was flawless and her auburn hair held up in the latest style; on the other hand, the matching pearl earrings and necklace she wore were impressive but old-fashioned, as was the plainly decorated but expensive dress she wore. The unworldly daughter of a wealthy Boston merchant, I decided, come to England to complete her education. I could not conceive that she would have any genuine interest in buying Thorpe Manor, but her beauty was enough to light up the room where the feeble candles could not.

For a moment, I almost kissed her hand then, in the nick of time, remembered I was in an English country dining room and not a French romantic novel and satisfied myself with briefly squeezing her fingers as I introduced myself. I had the terrible feeling that I had actually blushed, and in an effort to regain my foolishly departed composure, I looked around the table at the other diners.

There were nine in total, including Holmes and myself. Mr Reilly and Miss Schell I had already accounted for (there was an unattended place setting to the lady's left), and of Buxton's life I already felt I knew more than enough. That left a saturnine gentleman at the bottom of the table, who glared down his nose at me but did not return my nod of greeting, and the three other guests sitting alongside Holmes on the opposite side of the table (Buxton having taken the seat at the top, with obvious pleasure). All were presumably wealthy enough to purchase the estate, but beyond that three men could not have been more dissimilar.

To Holmes's right sat a slim, elderly gentleman of at least seventy, possibly a decade more. Small metal-rimmed spectacles sat in front of rheumy blue eyes, above a neatly trimmed white beard and moustache. That was virtually the only hair in evidence, however, for his head was completely bald, save for a sliver of silver at the top of each ear, which ran down the base of his skull at the back like the garlands reputedly given to Roman emperors. As he raised a water glass to his mouth, his whole arm shook and a little of the water spilled out and ran down the paper-thin skin of his hand. I was unable to hazard much about his background – a friend of the Thorpe family, perhaps, or one of Buxton's acquaintances, a local historian invited to make up the numbers at dinner. As a medical man, however, I was confident in my diagnosis that he would be better served tucked up in bed with a hot drink than sitting in this draughty and poorly lit dining room.

If this frail old man was an unlikely addition to our company, the figure to Holmes's left was a puzzle of an altogether greater magnitude. Thus far, everyone present had been – by my estimates, at least – the type of person one might expect to find at an estate sale. A colonial grandee, a wealthy New Englander, even an extremely elderly gentleman of uncertain origin; but this fourth newcomer was as much a fish out of water as I would be in a Bedouin tent.

Most obviously, he was a foreigner. His skin was brown, as were his eyes, and his hair, what I could see of it where it curled out from beneath a green turban, almost black. His jacket too was an emerald green and decorated with a gold medallion on the left breast. A gold earring hung from one ear. Physically, he was tall, at least as tall as Holmes, and broad-shouldered. He was in conversation with Buxton, but as I looked across at him he turned in my direction and I saw that his face was marred by a long scar, which ran from his left temple, across the corner of his left eye, to the edge of his mouth. The eye was not damaged, but the scar had puckered the skin enough to twist one side of his face very slightly, leaving him with a permanently leering expression. By his colouring, I knew he was not from Afghanistan or India, but other than that, all I could say was that he was from the east. What he was doing here in Thorpe Manor I could not begin to conjecture.

Next to him, however, was someone of whom I could confidently state that I knew not only his profession but even his name. The peculiarly christened Amicable Watt was as well known in certain London circles as any government minister, and considerably wealthier. The son of an itinerant pedlar who had named each of his many children after an element of character he hoped they would exhibit in life, Watt had made his fortune by the age of twenty-five, starting at fourteen with a wheelbarrow from which he sold pots and pans. He had recently been described in The Times as a modern-day King Midas and was reputed to have interests in businesses as diverse as mining, banking and shipbuilding. Less well known was the fact that he had been suspected in the murder of two rivals as a young man, though he had never been charged, far less convicted. He caught my eye as I looked over at him and winked, a huge grin on his rather florid face. If initial impressions were any measure, Amicable Watt seemed likely to live up to his name.

The same could not be said of the scowling gentleman who made up the last of our number. Dressed in an old-fashioned black suit, with a stiff, high-collared shirt, he watched his fellow diners in the same manner in which a crow might observe a group of rabbits. His long face was frozen in a look of disdain, which had not shifted in the whole time we had been seated. It was impossible to tell who he might be, but should he turn out to be either a hangman or the owner of a particularly poorly run workhouse, I would not have been surprised.

"Are you a doctor of medicine, sir, or – like our host – an academic man?"

Any further thoughts on the matter were interrupted by a question from Mr Reilly who, I now realised, had been watching me quizzically as I scrutinised the other guests. I was suddenly conscious that I had been doing so for longer than I intended, and must have looked quite rude.

"Medicine," I stammered; then, recognising that this lacked something as a response, went on to explain that I had trained in London and served with the army in Afghanistan, but was now in private practice back in the capital.

"You must have a very successful practice," he observed. "Is it in Harley Street, perhaps?"

It was an odd question, and I wondered what had prompted it, only belatedly realising that he thought me a potential rival for the purchase of Thorpe Manor. I hurried to disabuse him of that notion.

"No, no, I'm simply down with my friend for a change of scenery and to help out the Thorpe family lawyer with a... small task."

I was not sure, because we had not discussed it, but though Holmes had made no effort to disguise our particular interests from

Buxton, I thought perhaps he would prefer that the reason for our presence was not widely known. At the same time, I knew that my hesitation had sounded unnecessarily mysterious and berated myself for becoming distracted and thus not being prepared with a more ready reply.

Reilly gave no indication that he had noticed, however. "So, you are not interested in purchasing the estate? I may say, if it is not too ill-mannered, that that fact pleases me a great deal. I have spent most of my life in Malaya, and wish now to retire and spend my final years at home, in England. You will forgive me, I hope, for my pleasure in knowing there is one fewer bidder for the estate than I believed."

Mark one on the scorecard, I thought with satisfaction. A career spent in the colonies and now returning home with his fortune. Reilly was exactly as I had imagined.

"Two fewer, in fact," I corrected him with a smile. "My friend, Sherlock Holmes there, will also not be bidding. I assume Miss Schell, however…" I concluded, turning to the lady.

"It is Mrs Schell, Doctor," she corrected me in turn, and it was only now that I glanced down and noticed the wedding ring on her left hand. "But yes, my husband and I will most likely be bidding on this fine old property. We hope to open our first English sanatorium here, to match the ones we already own in the States."

So much for my unworldly Boston rose! "Your husband…?"

To my shock, she nodded at the geriatric gentleman on the other side of the table. And so much for my elderly friend of the family, I concluded ruefully. "Frederick, dear, say hello to Dr John Watson," she called. The greeting seemed to catch him by surprise; he gave a start and peered myopically across at his wife.

"Dr Watson is a friend of this fellow," he said, placing a hand on top of Holmes's arm. Unexpectedly, his voice was firm and clear, belying his physical frailty, even if his words seemed tangential to the general conversation. "Sherlock Holmes is his name. Comes from London, he says. Writes monographs. This fellow," he went on, pointing a shaky finger at Amicable Watt, "claims to be called... mm... Friendly or some such thing. Don't know the name of the other one," he concluded, shifting his attention to the dark-skinned man on the other side of Holmes. "Said it, but I didn't catch it."

Thus addressed, the final member of our party rose to his feet and gave an extravagant bow from his waist.

"Perhaps it would be easiest if I were to introduce myself," he began, in perfect English, with no trace of any accent beyond the slightly mannered drawl picked up in certain superior public schools. "My name is Alim Salah, and I have the good fortune to be the emissary of my uncle, the Sultan of Ghurid. Though Ghuridian by birth, I was sent by my uncle to be schooled in England and have lived here for many years. It is for this reason that I was chosen to conduct negotiations on his behalf for the purchase of Thorpe Manor and its attached estates and lands. If I may be frank, you have all wasted your time in coming to Thorpe Manor. Ghuridian pockets are far deeper than those of..." He hesitated, as though seeking the perfect description. "...shopkeepers, rubber farmers and women."

Salah's intention to cause offence was clear, and I felt Reilly stiffen in outrage at my side. "And what on God's good earth would an Arab want with an English estate?" he snapped. The same question had occurred to me, though I would have expressed it with less venom.

Reilly's tone appeared only to amuse Salah.

"For better reasons than anyone else seated at this table," he replied with a cold smile. "To right a great wrong committed by you English brigands against my people, in fact. For reasons of justice!"

Before Reilly could respond, Holmes interjected. "Or a past injustice, perhaps. Such as the theft of a precious ruby."

Both Reilly and Lawrence Buxton reacted with indignant exclamations to Holmes's suggestion. For perhaps thirty seconds, the table was a tumult of sound and fury as Salah furiously – and loudly – confirmed that Ghurid was indeed the historical source of the Thorpe Ruby, stolen by a villainous Crusader, and Reilly and Buxton noisily objected both to the description and to any claim which Ghurid might make. Frederick Schell appeared largely oblivious to the argument raging about him, but the other guests observed proceedings with, in order from Amicable Watt to Mrs Schell, amusement, contempt and a degree of nervousness. Holmes, as ever, watched on with a sort of fascinated detachment, his eyes flicking from one speaker to the next, missing little but contributing nothing beyond the initial stimulus.

I do not know how matters would have ended had a small serving girl not entered, bearing a tray of soup bowls – and, on her heels, a tall, slim figure who, stepping from the shadows by the door, was revealed as the missing final guest for dinner.

Captain Hopkirk was a dashing young man, though not perhaps so dashing as to bring the furious dispute to an immediate halt. That honour lay with the serving girl who quickly moved between the diners and deposited bowls of greasy soup before them. As she did so, I quickly took stock of the captain.

Like Salah and Holmes, he was of above average height and equally broad shouldered, dressed in a tweed jacket and cavalry twill trousers, with an open-necked Tattersall shirt. Short, flat hair, a neatly trimmed moustache and a pronounced upright bearing combined with what I was certain was a Guards pin in his lapel to give him a military air befitting his rank. When he spoke, his voice was friendly and engaging and I felt myself warm to him at once.

"My apologies for the late arrival, but I had an appointment in town which I just couldn't break. Regimental affair, you know."

He smiled and gave a small shrug, as though to suggest that he would have broken off the engagement if he possibly could. Buxton stood and quickly made the introductions, glad, I suspect, to see the assembled guests settle down. The glare he aimed in the direction of Alim Salah did not go unnoticed, however. The Sultan's emissary had certainly prodded a hornet's nest with his announcement, and there would be repercussions to come, of that I was sure.

In the meantime, Hopkirk took his place at the far end of the table, and conversation – and dinner – recommenced.

Chapter Four

Dinner for Eight

I had hoped to break the ice with Hopkirk by enquiring about his military service, but almost as soon as he sat down, Mrs Schell all but monopolised his attention. It quickly became clear that they were already known to one another and, in one of the rare breaks in their conversation, I was able to ascertain that the captain had met the Schells in San Moritz three years ago, while the American couple were on their honeymoon.

"Freddie and Julieanne were good enough to invite a tired old soldier like me to join them over drinks one night, and we soon became firm friends," Hopkirk explained. He lowered his voice a little and leaned across Mrs Schell in order that I might hear him clearly. "Sadly, Freddie does not keep in the most robust of health – something of a handicap in the owner of a collection of health spas – and he asked me to squire his new wife around, to show her the sights and what not. Of course, I was happy to do so."

"James could not have been more helpful," Mrs Schell confirmed, with a fond smile. "We have army officers back in the States, naturally, but none to compare with Captain Hopkirk. I would have felt quite terrified to venture out into the cities of Europe on my own, and the local guides were not to be trusted, so it was truly a Godsend when a gentleman like the captain crossed our path."

Was it an uncharitable thought, as I watched the two of them together, to conjecture that they would have been better suited as husband and wife than the young and vivacious Mrs Schell and her elderly and infirm spouse? She was a striking woman, but I struggled to imagine that her marriage was a love match. I was just wondering how to phrase that question delicately when talk switched to the various diversions to be had in the French Riviera (an area I had never visited) and though I tried to follow the conversation, it soon descended into a series of private jokes and reminiscences. With nothing to contribute, I turned my attention back to the rest of the room.

Conversation remained strained after the earlier emotional flare-up. Holmes was involved in a one-sided discussion with Mr Schell – I heard him mention Pasteur's experiments concerning food preservation, but Schell gave no sign of noticing – while Buxton and Reilly were muttering to one another in conspiratorial tones and casting venomous glances across at Salah. Amicable Watt was attempting to engage his unfriendly neighbour in conversation, with little success. I heard him say, "Well, Judge Pennington…" however, so at least I now knew his name and profession. I had not been too far off the mark with my guess of hangman, after all.

As for the man who had started the argument, Alim Salah sat in splendid isolation, exhibiting no sign that he regretted his words or their consequences. On the contrary, a half-smile played on his lips as he looked about the room, and I found myself wondering what he had intended to achieve. Perhaps his aim had simply been to discomfit the people against whom he would be bidding?

The serving girl had just entered with the main course of mutton and potatoes, already plated, and before she could lay them out before us, I took the opportunity to swap seats with Buxton and introduced myself to the scar-faced Ghuridian.

"It is a difficult thing to hear, that your countryman has behaved dishonourably," he said, prodding at his food without enthusiasm, "especially after so great a time has passed. But the people of Ghurid have long felt the shame of the loss of the ruby, and though the purchase of the thief's lands will not erase that shame, my uncle believes that it is important symbolically."

His measured tone suggested that his earlier insults had indeed been deliberately calculated to antagonise his competitors in the purchase of the Thorpe estate. "I was told a local legend today that the ruby is still hidden somewhere in the house," I said, and was not surprised that Salah too had heard the story.

"Of course, that is part of my uncle's thinking. Primarily, we intend the manor house to be used by our diplomats and members of the royal family on visits to England, but we will also certainly have every inch of the house and grounds searched."

"So the legend is true, then? Insofar as it relates to the ruby being stolen from a temple and brought back to England?"

"It is."

"And the band of assassins sent to Thorpe Manor to kill him and retrieve the stone? Is that also true?"

"It is as true as any other story from almost a thousand years ago, Dr Watson," Salah chuckled. "But the Ghuridian legend matches the English one in every respect, which must count for something. It says that the sultan of the time sent a quartet of highly trained fida'i – assassins, you would call them – to hunt down the desecrator of our holy places and bring back the temple ruby. They tracked him across desert, forest and sea to the home of the infidel, but he would not say where he had hidden his prize, in spite of the most fearsome tortures. The fida'i returned to Ghurid empty-handed, and they and their entire families were put to death for their failure."

I swallowed at this final bloodthirsty detail. "The version I was told this morning omits that last part, obviously, but yes, otherwise it accords exactly with your own."

"Personally, I do not hold out any great hopes," Salah confided. "If the gem were capable of recovery, it would have been found by now. But as a symbol of the resurgence of Ghurid, even the possibility of its return exerts a powerful hold over the common people, and my uncle is wise enough to harness that power to his own ends. And, of course, were I to be the man to find it, well... the laws of Ghuridian succession are a tangled, and thus infinitely flexible, mess."

I nodded. The specific politics of Ghurid were unknown to me, but the generally fragile governments endemic to the region and the ease and frequency with which they were replaced was a constant theme of international reports in The Times. Anything which helped shore up a ruler in the area would be assiduously promoted.

Holmes, too, was nodding. Evidently having exhausted all possible avenues of interest with Mr Schell (who was now apparently asleep at the table, his meal going cold in front of him), he had turned his attention to Salah.

"I could not help but overhear, Mr Salah. I wonder, does the legend in your country say exactly where the torture of the Baron de Trop took place?"

"Only to the extent that we were able to identify Thorpe Manor."

"That is a shame. If you knew where exactly he died, it would perhaps narrow down your area of search."

"It would, yes, but this is not so large an estate, and I intend to explore as much of it as I can while I am here. Perhaps I shall find it myself."

Holmes laughed and applauded softly. "I respect such self-confidence, Mr Salah, so long as it is not misplaced. But surely you will only be here a few days, and I believe that Mr Buxton has various tours planned for us all."

Salah laughed too. "We Ghuridians are a race as comfortable in the night as the day, Mr Holmes; even those of us who have spent years away from home. The heat of the desert sun is in our bones. I shall have many hours when you are all safe in your beds to explore the house and gardens. Who knows what success I might have?"

He fell silent, considering the task ahead of him, perhaps. Just then the same girl as before entered to clear the plates, and I realised that I had seen no other servants at all since our arrival. I remarked on this fact to Buxton.

"No, apart from a man who comes by rail from Browerby, the next stop up, to do the garden once a month, Alice Crabtree is the only villager who was willing to come and serve at the house tonight. The late Lord Thorpe was not a popular man locally, you see, and kept no servants of his own. In fact, I believe the delivery of meat and vegetables this morning was the first such to the house in forty years. While his Lordship was alive, nobody local would sell him so much as a carrot, and he was forced to order his provisions in from Stainforth." He leaned towards me conspiratorially. "Mr Thompson, the lawyer, paid Alice a sizeable fee to cook and serve dinner this weekend, or we would have been reduced to whatever cold sandwiches I could have contrived to put together. Not that the food we have been served has been much better!"

The food had been less than impressive, it was true, but given the circumstances, it was plain that we should be grateful to have been fed at all. As Alice leaned past me to place a bowl containing what I hoped was custard on the table, I gave her a thankful smile. I wondered if she knew what had made Lord Thorpe so unpopular, and would have asked, but she hurried past me and onto my neighbour before I could do so.

The table had gradually fallen quiet, I realised, with only Hopkirk and Mrs Schell still engaged in anything more than the most desultory of conversations. I could just make out the sound, if not the content, of their murmured chat, but apart from that, and occasional requests to pass the salt, the meal continued in silence until its end. A wind had whipped up outside and I could hear it clearly. Heavy grey clouds had gathered too, and I wondered if we might have been better taking our chances with the London smog.

Finally, Alice cleared the last bowls and cups, and we each rose and awkwardly bade one another goodnight. I should have liked a nightcap but as Buxton had left for his own cottage across the fields, there was nobody to offer one, and so I made my way to bed, still somewhat hungry and in a vague ill-humour.

Chapter Five

The Silent Man

I was woken the following morning by the sound of a curtain flapping in the window of my room and a sudden realisation that the air was freezing cold. I had closed neither window nor curtains fully the night before, but even so, little light, and no sound, intruded from outside. This, combined with a certain dull quality to the air, could only mean one thing. I padded over and pulled the curtains open wide and sure enough, outside everything was blanketed in fresh white snow.

Heavy flakes – the size of sovereigns – were still drifting lazily to the ground, the uniform whiteness of which was interrupted here and there by fallen branches, some of them quite large, suggesting the storm I had evidently slept through had been a heavy one. A patch of clear blue sky to the west hinted that the worst was over; as far as the eye could see, however, the fields and hills were hidden under thick drifts. Shivering in the cold air, I washed and dressed quickly and made my way downstairs, and through to the dining room where Buxton had said breakfast would be served.

Perhaps because the weather was so vile outside, the curtains were drawn and candles had again been lit. In their unsteady light, I was dismayed to see that the only other person present was Judge Pennington, the disagreeable diner of the night before. He was sitting with an untouched plate of eggs and bacon in front of him, smoking a cigarette and staring into the distance. As I entered he glanced across and, to my surprise, beckoned me over.

"We were not introduced last night," he said, holding out his hand. "My name is Mark Pennington. And you are Dr John Watson." He coughed and stubbed out his cigarette. "I am a circuit judge," he explained, "and your name and that of your friend Mr Holmes are not unknown to me."

"How do you do," I said automatically. The judge's manner, while not unfriendly, was brusque, and I had the sense that in introducing himself he was merely fulfilling a social obligation.

"Is Mr Holmes a late sleeper?" he asked after a moment.

"He can be," I replied. "Though at other times he can be up all night and not go to bed for days."

Pennington nodded and we sat in silence for an uncomfortably long time. Finally, as a precursor to making my excuses and going to get my own breakfast, I asked if he intended to retire to the manor, should his bid for the estate win the day.

At this he scowled. "That was my intention. I have travelled around the country for thirty years, sitting first in the Northern and then in the North-Eastern Assizes, and have long desired to settle in this area and write my memoirs. The life of a circuit judge is a fascinating one, but by its very nature peripatetic."

"I'm sure it is," I murmured sympathetically, if not entirely truthfully.

"But if Mr Salah's claims last night are to be believed, I doubt that I will be successful. I am not a poor man, by any means, but nor do I have endlessly deep pockets." The scowl that seemed rarely to leave his face deepened. "It really is unconscionable that England's very heart is being sold off piecemeal to foreign potentates," he grumbled. "What purpose is the Empire if all we succeed in doing is to raise primitive nations to greater wealth than our own citizens!"

He glared at me, once again the angry crow of the previous night, clearly waiting for a positive response. Fortunately, I was saved from supplying one by Holmes's voice, which preceded him into the dining room by a second.

"There you are, Watson!" he exclaimed. "I have been looking for you everywhere." He pulled out his watch and examined it briefly. "It is almost nine, but the only person I have seen is the girl from last night, carrying what I assume were those dishes." He pointed across at a sideboard, on which were arranged a selection of silver dishes, each of which promised some much-needed sustenance. "She asked me to pass on the message that Mr Buxton would be unlikely to get across the fields from his cottage this morning, so it seems our tour will be delayed."

He appeared to notice Pennington for the first time. "Ah, Judge Pennington," he said, with a nod of greeting. "I had hoped to speak to you at some point. I take an interest in the proceedings of the various assizes, and there are one or two errors of law which you have made recently, which I would be delighted to go over with you."

Pennington's face flushed bright red. He had finally begun to eat his breakfast and had just taken a forkful of bacon and eggs, which prevented him from replying immediately. While he frantically chewed, however, Holmes took me by the arm and guided me away, towards the sideboard. "That is why I was looking for you, Watson," he said, but I confess I was barely listening. A good night's sleep had restored both my humour and my appetite, and I was privately delighted that I would not be expected to listen to another lecture on the history of the manor house. A good breakfast and a morning in front of the fire with the newspapers sounded far more what the doctor ordered, so to speak. Unfortunately for those minor ambitions, I had failed to account for the possibility that Holmes might have other plans.

"There is little to be gained at this stage in remaining sedentary," he declared, lighting a cigarette. "What we need just now is the testimony of witnesses."

"Witnesses to what, Holmes?"

"To the ghost, of course!" He grinned suddenly. "Obviously, there is no such thing, which begs the question: why do the locals think there is? The village is only a short walk, after all."

This was certainly not how I hoped to spend the morning. I had however spotted what I believe was a legitimate objection.

"You have not allowed for the snow, Holmes! If Buxton could not make it to the house, I very much doubt that we will be able to effect the same journey in reverse."

I should have known that Holmes would have taken this into account. "Mr Buxton has a cottage to the west of the house, across a considerable distance of rough ground. The village on the other hand lies east, at the end of a well-sheltered pathway. How do you think the maid contrived to be here to serve breakfast?"

I groaned inwardly, seeing my comfortable few hours slipping away from me. A hurried breakfast, then a forced march to the village, would, I expected, be the disappointing sum of my morning.

In fact, I pulled out a seat just as Holmes, with a cry of "Well, stop lollygagging, Watson!", strode in the direction of the door. With a last sad glance at the covered dishes on the sideboard, I followed him, pausing only to grab my hat and coat from the stand. From behind us, I heard the indignant voice of Judge Pennington calling on Holmes to stop, but he was already out of earshot.

Our walk to the village covered much of the same ground as our trip from the station on the previous day but was considerably less pleasant. A fiercely gusting wind negated the negligible warmth of the sun, which was now weakly shining through the clearing clouds, and the ground underfoot, though navigable, was comprised of, in equal amount, snowdrifts a foot deep, and wet, slippery mud. Even though the distance cannot have been more than half a mile, by the time we arrived on the outskirts of the village I was chilled to the bone and soaked from the knee down.

To Holmes's disappointment, there was not a soul to be seen, and, for want of anywhere else to go and keen to find shelter from the wind, we soon found ourselves at the door of the local hostelry, The Silent Man.

It was still a little before ten in the morning, and I expected it to be closed, but Holmes gave the door a hearty push and it swung open, allowing a very welcome warmth to wash over us. He stood for a second in the doorway, then moved inside.

The interior consisted of a single irregularly shaped room, with rough, whitewashed stone walls, stained yellow by smoke. Directly in front of us were a table and some chairs, with a mirror above, fastened in the angle where two walls met. A wooden bar ran almost up to this table, stopping only a few feet away, but taking up the rest of the length of the back wall, with another half dozen tables ranged in front of it. The entire room was laid out in dogleg fashion, and as we walked towards the deserted bar, more tables hove into view. I was not surprised, even at so early an hour, to see a figure hunched over a drink at the far end. I had never known a country pub which did not have at least one near resident present from opening to closing each day. I was surprised to recognise the man, though. It was our companion from the train the previous day, Simeon Forward. As we approached, he glanced up and nodded a greeting but otherwise seemed disinclined to talk.

The lack of patrons and the muffling qualities of the snow outside gave the place a peculiarly empty sensation and I was just about to say to Holmes that perhaps we should leave, when a door behind the bar swung open and a man I assumed to be the landlord appeared from the back rooms.

He was plump and of medium size, with a red face and a head of curly brown hair, which fell over his collar and past his ears. He wore a grey shirt, the sleeves rolled up to the elbows, with heavy brown leather strapping at each wrist. He smiled with pleasure as soon as he saw us, hoping, I expect, that we would prove to be new customers.

"Good morning, landlord," Holmes said, as he removed his coat and draped it over the back of the nearest chair. "An uninviting day, is it not? Enough to keep your regulars indoors, I imagine."

The man hesitated before replying, and his eyes flicked towards Forward, who gave no sign he was even aware that anyone was speaking. Finally, he appeared to come to a decision and agreed with Holmes that yes, the snow and wind could be a trial, even to the locals, at this time of year.

"But how can I help you gentlemen?" he continued in an unexpected strong London accent. "Perhaps a warm toddy to keep the chill out – but even if you've no mind to a drink, you're very welcome to warm yourselves by the fire until you can feel your fingers again." His eyes flicked towards Forward once more. "Indeed, I'd be glad of the company."

I had failed to notice the fireplace when first we entered, as it was hidden away in the deep alcove which comprised the other end of the room's dogleg. It was small and unimpressive and, I suspected, would give off little heat. Above it, a faded pennant, celebrating some long-forgotten triumph, and another mirror were the only decoration. However, as I hurried across, keen to warm myself as much as possible, I realised that it was flanked by the most extraordinary woodcuts, one on either side of the wide hearth.

The details were difficult to make out, for the wood was obviously ancient and had been rubbed smooth over the centuries, but the left-hand woodcut seemed to show a series of images: a man making his way through a maze, a shining light in one hand and a sword in the other. Behind him clamoured a mob armed with curved weapons, seemingly bent on his destruction.

The second woodcut was better preserved, and showed a man – the same one, presumably – on his knees, with several blades transfixing his body and what I took to be blood pouring from his mouth, then on his back, presumably dead.

I pointed out the carvings to Holmes, though he could hardly have missed them.

"Edouard de Trop, I suspect," he said, tracing a finger across a crusader's cross marked on the breast of the figure on the first carving. "But as to what he is doing…

"Landlord," he called across, "could you spare us a moment?"

The man, I noticed, was watching us keenly. In response, he willingly dropped the towel he had been desultorily wiping across the bar counter. "As you can see, gents, I'm not exactly rushed off me feet," he said, "and like I said, I'm glad of the company."

He came round from behind the bar and stood beside us.

"Ah, it's those woodcuts that's caught your eye, eh? Been there for ever, the locals say."

"You are not a local man?" Holmes asked with a smile.

In turn, the landlord's face split into a wide grin. "How could you tell? No, no, I'm no Yorkshireman. Born and raised in London, and only moved here a few years ago, on account of me lungs." He held out a broad hand. "Walter Robinson, pleased to make your acquaintance."

We each shook his hand, and Holmes introduced us (his own name eliciting no response from Robinson, to my surprise) before gesturing to the woodcuts once more. "Perhaps you could tell us what they show?" he asked.

"I'll do me best, sir, but I can't say as I know as much as I should, them being in me bar and all. This one," he said, pointing to the left-hand panel, "is the evil Lord de Trop. The locals claim that he went crusading against the Musselmen back in olden times. As I heard it, that shows him being chased by a crowd of heathen through the caves round here – the catacombs, they call 'em. And that's the jewel he stole from the heathen king in his hand, they say, and the sword he took to the Holy Land in the other."

"The catacombs?"

"Aye, least the locals call them the catacombs, though I can't say what their right name would be, if they ever had one. Underground caves, anyway. They're all round the place in this neck of the woods. They even run underneath Thorpe Manor, I heard." He scratched at his neck thoughtfully. "The catacombs are famous round these parts. The late Lord Thorpe – him that's just died – spent a pretty penny in his younger days excavating them. They say that's where the ghost spends his days, walking the maze of caverns, searching for his lost jewel, and only coming out to terrify good Christian folk when he's tired of searching." His voice had fallen to a sardonic whisper as he ended his tale, and he glanced again at Forward, who I noticed had half turned on his stool.

"You are not a believer, Mr Robinson?" Holmes enquired.

"I grew up in the East End, sir. I seen enough of the rottener side of human life as a kid, that I've no need to make up worse now that I'm grown. But that's the tale the locals tell, and you can take it or leave it, as you see fit."

"And I'd advise you to take it, if you want to keep a grip of your soul!"

Forward's voice broke across Robinson's like a clap of thunder. "I saw you two gents on the train yesterday, did I not? And I told you then, the ghost is real as you or me."

He slipped from his stool and moved to the fireplace, his pint jug still in his hand.

"Now this," he said pointing to the left-hand carving, "is what he says it is. It's the Baron de Trop – there weren't no Lord in them days – in the catacombs that run under the manor. The top part shows him escaping from the heathen and hiding the ruby he'd stole from their godless temple. And t'other," he indicated the right-hand side, "is the Baron riddled with swords, after they cornered him in the main hall and he wouldn't speak a word to them."

Holmes leaned forward in interest. "Is the legend so exact then, that it specifies exactly where he died?"

"Don't know about exactly, but the truth is that once he finished whatever he was up to in the catacombs, he came back to the manor house to make his stand. Course he were only one man, and them a horde, so he never had a chance. But he said not a word to the buggers who had him. He never told them where he'd hid the jewel, though he were covered in blood and run through with steel. Bit his own tongue out, rather than talk." Forward smiled thinly and tapped the middle of the right-hand carvings. "A right Yorkshireman was the Baron. Knew what was right and what wasn't, and there weren't no foreigner could make him do something if he'd set his mind not to."

"You know, I believe you may be right, Mr Forward."

Holmes's reply, though barely audible, was loud enough that Forward heard it and grunted with satisfaction. "Course I am," he muttered with ill grace. He drained his jug in one long draught and placed it carefully on the table. "There's few know more about this area than I do," he continued, turning the jug by its handle as he did so.

Holmes could take a hint as well as the next man. "Another drink for Mr Forward, landlord."

I wondered if Robinson was put out by Forward's interference; he glowered at the older man before picking up the jug and heading back to the bar. A moment later he dropped it on the table again, filled with ale, but he did not rejoin our company.

Instead, he picked up a cloth and, positioning himself behind the bar directly opposite us, began to polish some glasses.

"Now, what else can you tell us about the catacombs? Mr Robinson said that the late Lord Thorpe investigated them some years since?" Holmes asked.

Forward drained half his glass before he said another word.

"He did. Forty years ago now, when he was a young man. It's the tradition, see, or was then. Every new Thorpe, when he becomes a man, adds something to the manor. That's another tradition that's finished now, though, on account of him having no children.

"His Lordship said he was going to turn the caves into something. He never said what, though, and it came to nothing in any event." Forward's voice was bitter and hard. "Like everything he touched."

"We heard that Lord Thorpe was not a popular man."

"I'll not speak ill of the dead, even one such as him, but I will say this, and you can judge for yourself. Ten years Walter Robinson's run this pub, but he isn't popular round these parts, just on account of him selling ale to the manor house."

"Why should he not do that?" I asked, astonished. "He is a publican, after all. Selling beer is his trade."

"That's not for me to say. But he's lucky there's but the one pub in the village, or he'd be out of business long since."

Holmes had observed this exchange in silence, but now he spoke up. "Lord Thorpe chose to stop his operations in the caves? Or did something happen that prevented further exploration?"

I thought I knew what Holmes was thinking. "Do you think he might have been seeking the ruby, Mr Forward, and having found it, ceased his endeavours?"

The effect of my words on Forward was as immediate as it was unexpected. With a curse, he jumped to his feet, knocking the table and causing his glass to tip on its side, spilling ale onto the floor.

"Who knows what he was looking for, or what he found!" he snarled. "He were a weak man, and a fool, and everyone who crossed his path ended up the worse for it. All I know is there were plenty of us went to work for him, digging all day, neglecting our own work, and then one day he upped and sacked every man, and locked himself away. That was a hard year for lots of families hereabouts! And that's all I have to say!"

Holmes and I made efforts to placate him, but he was not to be calmed. With a final angry growl, he pulled a hat from his pocket, jammed it on his head, and strode out of the pub.

I confess I was at a loss. Holmes, too, seemed bemused by the old man's reaction and merely raised an eyebrow when I wondered aloud what had prompted him to react so violently. The answer – or at least an answer – came from the unexpected source of Walter Robinson.

"Forward was the gaffer of the team that worked the caves for Lord Thorpe all those years ago. He was the one who convinced the men to leave the fields and come and help with the excavations. Looks like you touched a nerve with your talk of his Lordship finding the lost ruby. If anyone knows that, it'd be him." He sniffed and looked across at the door through which Forward had exited. "I heard him tell you I'm not well liked hereabouts, on account of selling the manor house a barrel of beer or two every month. And no more I am – though I'd like to know how they think a publican can make a living in this tiny place without selling where he can.

"But Simeon Forward's not held in much higher esteem neither.

He sits in here most days by his self. His wife and daughter's dead, and he's no friends, for they blame him for the bad year that followed the cave workings closing down. And they blame the old Lord for closing them down, and they blame me for selling ale to the man who closed them down." He placed a final glass on the shelf and folded his cloth neatly before stowing it under the bar. "They don't have much round here, Mr Holmes, but it seems to me there's always enough blame to share around."

With that, he fell silent. We finished our drinks and, the wind having died down a little, we left the little hostelry and stood in the street once more. Looking back, I thought I saw Robinson watching us through a window, but it was only for a moment and it could as easily have been a shadow.

Holmes spoke suddenly, and I refocused my attention on him. "An interesting encounter, but now back to the manor, I think, Watson. I believe a tour of its more unusual features is in order. Perhaps the little maid can act as a surrogate guide in Buxton's absence."

Chapter Six

The Crystal Palace

The walk back was no more pleasant than the journey to the village. The wind came in gusts which bit through our thick coats, and even with gloves on and my hands rammed deep in my pockets, I felt my fingers go numb with cold. Holmes trudged through the drifts in front of me, whistling a low tune which I could not quite make out.

The sight of the manor house ahead of us was, therefore, most welcome. The curtains were still drawn, I noticed, but at least one other guest was up and about, for Reilly stood in the doorway, wrapped in an enormous fur coat and with an unusual fur hat on his head, from the sides of which large flaps fell down, covering his ears and tied beneath his chin. Even so, and in spite of the fact that technically he was still inside the house, I could see he was shivering from ten yards away.

"You would be better off in the dining room," I suggested to him, but he shrugged and shook his head.

"It makes no difference, Dr Watson. Whether I am in the dining room or out in this icy wasteland, the cold is like nothing I have ever experienced. The water in my bedroom was frozen over!" He shook his head again. "I had thought that these garments–" he indicated his coat and hat "–would be enough to keep me warm, even in England's notoriously cold climate, but apparently they are insufficient. It is simply not possible to stay warm here!"

He stamped his feet – I noticed with amusement that he wore enormous fur-covered boots too – and glared past me at the snowy fields, as though they had personally offended him.

"And the man Buxton informs me that this is not unusual for the area at this time of year! I must admit, Doctor, that I am having second thoughts about spending my twilight years in Thorpe Manor."

"Buxton is here?" Holmes asked, ignoring Reilly's other comments entirely. "That is capital news."

"He is," Reilly responded sourly. "He is in the main hall with that impertinent foreigner. That is my only consolation," he added with an unpleasant barking laugh. "Salah finds the cold even more painful than I do. If I thought he would have to live here himself, I might even let him win the auction, just to teach him the lesson that pride comes before a fall. But that seems unlikely, so I am even more determined to ensure the estate does not fall into alien hands."

The thought appeared to embolden him. "Perhaps a walk around the house will get my blood flowing again," he said. "If you will excuse me, gentlemen."

We watched him tramp off along the path that ran beside the house, then Holmes expressed a desire to speak to Buxton at once and, glad to be out of the snow, we went inside.

* * *

Whatever business Salah had with Buxton was over by the time we made our way to the main hall, and of the two only the historian remained, now speaking to Mr Amicable Watt. I doubted it had been a convivial meeting, for Buxton's face was flushed with anger and Watt was plainly doing what he could to calm the older man down. We had barely taken our seats when Buxton launched into an impassioned tirade.

"The cheek of the man!" he began, banging his fist against the arm of his chair. "The confounded cheek! Do you know what Mr Salah has just had the effrontery to say to me, Mr Holmes? I, who have dedicated years of my life to building a detailed history of Thorpe Manor and its people? A history which, I hope I may say, will be of immense utility to future scholars. A history which encompasses both low and high, great men and peasants. Which..." He stumbled to a halt, apparently having lost his thread of thought. "Do you know what he said?" he repeated, then answered himself before we could say a word. "He said that he considers my work – my notes, my essays, my papers – to be part of the property of the estate and that, as such, he will take possession of them in toto, in the event that he wins the auction." Buxton's fingers dug into the arm of the chair until his fingers whitened, and small specks of saliva formed at the side of his mouth. "And then he said... and then... then he said that his people would extract any information relating to the ruby and the remainder would be burned!"

The effort of spitting this final word out was too much for the man, and he fell back in his chair, eyes bulging.

I have remarked before that Holmes, while often monomaniacal when involved in an investigation, was capable of great feeling for his fellow man, and so it proved on this occasion. He leaned forward and laid his hand on Buxton's arm. His voice was soothing as he reassured the distraught historian that he was certain such an outcome could be avoided.

"I cannot be specific, since Mr Thompson requested our circumspection regarding the precise reason for our presence here, Mr Buxton, but you are aware that we are not interested in purchasing the estate, and so I think I can rely on your discretion to a certain degree." He turned to Watt, who cupped his hands around his ample middle and smiled widely. "I hope I can similarly rely on you, Mr Watt?"

Watt's smile grew wider. "You can that, Mr Holmes. If there's one thing I'm good with, it's a secret. You don't get far in business if you're a blabbermouth."

Holmes appeared satisfied with this assurance. "Very well," he said. "Rest assured, Mr Buxton, that I will do everything in my power to ensure that there is no question of Mr Salah, or anyone else, looking for the Thorpe Ruby, no matter who wins the auction next week."

I cannot say that I saw hope rekindle in Buxton's eyes, but Holmes's words certainly had a positive effect on the man. He sat up straighter and ran his hands through his hair, before blowing his nose noisily on his handkerchief.

"It is good to hear that, Mr Holmes," he said earnestly, "I cannot deny it. And in turn, I can admit to you now that I am not entirely in the dark concerning yourself and Dr Watson. I myself pay little attention to events beyond the local area, but Mr Watt was kind enough to share with me the information that you are a well-known figure in London circles. A type of policeman, he said?"

Only one who knew Holmes well would have noticed the slight flicker in the corner of his eye at that moment.

"A type of policeman…" he repeated coldly. "That is one way in which an ill-informed man might describe my role, I suppose, though it is not an accurate one. Better to say that I am able to assist the police force from time to time in their more important cases. The current situation is not, I would stress, such an occasion, but rather is by way of a private commission." He held up a hand to forestall any questions. "I can say no more than that, I'm afraid, but I will repeat that I have every hope that there will be nobody in need of your notes, next week or any other."

Buxton, aware that he had made a gaffe of some sort, but uncertain as to exactly what, nodded his thanks. "That's all I need to know, Mr Holmes. But is there anything I can do to help you in your… investigations?"

"A tour of the house and its grounds would be most helpful," Holmes replied. "We have been told that there is, or perhaps was, a tradition incumbent on the male heir of the Thorpe name upon reaching his majority? One which led the late Lord Thorpe to excavate the catacombs, which riddle the nearby countryside. Perhaps you could shed some light on that, to begin with?"

"That I can," said the historian eagerly, automatically reverting to a lecturing tone as he was asked to expound on his area of expertise. "You must understand that the Thorpes have always been an eccentric family, though it would not have done to say that to his Lordship's face. They were all given to puzzles and games and the like, if you take my meaning, and that extended early on to architectural fancies, such as the pillars you noticed yesterday by the front door. Those were installed by the ninth baron in 1356 when he assumed the title. Over time, the idea evolved until it became the rule that the eldest Thorpe scion should create some new addition to the estate by his twenty-first birthday.

"Some of the improvements were remarkably modest – a new ice house, for example, but most were more… fanciful. We have a boating pond in the shape of a ruby, a maze with two miles of paths within it, and a statue of the third Lord Thorpe dressed as a Roman senator.

"Robert Thorpe, his late Lordship, came into his majority already Lord Thorpe, following the untimely death of his father. He was apparently a young man of exceptional intelligence and drive – this was before my time, you understand, so I am merely repeating what I was told – and had just completed his undergraduate studies, though he was not yet twenty-one. He returned to Thorpe Manor and announced that he would contribute to the family tradition by having the catacombs that adjoined the house opened up and made accessible to all. This made him popular locally, as he employed local men to do the work, and all seemed well. Until one day, with the work only partially complete, he sent all the workmen home and, the project abandoned, brought in a firm from London to build something else…"

"Something else?"

Buxton smiled, with the pleasure of a teacher able to surprise his pupils.

"Indeed, Mr Holmes. But I think it would be advisable to show you, rather than try to explain. It is no great distance, but the snow is deep in the grounds, so you had best borrow some Wellington boots."

* * *

It was certainly more comfortable to traipse through the thick snow to the rear of the house in Wellington boots, and I silently cursed that we had not thought to ask for them before setting off for the village (I feared my brogues were ruined).

In daylight, the irregular shapes I had seen shadowed by the glimmer of dusk were revealed to be a collection of the most extraordinary buildings. Without obvious pattern, each one had been constructed with no thought to the others, either in terms of location, size or type. A Chinese jade pagoda stood cheek by jowl with a mock Cleopatra's Needle, a Greek temple was flanked by a bridge to and from nowhere and, in the near distance, what appeared to be an ancient and ruined monastery turned out, according to Buxton, to have been constructed from whole cloth only a century before. There was even, as he had promised, a statue of a portly man with extravagant side whiskers in a Roman toga.

Watt, who had invited himself along with us, whistled at every new exhibit. "So this is how the idle rich spend their money?" he chuckled as we passed the entrance to a maze, carved in the shape of a giant head. "I always wondered."

He appeared to take genuine delight in everything he saw, and to wish everyone in his company to share in that delight. It was both an appealing and a wearisome characteristic. There is only a finite amount of bonhomie that any man should be expected to suffer, and after Watt's booming laugh punctuated a fifth eccentric building in as many minutes, I began to wish that I had left Buxton to walk with him and had taken my customary place at Holmes's side.

We had been walking for fifteen minutes at least, and I was beginning to wonder if we would ever reach our destination, when Buxton suddenly left the path entirely and trudged off into deeper snow. We followed him for a further few minutes, then he stopped and pointed straight ahead, announcing grandly, "Robert Thorpe's Folly!"

Through a stand of tangled elm and beech I made out a strangely familiar glass and stone edifice half hidden by ivy and fallen branches. Taken out of context I could not put my finger on what was so familiar about it, but Holmes had no such problem.

"The Crystal Palace," he murmured in my ear. "It is a scale model of the Crystal Palace."

Now that he had given a name to the building, I could see it clearly. The two stepped sides of layered glass flanking a central column surmounted by a semi-circle of glass were unmistakable. The original, built to house the Great Exhibition of 1851, had been torn down before I was born, but I had visited the rebuilt version at Sydenham and, with the exception of the middle column, which was made of solid stone rather than glass, this miniature version was an extremely close likeness. What I could not understand is why anyone would build it here.

I wondered if Holmes was thinking the same thing. He walked along the front of the structure, cupping his hands now and then to see through the glass (I could have told him from where I was standing that there was nothing between them but a plain stone floor). Then he walked back again, stopping only once to run his hands carefully across the central stonework, which had been carved in the shape of the same panes of glass, each six inches square, that made up its two wings. Presumably due to its sheltered location, the carvings remained recognisable, though coated in grime and mould, even after the best part of half a century in the garden. Holmes traced a finger around those "panes" he could reach and peered upwards for several seconds. He took several steps away from the building, the better to see the roof, until his back was flat against the nearest tree. Suddenly, in a flurry of unexpected movement, he reached above his head and pulled himself up into the branches. The snow had not penetrated beyond the tree's higher reaches so he was in no danger of slipping, but as he levered himself into a standing position, holding fast to the next highest branch, I wondered how long that would be the case. Snow fell from the tree, showering us all, as Holmes stretched on tiptoe to examine the very top of the Crystal Palace. I heard him mutter something to himself then, without warning, he leapt back to the ground.

"Holmes!" I berated him, but he paid me no attention. He stalked back to the central section and ran his hands over the wall again. After a minute of this, he frowned in disappointment and stepped back from the model palace, brushing dirt and mould from his hands.

"Did Lord Thorpe ever explain why he chose to recreate this particular building?" he asked Buxton.

"Unfortunately not. From the date of its construction, he effectively cut himself off from human contact, dismissing almost all the servants, closing down the east wing, and having his food and drink delivered from the village. He never left the manor house again; and until he contacted me and asked me to write a history of the family, I do not believe anyone had spoken to him in four decades.

"I did ask him on one occasion when the matter of the various follies came up in our conversation, but the question raised an ire in him such as I had never witnessed before, and he as good as told me that should I ask again, it would be the last time I set foot in the house.

"Lord Thorpe could be a difficult man." He shook his head at the memory and sighed. "It is hard to believe that he was ever as young and carefree as the painting above the great fireplace suggests."

Holmes raised an eyebrow. "His Lordship is one of the figures in the painting?"

"He is, Mr Holmes. He can be seen throwing the ball on the right-hand side of the painting, in front of his parents. The other boy, the one with the bat, is his younger brother, who pre-deceased him by a half a century, while the baby on the grass is Lady Jane Thorpe, who was sadly killed in a horse-riding accident at the age of fourteen. It was not a fortunate generation."

He kicked at a tree stump to dislodge packed snow from the tread of his boots. "I had thought this might be a good starting point for... well, whatever is that you are investigating, Mr Holmes. But I am entirely at your disposal. However, I suspect we might be best to postpone any further exploration of the grounds for the moment." He pointed through the cluster of trees to the lawn. While we had stood under the protection of the little grove, fresh snow had begun to fall in heavy, slow flakes.

I had no desire to stay out in a snowstorm if I could avoid it and so, before Holmes could say a word, I hurriedly agreed with Buxton that returning indoors was definitely the order of the day. I thought for a moment that Holmes would object but instead he gestured that Buxton should lead the way. I allowed Amicable Watt to go before me, and quickly fell into step alongside Holmes, in the direction of the manor.

Chapter Seven

Arguments

We arrived to find Stephen Reilly just setting out to look for us.

"Buxton!" he called from the doorway as soon as we came into view. "Buxton! A word with you!"

He was still wearing the fur coat and flapped hat that he had had on when we left him, but now his normally tanned face was red with fury.

"Is it true, Buxton? Is what Mr Salah told me true? Is the railway line closed?"

I heard Buxton tut to himself at my side and then mutter something under his breath. Holmes, on the far side of him, must also have heard the noise, for he stopped Buxton by the arm, still twenty yards from Reilly.

"Is it true?" he asked. "Presumably by more than mere snow, though, or it would not have been worth mentioning. A tree down onto the tracks from the storm last night seems more likely."

"More than one, Mr Holmes. I saw Bert, the station porter,

on my way here, and he asked me to pass on the message that several trees have fallen on the tracks and with the snow blocking some of the roads, it might be Tuesday before the train to Thorpe-by-the-Marsh is running again. I first approached Salah to tell him, but in the excitement following his outrageous threat, it completely slipped my mind to mention it to anyone else. If you will excuse me."

He hurried forward to speak to Reilly – and to Hopkirk and Mrs Schell, who had appeared at his shoulder, drawn by the shouting. With Watt – who I was beginning to think could not bear to miss out on anything of potential interest – bringing up the rear, they disappeared into the house as Holmes stopped to light a cigarette.

"As late as Tuesday," he said, blowing smoke rings into the air. He sounded extremely pleased. "Why, that is excellent news, Watson. That will prove most convenient."

"Do you believe you will complete your investigations by then, Holmes?" I asked in wonder. If, in the space of a mere three days, he managed to locate a gem missing for the greater part of a millennium or a cache of missing artwork, it would rank among his most impressive work, in my opinion.

"My investigations, Watson? I am not sure they are worthy of quite so grand a title yet."

"Not sure…? Holmes, I think that if you have the ruby to hand by Tuesday that will be a near miraculous achievement."

"The ruby…? Why, my dear Watson, you surely do not think that I refer to that trifling matter?"

"What else, Holmes?"

"Why, I already know exactly where the missing ruby is to be found. That puzzle was barely worth the effort of coming into the country at all. But I may have stumbled upon something far more interesting."

I was astonished by Holmes's claim, and was about to enquire further, when a loud crash from within the house, followed by a female voice crying for help, caught both my attention and his and we ran inside.

The sight which greeted us was one better suited to the streets of Whitechapel on a Saturday night than the hall of a great country house.

Captain Hopkirk had Alim Salah's emerald jacket bunched in one hand, and was endeavouring with the other to land a series of punches to his opponent's midriff. Salah, meanwhile, had torn the collar from Hopkirk's shirt and, if the livid red mark across the captain's cheek was any indication, had landed at least one significant blow himself. An occasional table had been knocked over in the struggle and the vase that had stood on it now lay strewn across the floor in a dozen jagged pieces. Buxton and Julieanne Schell stood at the bottom of the stairs and the little maid Alice in the doorway to the dining room, her hand to her mouth, about to scream again for help.

"You will take back that slander, sir, or by God, I will kill you where you stand!" Hopkirk was shouting into Salah's face as we entered.

In response, Salah pulled his head back and thrust it hard into Hopkirk's, striking him flush on the forehead and knocking him to the ground. Instantly Salah was on top of him, his fingers digging into his opponent's throat. Bad enough, but to my horror

Hopkirk's flailing hand reached out for a broken shard of pottery and, finding one within reach, grasped it tightly and swung it in an arc, wickedly jagged point to the fore, towards Salah's neck.

Holmes took two quick steps forward and kicked the weapon from Hopkirk's hand. At the same time, I grabbed Salah by the shoulders and heaved him to one side, breaking the deadly hold he had on his opponent's throat. Hopkirk gasped and rolled onto his side, breathing heavily. Salah pushed himself against the wall and glared across at me. He rose slowly and pulled the hem of his tunic sharply to straighten it, but the garment was ruined, ripped at the collar and sleeve. He ran his hands across his thick black hair and looked carefully around the room, finally focusing his attention on Hopkirk, whom Holmes had helped to his feet.

"The story of English manners is famous the world over," he said, still a little short of breath, "but in my experience," and here he unconsciously ran a finger along the scar on his face, "the fiction and the reality are often two different things. So it has proven today. If I were in London, I should be contacting both the police and my solicitor and reporting this assault, but as we are not, I will satisfy myself with purchasing this house and its lands for Ghurid, and then take great pleasure in having all of you thrown off the estate as trespassers!"

He pushed past Reilly and Mrs Schell, then stopped at the top of the stairs for a final word. "I intend to change out of these rags and go down to the village, where I will send a telegram to my uncle's representatives, informing them that we should spend whatever is necessary to purchase Thorpe Manor. And I think you will find that Ghurid has deeper pockets than any of you!"

In the pause that followed this announcement and Salah's

departure upstairs, all I could hear was Hopkirk's laboured breathing. I was reminded that damage could be done by even a brief compression of the throat and offered to examine him, but he angrily shrugged my hand from his arm and, with little more grace than Salah, bundled past the figures on the stairs and scurried up to his room. I heard his door slam and the sound echoed round the hall. Mrs Schell, who had not moved since we had come through the front door, gave a start at the noise and, without saying a word, also turned and fled upstairs.

"I'll just get a brush and pan and sweep this up, sir." Alice the maid gave a little bob in our general direction and left for the servants' area, behind the main staircase. Suddenly, where all had been riotous noise mere moments before, the hall was quiet, and only Reilly remained alongside Holmes and I.

"What can you expect of a damned foreigner!" he declared angrily. "Did I not say that he was an impertinent upstart?" He walked towards us and dropped his voice somewhat. "I did not hear exactly what was said, but I understand from Mrs Schell – who was quite shocked, and rightly so – that Salah made a most improper suggestion concerning an innocent stroll she and Captain Hopkirk took around the grounds this morning. I personally don't understand the appeal of tramping about in the snow, but young people like that sort of thing, I believe."

He made a small noise in the back of his throat which was either an amused laugh or a snort of derision at the foolishness of the young, then remembered something which caused his brow to furrow in undoubted irritation.

"More important, though, is the news of which Buxton belatedly informed me, that there will be no trains back to London for several days. That is extremely inconvenient. I had intended to leave in the morning."

"So soon?" Holmes made no attempt to hide his surprise. "I understood from our conversation this morning that you intended to bid on the estate?"

"I did. But my walk in the garden did much to open my eyes to the fact that I am not suited to living in England. It is too cold and too wet for me, Mr Holmes." He tutted to himself. "And now I must brave the cold and the wet again and go down to the village to send a telegram to reschedule my passage home." He checked the time in the clock in the hall. "The post office closes in half an hour, so if you will excuse me…"

He nodded a goodbye, and went upstairs, leaving Holmes and me alone in the hall. We went through to our already familiar seats by the fire and each lit a pipe.

I was impatient to hear Holmes's views on the recent goings-on. "Well, what did you make of that?" I asked as soon as we were comfortable.

"I think that this weekend shows every sign of being a less relaxing break from London than you had hoped, Watson," Holmes gently mocked me. "I fear that your old wound will not be getting the rest you so desired."

"I shall endeavour to cope, Holmes," I replied with a matching smile. "But I mean the scuffle between Hopkirk and Salah, as I'm sure you know."

"If Reilly is to be believed, it was simply a case of the good captain defending a woman's honour."

"If Reilly is to be believed? You think he might be lying?"

The thought had not occurred to me, but I recognised in myself a willingness to assume the best of a fellow army man, and Reilly's testimony had suited that tendency well.

Holmes blew smoke rings towards the ceiling and watched them float for a moment before replying. "I did not say quite that, Watson. He did after all only report what Mrs Schell had told him. But a lady's honour may be impugned with cause, and a man may react violently to the imputation without necessarily acting from good intentions."

"Captain Hopkirk and Mrs Schell? Involved romantically?"

I consider myself a man of the world and was not shocked at the suggestion in and of itself, so much as by the fact that such an affair of the heart was being conducted essentially under the nose of Mr Schell. The risk of exposure was great, and that to her name and his career (though I was suddenly aware that I knew nothing about the latter, even to the extent of knowing if he was still on active service) greater still.

"Do you have any evidence to support such a claim?" I asked Holmes uncertainly.

"The evidence of my own eyes is enough in this case, Watson. At dinner, they acted the very image of young lovers, cutting out all their fellow diners in favour of exclusively private jokes of their own. That is the behaviour of a couple who are more than friends."

I had noticed the pair's swift recourse to topics into which no outsider could intrude, and the easy familiarity with which they had spoken, like two old friends re-commencing a conversation only interrupted by time apart, not ended and now begun anew. Even so, I would not have considered this to be evidence of improper behaviour, were it not for Holmes's certainty. For a man who did not welcome romantic dalliances of any kind, he had a keen eye for them in others.

"And Reilly would naturally assume that Salah was in the wrong, and so believe Mrs Schell," I mused aloud. "He has made no secret of his dislike of him."

"Indeed. Though Reilly's honesty, too, is suspect."

Holmes's earlier comment regarding Reilly's honesty had been open to misinterpretation. This, however, was a statement allowing of no such ambiguity. I remembered, too, his claim that he had found something worthy of his attention, and hoped he was not creating a mystery from whole cloth simply in order to give himself some affair to investigate. I gave myself a moment to consider my reply by slowly re-lighting my pipe. "How so?" I said finally, hoping that any hesitancy was not evident in my voice.

I was not wholly successful. "You doubt it, Watson?" Holmes chided me. "Then you must consider why Reilly had already booked passage home for tomorrow, when he says that his decision to leave early was only made today."

I was annoyed with myself for failing to notice the same thing, but I could think of one relatively comprehensible excuse for Reilly's lie. "Perhaps he did no such thing, but rather wants to telegram his bank about the bid he will make for the estate, in similar fashion to Salah? It is not unreasonable to suppose that he would prefer his opponent to remain unaware of that fact."

Holmes shrugged. "That is certainly possible, Watson. But if Reilly is not keen for Salah to know his business, it is strange that they are even now standing together in the hallway, about to leave together to send their telegrams."

I twisted round in my armchair to obtain a view of the doorway into the hall and, sure enough, Alim Salah was standing holding the front door open, the Wellington boots he wore at odds with his scarlet tunic. Beside him, Stephen Reilly, wrapped in his voluminous furs, had plucked a walking stick from a stand by the door and was swinging it back and forth impatiently. If the look on Salah's face was any indication, he was at best a grudging companion for the older man (neither was Reilly wreathed in smiles, to be fair), but there was no doubting that they intended to walk down to the village together. Now suitably shod, they passed out of sight behind the wall and a second later the front door slammed shut.

There was no hot meal that evening. Alice did not work on Sunday afternoons, but she had prepared sandwiches, which Buxton laid out in the main hall. Reilly and Salah had returned from their trip to the village in exactly the sort of sullen bad temper that I should have predicted would be the result of prolonged time in each other's company. Both men took a plate of sandwiches to their rooms, barely uttering a word to the rest of us.

Mrs Schell reported that her husband continued to be unwell and would skip dinner entirely, while she and Hopkirk went for a moonlit walk around the lawn. Now that Holmes had pointed out their relationship, it was difficult for me to miss the little indications of their affection.

Unexpectedly, Amicable Watt turned out to be a keen chess player, and challenged Pennington, who was also an enthusiast, to a game. Within half an hour Watt had won three times and the judge, apparently not a good loser, had stormed off to his bed. Watt, with nobody else willing to play, did likewise soon after. Any hopes I had harboured of a few convivial evenings in the country were rapidly evaporating.

Even Buxton deserted us, pleading the need to return to his history, though he did promise to show us the remainder of the estate's more interesting features first thing in the morning.

Left to our own devices, Holmes and I quickly settled into a mirror of our life back in Baker Street. We sat on either side of the fireplace, whisky to hand, and smoked our pipes, talking over old cases. The snow was still falling outside, and the warm room felt far more inviting than it had done the previous night. Only when I heard Hopkirk and Mrs Schell return and go upstairs did a less agreeable recollection come to mind.

"I believe that Hopkirk would have killed Salah with that pottery shard, Holmes. Admittedly, Salah had his hands on his throat, but a man of his military training could easily have broken free without recourse to deadly force." I leaned forward and tapped out the bowl of my pipe against the grate. "There was real hate in his eyes. I think he had so lost control that he wanted to kill him."

"In the heat of the fight, both men had lost control," Holmes agreed. "Has Hopkirk seen action, do you know? It might be that he has experience of battle in the farther-flung reaches of the Empire, and this has left him less sensitive than most to the taking of a life."

"That is no excuse, Holmes!" I countered, a defensiveness on behalf of my fellow soldiers animating me to protest. "Exposure to the worst of mankind does not require one to join their throng."

"You are quite right, Watson, and I apologise for any offence caused. I simply wondered if perhaps – with his blood running hot – Captain Hopkirk might have associated Mr Salah's face with that of the enemy, and so reacted without rational thought? But that question lies most properly with either a military or a medical man, so you are certainly best placed to judge." He smiled, defusing any remaining tension between us, and stretched out his hands to warm them at the fire.

I sat forward in my chair, reaching for my tobacco pouch where it lay on the floor. "Perhaps I could engage Hopkirk in army shop talk in the morning?" I suggested, lazily settling back into my seat. "It has always been my experience that young soldiers, even more than old, need little encouragement to discuss their past victories."

Holmes nodded. "If the chance arises, why not, Watson? It is a trivial matter really, but though Mr Salah is not an especially likeable man, I would not have thought him so reprehensible as to invite murder so easily."

He rubbed his eyes, and climbed slowly to his feet. "For now though, I must leave you to your own devices. This country air is exhausting for those of us used to London, and I am in need of sleep."

I bade him good night, then sipped at my whisky and lit a cigar, watching the flames dance in the fire, content in its warm glow. Soon afterwards, I felt my eyelids begin to droop and my head to loll back. The clock chimed a quarter to midnight, and I emerged from a half-doze with a start.

Pausing only to drop my cigar butt in the ashes of the fire, I grudgingly heaved myself to my feet and shuffled towards the door. As soon as I ventured a few feet from the warmth of the fireplace, however, the room turned icy cold, and I increased my pace and hurried into the gloom of the unlit hall, keen to reach my room as quickly as possible.

The combination of haste, poor lighting and my own drowsiness meant that I failed to see Alim Salah until I was almost on top of him.

He stepped unexpectedly from the shadows at the side of the staircase, muttering to himself in his own language, and I barrelled into him, neither of us able to stop our forward progress in time to prevent the collision.

I began to apologise, but he uttered a curse and pushed me hard in the chest. Caught unawares, I stumbled backwards across the hall, all my efforts now expended on maintaining my balance. I banged painfully against an umbrella stand and muttered a curse of my own. Rubbing my hip, I strode back towards Salah, my initial intended apology forgotten in view of the excessive force of his reaction.

Again, however, anything I wished to say was curtailed by Salah's intemperate actions. I was still several feet away from him when he swung a thick wooden walking stick in my direction.

I jumped back, wishing I had a weapon of my own, for clearly the fellow was either mad or drunk. He did not press his advantage, however, but stood where he was, the stick still grasped in his hand but now pointed to the floor.

"Must I be expected to turn the other cheek to every Englishman who assaults me!" he snarled in the darkness. "I am no Christian, sir, and will not act like one!"

I could not see his face, but I caught a whiff of whisky in the air and was slightly reassured. A drunk can be more easily reasoned with than a madman, all things considered.

"Salah..." I began, but for the third time in as many minutes the words I wished to say went unspoken. Without warning, he pushed past me and set off up the main stairs. I considered allowing him to go, but considering his words in light of his recent fight with Captain Hopkirk, it would have been remiss of me to allow him to proceed upstairs, possibly drunk and certainly armed.

"Why don't you give me the walking stick, old chap," I said. "You won't need it tonight, will you?"

He stopped and turned back towards me, staring down at the stick in his hand as though seeing it for the first time. Then he loosened his grip and let it fall onto the carpet, where it slowly rolled down the steps until it lay at my feet. Without another word, he turned his back and disappeared into the shadows at the top of the stairs. A moment later I heard a bedroom door slam shut, and then nothing more.

I picked up the stick and dropped it in the umbrella stand. My hip had begun to ache painfully, and I stood rubbing it in the darkness, toying with the idea that I should take a glass of whisky up to my room in case I needed to numb the pain during the night.

I was forced to acknowledge that there was little legitimate medicinal benefit to be had from such a plan, however, and I had just placed my foot on the bottom stair when an unusual sound disturbed the silence. It reminded me of something, but try as I might I could not place it, not until Alice the maid slowly emerged from the darkness of the kitchens, with a lantern in one hand and the other wrapped around the handle of a voluminous canvas bag, which she was dragging laboriously towards the staircase.

I hastened to help her, taking the handle from her grip and heaving the bag towards me. The pain in my hip flared with every movement, but within a minute at most I had it positioned where she required, at the foot of the stairs.

"What on earth have you got in here, my dear?" I asked.

In reply, Alice handed over the lantern, and wordlessly gestured that I should see for myself. I bent down and angled the light into the top of the bag.

Somewhat prosaically, it was full of boots. Half a dozen pairs at least, of varying types and sizes. I recognised the pair that I had worn earlier.

"I've been cleaning them, sir," the girl explained quietly. "On account of the snow."

"Can I take them anywhere?" I asked.

In the half-light cast by the lantern I was just able to make out the shake of her head. "I've not finished yet," she said. I placed the light on the table that had until recently held a ceramic vase, and bade her goodnight. It was late for so young a girl to be up and working, but with only one servant in the house it must be a long day for her. At least she was being well paid for her troubles, I thought, as I climbed the stairs, yawning and eager for sleep.

It was only once I was in bed and on the verge of sleep that I realised I had completely forgotten to ask Holmes what he had meant when he said he had found the Thorpe Ruby.

Chapter Eight

The Mausoleum

The next morning dawned bright but cold. The snow had finally stopped during the night but still covered the land as far as the eye could see. Alice had evidently been busy, for there was a pair of boots outside every door. As Holmes met me in the corridor, I handed him his pair.

"Buxton's doing, I assume," he said with a smile.

"Indirectly," I replied, and recounted my meetings with Salah and Alice the previous night. He shook his head at my description of Salah's antics, but made no comment.

Buxton was already in the dining room when we entered, halfway through a plate of sausages and eggs.

"Excellent," he exclaimed when he saw the boots we carried. "I hoped that Alice would remember to put those out for everyone. In spite of everything, I should like to make an early start!"

We quickly filled our plates, and took seats beside him. Almost before we had sat down, however, he blurted out a question which had obviously been troubling him.

"I must ask you, Mr Holmes, if you were serious yesterday when you said that you might be able to prevent Mr Salah from buying the manor house? The idea of handing over all my notes to him has kept me awake half the night. It has left me in a terrible state, I'm not ashamed to admit."

Now that I was able to study him more closely, Buxton was looking rather ill. He was exceedingly pale, his eyes were bloodshot, and his fingers tapped incessantly on the table as he spoke. He had not shaved – or rather, he possibly had, but so unevenly that there were patches of his face which looked untouched, alongside others still marked with drops of dry blood where the razor had nicked him.

I glanced across at my friend. He gave a tiny nod – he too had noticed the change in Buxton.

"I did not say quite that, Mr Buxton," he began, in a quiet, measured tone. "I simply said that I hope soon to be able to answer the question of the lost Thorpe Ruby. Having done so, Mr Salah will have no need of your notes."

Buxton shrugged unhappily. "I can only pray that that is the case. That history is my legacy, Mr Holmes. Without it, the years I have spent here will have been entirely wasted." He let his fork fall noisily onto his plate and crumbled a bread roll in his hands. "As I mentioned last night, I had hoped to conduct a formal tour of the house and grounds for all interested parties this morning. However, it seems the snow has rendered that prospect less appealing than it might otherwise have been. Mr Schell has asked his wife to stay here with him, so they will not be joining us, and Mr Reilly says he has seen quite enough of the grounds."

"And the others?" I asked.

"I have yet to speak to either Mr Watt or Judge Pennington, and I am pleased to say that Mr Salah will not be joining us. But Captain Hopkirk says that he will meet us here in half an hour. He is not yet dressed, he says, and has still to shave, but is very keen to see the mausoleum."

"The mausoleum?"

Buxton nodded. "The family mausoleum. Every generation of Thorpes, from the first baron until the middle of the last century, was interred in the oldest building in the grounds, the Thorpe Mausoleum. In recent years, however, the family have been buried in a small graveyard in the East Gardens." He sniffed sadly. "Nothing is as it once was." He stood and brushed crumbs from his waistcoat. "But if you will excuse me, I have some work to do. I shall meet you in the hall in half an hour, if that is acceptable?"

"It is," Holmes confirmed, then continued, "I had hoped to have a little time in which Watson and I might return to the model Crystal Palace, in any case. I have been thinking about ghosts, you see."

The look Buxton gave him was a mixture of sudden anger and disappointment. "Ghosts, Mr Holmes?" he snapped, his temper flaring. "I had thought you were earnest in your claim that you could help, but if this is your idea of a joke, I assure you it is in very poor taste!"

Holmes was placatory. "Not at all, Mr Buxton. I am entirely serious, I assure you. Watson will confirm that I rarely joke, and never about an investigation."

I nodded, though I was as much at a loss as Buxton. For his part, he looked between Holmes and me for a moment, then his shoulders sagged as though all fight had gone out of him again. He gave Holmes one last imploring look, then turned and shuffled from the room. I listened to his heavy tread on the stairs, and watched Holmes chew on a piece of toast.

"Really, Holmes?" I said eventually, "Ghosts?"

In reply, Holmes merely took another bite and smiled.

So cold was it outside that I almost decided to stay in the house by the fire. Only Holmes's direct request that I accompany him convinced me to don boots and a heavy coat to tramp once more far across the snow-covered garden.

Not unexpectedly, the palace was unchanged since the previous day, which made the reason for a second visit so soon after the first perplexing to me. I said as much to Holmes, as he led us on a complete circuit of the peculiar structure, before coming to a thoughtful halt at the front, directly in front of the building's stone section.

"We have returned because this building hides its mystery in the open for all to see, but even so I fail to see it. I am like a newly deaf man to whom a friend wishes to tell a great secret. He shouts and shouts but is not understood. This Crystal Palace shouts to me, Watson, and it irritates me greatly that I cannot hear it."

"It shouts to you, Holmes? In what way? And what is this mystery that you cannot see? I must admit that, to me, it appears much as the same as every other oddity in these gardens; a ridiculous folly constructed to amuse those who should know better."

"It can be both, Watson," Holmes chided me. "Both a folly and a mystery. But what it is not is the same as the lake and the maze and the others. Their purpose is solely to entertain, in one way or another. Consider this Crystal Palace, though," he said, waving his hand in a wide arc to encompass the whole structure. "What stands out so clearly that it cannot be ignored?"

I looked, but as before it appeared to be nothing more than a copy of the marvellous glass edifice I had seen at Sydenham. "If you are deaf, Holmes, then I must be blind into the bargain, for I confess I can see nothing," I said.

"But its very name gives it away!" he cried in exasperation. "It is a palace made of crystal. Every inch of the original is comprised of clear glass panes, and yet this imitation only mimics that in part. The wings," he gestured left and right, "are as expected, and if you peer through them you can see there is nothing inside. But the centre section... why build that of stone, if the intention is not to hide something within it? And if there is a vault inside, it must be possible to gain access to it." He groaned and kicked at the moss-covered ground in frustration. "I thought that approaching the matter afresh this morning might provide new insight..."

His voice tailed off and his eyes took on the hooded aspect that was a reliable indicator he was now deep in thought. He pressed his hands against the stonework, then his face, pushing his cheek hard against the brick as his fingers slowly stepped from stone to stone. I edged towards him, curious to see what he was doing, and he hissed for me to be still. So intense was his concentration that I found myself holding my breath as he shut his eyes and continued his exploration of the palace.

"It is a lock!" he cried at last, stepping back from the wall. "This whole section is a lock!"

I heaved in a deep breath with some relief and raised an eyebrow. "How so, Holmes?" I asked. "What kind of lock?"

He laughed with the delight of discovery and beckoned me

towards him. "Come closer, Watson, and rest your ear lightly on the brickwork here," he said, indicating a spot to his left. "Now listen very carefully."

I did as he asked. Slowly, he laid the palm of his hand on the nearest of the stone "panes" which decorated the palace's central section, and gently pressed inwards. Faintly, as though the sound were coming from far away, I heard a soft click, followed by a brief and swiftly cut off ticking sound. Holmes moved his hand to the next "pane" and repeated the exercise, with the same results.

"Six rows of four squares mimicking individual panes of glass," he said, "plus two more at the bottom, representing the doors in the original structure. And twenty-six letters in the alphabet. This is a coded lock, Watson, I am sure of it. It obviously works on the same basis as the combination of a safe, only using letters rather than numbers. Once you press the panes in the correct sequence, a mechanism opens an entrance of some sort." His admiration was plain. "Quite ingenious, and virtually impossible to crack, as we have no way of knowing the combination, nor even how long it need be."

"Could we not break it open?" I asked. "I assume you think that the missing art collection must be hidden there. Or the Thorpe Ruby!"

Holmes laughed. "Not the ruby, Watson. This was only built forty years ago, remember!" His face clouded. "As for breaking it open, I am not sure that would be a good idea, even if it were possible. These walls are thick, and a great deal of force would be required to break through them. If, however, the missing works of art are indeed inside, the risk of damaging them would be equally great. No, I think it best that we report our findings to Mr

Thompson when we leave, and allow him to take such action as his employer directs."

While he spoke I had idly been trying some of the more obvious combinations, and now I saw that Holmes was observing me with a sardonic smile playing about his lips.

"I very much doubt that Lord Thorpe would use either his own name or the word 'ruby' as the code, old friend," he said. "But we should hurry back, in any case. Buxton said half an hour, and he strikes me as a punctual man."

Holmes was right on both counts, of course. I brushed the dirt from my hands and struck off towards the house, with Holmes bounding ahead of me in excellent fettle.

Holmes's discovery of the stone lock at the Crystal Palace had the effect of re-energising him entirely. He pushed his way through the trees and onto the path with fresh vigour, and strode back to the house as though there were no snow on the ground at all. I followed behind as well as I could, but I admit that in my case the distance seemed no shorter.

Buxton was nowhere to be seen when we arrived back at the house, but Hopkirk was standing at the bottom of the stairs, wearing heavy hiking boots with thick socks, which covered the bottom of his trousers.

Holmes cast a quick sidelong look at me, then announced that he needed to change his trousers, and bounded up the stairs, leaving me alone with the captain. It was my first opportunity to speak to the man, and recalling my conversation with Holmes the night before, I determined to draw him out about his army career.

I began in time-honoured English fashion.

"I don't think I've seen such snow since I was briefly stationed at Michni Fort in Afghanistan in '79. It was cold enough then to freeze the chai in your cup!"

It was true – it had been bitterly cold on the Karapa Pass, and I had been glad to leave after only a few days, but though I had yet to meet a British soldier who would pass up the chance to compare experiences of severe weather abroad, Hopkirk offered up no reply beyond a drawled, "Really?"

"Did you ever see service in Afghanistan?" I tried again, more directly.

Hopkirk seemed suddenly to come to life as he considered the question. "Forgive me, Doctor, I've a lot on my mind just now, what with one thing and another, but that's no excuse for rudeness! No, I never have served in Afghanistan, nor anywhere in that neck of the woods, truth be told. I've spent most of my time pottering about Old England, I'm afraid."

His grin was an infectious one and I immediately found myself smiling back.

"No matter," I said. "This is just as cold as any corner of the Empire."

He laughed and pulled a cigarette case from his jacket pocket. "Unfortunately, I shall need to brave it, nonetheless," he said, lighting one. "These can be quite nasty and I don't want to stink out our host's hallway."

With a wave, he stepped through the door and closed it behind him. Just then, Buxton strolled out of the dining room with Pennington at his side and explained that Amicable Watt would not be joining us. Forced to choose between following the soldier and speaking to the historian, I reluctantly decided that manners decreed that I converse with Buxton. My chat with Captain Hopkirk would have to wait.

The mausoleum was quite a distance from the house, across a steep dip in the ground and at the far side of a small lake. By the time we reached the steps leading down into it, I was quite fatigued and beginning to wish we had never left our armchairs.

Not that it was an unremarkable building. Unlike most of the other structures in the grounds, there was no hint of the fake or the frivolous about the large, round (or more strictly, I later learned, hexagonal) edifice that stood in front of us. Even with snow piled up against it, there was a real sense of solidity in the high stone walls, and the door which Buxton slowly pushed open seemed to have the weight of history behind it.

In contrast to the still blustery weather outside, the interior was quiet and still, the light sandstone of the walls clean and somehow calming. A short flight of stairs led down to a rectangular space lined by niches in the wall, in the shadows of which I could make out what I took to be coffins. Four further caskets, these built of stone with a figure carved on each lid, were laid out, two to each side of the room. A doorway was built into the long wall directly opposite us, and it was to this that Buxton led us.

"The inner crypt," he said, pulling open the door. "There is an admittedly rather stylised likeness of the third Baron de Trop on the wall, and of course his figure is carved more accurately on his sarcophagus."

Pennington groused that tombs were no place for the living and that he would wait in the outer crypt, but the rest of us willingly followed Buxton. The interior of the inner crypt had been designed in a pentagonal shape with long, narrow windows set high up, through which the blue sky could be seen like slashes of paint across the otherwise pale stone. In the centre of the room sat three imposing sarcophagi, eight feet or so in length apiece, and each topped with a life-size carving of its occupant, depicted in repose with his arms crossed over an impressively wrought broadsword.

On each facing wall was a painted mural, still in good condition in spite of the centuries. Upon close examination, I discovered they were all of the infamous third baron. Of his early years, there was no sign: the first panel showed a knight in full armour kneeling before a figure wearing a crown whom I took to be the king. The king's hand rested on the knight's in a benediction. The second panel – presumably the one Buxton had mentioned – showed the knight with no helmet, in Crusader's garb riding alongside other Christian warriors in battle. The final panel was a more detailed version of the carving we had seen in The Silent Man and depicted a tableau of a horribly wounded knight holding off a dozen men with scimitars, blood pouring from a multitude of wounds to his face and body. Grotesquely, what was clearly intended to be the man's tongue lay in a pool of blood to his side. I shuddered, and Holmes walked across.

"Hmm, that is rather vivid, Watson," he commented, though with no real interest. He examined each panel briefly, then stood and stared up at the windows, twenty feet above us.

"This crypt dates back to the time of the first baron, I believe you said, Mr Buxton? Yet these panels each relate to the third?"

"Yes, Mr Holmes. The murals were added during the Reformation as the coming-of-age contribution of the Thorpe heir of the time. The third baron is quite famous locally, of course," he explained.

"And which of this trio of caskets contains his remains?"

Buxton pointed to the far right-hand side.

Holmes immediately strode across to the sarcophagus indicated, pulled out his magnifying glass and knelt down before it. He shuffled around the entire length and breadth of the Crusader's last resting place, then repeated the exercise on the other side, pausing occasionally to dust at the stone with his fingertip. Apparently satisfied, he rose and did the same with the other two caskets. Finally, he stared at the windows again, reaching his hands into the air as if he thought he could leap up to them.

"Everything seems in order," he eventually declared, though I could not say what he had expected to find out of place. Surely he had not seriously thought to discover evidence that de Trop's restless spirit had indeed ever left its tomb?

He glanced quickly around the walls once more, but seemed already to have lost interest in the mausoleum. Hopkirk stood in the inner doorway smoking, and as Holmes strode towards him, turned and led the way back through to Pennington and from there to the snowy grounds outside.

Chapter Nine

Death in the Cellar

The manor house was considerably busier on our return than it had been on our departure.

The Schells were in the main hall, where Mrs Schell was reading Scott's Ivanhoe to her husband, who sat before the fire with a rug on his lap. Reilly was in the dining room, drinking tea, the empty plate that had once held his breakfast before him. He looked up as I popped my head around the door and gave a nod of greeting. Like Buxton earlier, he looked tired and out of sorts, and I found myself agreeing with his own earlier claim that his constitution was perhaps not well suited to English weather. Watt was seated at the other end of the table, so absorbed in an enormous pile of sausages and eggs that he did not even acknowledge my presence. Of Salah there was no sign, but given that Hopkirk had settled himself by the window in the main hall, I was not overly disappointed by his absence. A repeat of the previous day's violence was to be avoided if at all possible.

Holmes had taken himself off to his room, and Buxton informed me that he had some preparations to make in the cellars for an afternoon tour of the catacombs, which the solicitor Thompson had asked him to conduct. At a loose end, therefore, and having no wish to interrupt Reilly's gloomy reverie, I lit a gasper and stood in the main doorway, watching a family of small birds cavorting in the eaves.

I had just finished my cigarette and flicked it into the snow, when I heard the heavy sound of running footsteps behind me and then felt a hand grip my arm.

"Dr Watson!" Buxton gasped loudly in my ear. "You must come at once! There has been the most terrible accident!"

Behind him, the other guests – roused by Buxton's obvious panic – had begun to gather. Captain Hopkirk, used to command, was the first to react.

"An accident?" he asked. "What kind of accident?"

Buxton's face was white as chalk and his mouth trembled as he spoke. "It is Mr Salah. I fear he is dead!"

I heard Mrs Schell gasp from the door of the main hall, and then her husband's voice, calling from within the room, asking her what was going on. She went to tell him, which was for the best, as Buxton went on, "He is in the cellar, with his head split to the bone!"

The tumult had plainly reached the upstairs rooms, for at that moment Holmes came down, with Pennington close behind, just in time to hear Buxton's description. He did not break his stride, but quickly moved past the little crowd of people and headed for the door behind the main stairs, which Buxton had earlier told us led down to the cellars.

* * *

The cellar was accessible from within the house by a staircase that began at the rear of the deserted servants' quarters and came out in a musty, dark space. Buxton edged past us with a muttered apology. "There is no light down here, I'm afraid, Mr Holmes. If you will wait here for a moment?"

He laid his lantern down on the ground and attempted to push open a pair of wooden doors on the right-hand wall. The weight of the snow outside was sufficient, however, that it was not until Captain Hopkirk and Mr Watt added their strength that they were able to force them ajar. Fresh air and natural light entered the room but, even then, the sunken position of the cellar meant that only the area immediately in front of the doors was illuminated.

Not that there was a great deal to see. The room was heaped with rubbish, and almost entirely covered in mould and dust. As Buxton raised his lantern and moved further inside, I made out the shapes of rusted machinery and heaps of rotting wood which had been dumped against the walls, and some old chairs, missing legs and backs in most cases. Wooden barrels were stacked on one side of the door and what appeared to be an old sideboard on the other. In other words, the common detritus of a country estate that had been all but abandoned for half a century.

Through the open doors I could see a stone wall with a metal railing at its top. Presumably there were stairs at the sides providing access to the rear of the house. The only other exit, save the one that we had used, was through a smaller door in the far corner.

"The body is just here," Buxton said, pointing to the other corner, behind a collection of metal parts, at whose original purpose I could not even begin to guess. Holmes took the lantern, which he held aloft for additional light, and we gingerly made our way across the damp stone floor to examine poor Salah's remains.

He was dressed in a long coat and boots, much as he had been when last I saw him, standing at the front door with Reilly. Now, however, he lay on his back with his arms splayed and his legs crossed over one another. His head was turned to one side and, as Holmes leaned across and the lantern light shone directly on his face, it was easy to see the wicked gash on the back of his skull and the pool of blood underneath.

"If you could hold this," Holmes said, handing the lantern back to Buxton. I watched as he steadied himself with one hand then climbed gingerly over the rusted metal. Once on the other side, he retrieved the lamp and knelt for some time in minute examination of the corpse. Only after several minutes had passed did he stand and announce himself satisfied, and Hopkirk scrambled over to help lift the body across the clutter of the room and lay it out on a clear patch of floor by the double doorway.

There could be no doubt that the gash on his skull was the cause of death. It was deep and wide and the collar of his shirt and coat were heavy with blood. It was not, however, the only mark of violence on Salah's head. Several more shallow abrasions surrounded the main injury, extending to the top of his neck.

"What could Mr Salah have been doing down here?" Buxton asked querulously. "The only thing of interest is the entrance to the catacombs." He pointed to the small door in the corner. "He should have told me, if he wished to view them."

He seemed already to have forgotten his earlier anger with Salah, and his fear that the man would steal his research from him. Or, perhaps, wished us to do so.

Holmes's voice was scathing. "I very much doubt that he came into this cellar of his own accord – or under his own steam, for that matter."

"Not of his own accord?" I had not noticed that Reilly had joined us, but he nudged Buxton out of his way and bent over the body. "Are you suggesting he was brought down here? And then killed?"

"I cannot be quite so precise at the moment, Mr Reilly," Holmes replied. He crouched on his haunches by Salah's waist and grasped a portion of his coat in his hand. He squeezed, and a thin stream of water trickled from it to the floor. "As you can see, Salah was dressed to go outdoors, and the fact that his coat is wet indicates that he did so. It was not snowing last night, so he would not have become this wet by simple walking, thus I suggest he fell in deep snow at some point and the snow became trapped inside his coat and afterwards melted.

"Had he done so and then later been inveigled into coming to the cellar, he would surely have changed out of his wet things first. That he came – or, I suggest, was brought – to this place through the house and not directly from outside via these cellar doors is indisputable: we all saw how difficult it was for you to open them against the snow that has built up outside. No, he was carried here, I believe. Whether he was already dead when this happened, or merely about to die, I cannot say for certain."

In the dim light, it was impossible to see clearly the expression on anyone's face, but Reilly muttered something I could not make out as Holmes concluded his summary, and Buxton took a step backwards, as though to distance himself from the body. Hopkirk, I realised, was nowhere to be seen.

He could be heard behind us, however. "See here, Mr Holmes," he called. "There's blood on this cutter."

He was crouched over a sturdy iron pipe from which protruded a series of curved metal blades. As we came over, he dropped his lantern to the outermost blade. In its light, I saw a line of blood running down one blade, largely dried but as I discovered when I reached down, still tacky to the touch.

"It's quite fresh, Holmes," I said quietly. "It's been there no more than a few hours, I'd say. Certainly since last night."

To my surprise, Reilly suddenly laughed. There was a definite note of hysteria in the sound. "Well then, Mr Holmes," he said, "it seems that your guess has gone astray!"

"How so, Mr Reilly?" Holmes replied.

Reilly was still chuckling. The sound rang hollowly in the large empty space. "Why, surely, it's plain enough? Mr Salah admitted he wished to discover the lost ruby. Believing it to be in the catacombs beneath the house, he dressed for exploring and sneaked down here in the dead of night. He had already said that he intended to stroll the grounds at night – but, not wishing to alert anyone to his specific actions, he brought no lantern and stumbled in the darkness, banging his head on this machinery. Disoriented and confused, he stumbled further into this death trap of a cellar and fell again, expiring where we found him."

"And the wet clothes, old man?" Hopkirk asked.

Reilly paused for only a second. "Perhaps he intended to come in by way of the cellar doors. Finding them impassable, he was forced to re-route via the main house. It would be easy enough to slip on the path to the back door."

Holmes said nothing, but Hopkirk caught my eye and smiled. "That seems a trifle far-fetched to me," he said, shaking his head. "Don't get me wrong; I've seen more than my fair share of men groggy from a head wound, and they can do funny things. But even if we were to accept that anyone would come down here without a lantern – and I, for one, have my doubts about that – even if we were to accept that, I won't have it that anybody who measured his length in a dark room would press on, rather than just heading for home with his tail between his legs!"

Holmes shook his head. "I am sure that what you say is true, Captain Hopkirk, but I do not think we need concern ourselves with anything so imprecise as individual human responses to refute Mr Reilly's contention. The shape, thickness and direction of the stain on the blade all point to a heavy drop of blood falling from a height and catching its edge rather than the smaller amount that would be deposited should someone have fallen and cracked their head against it. Or," he went on in the same measured tone, "someone barking their shin against the metal while carrying a heavy object inside."

"Like a body!" exclaimed Buxton in alarm.

"Indeed," confirmed Holmes. "Which is unfortunate for us, as the killer would be considerably easier to identify if all we had to do was ask everyone to roll up their trouser legs. In any case, we need to take Mr Salah's body up to his room. Mr Buxton, how can we best contact the authorities?"

Buxton frowned. "There is no policeman in the village, Mr Holmes. The nearest one is in Stainforth, which is the next station up the line. We can telegram, but if the track's still blocked, they'll need to come by road and that could take some time."

"If you could see to the telegram as soon as possible, then, that would be excellent. And perhaps another to Mr Thompson, apprising him of the situation?"

"But what shall I say, Mr Holmes?" The little historian actually wrung his hands in anguish. "I'm afraid that I'm more comfortable with murders where everyone has been safely dead for centuries."

"I quite understand." Holmes placed a hand on his shoulder. "If you can provide me with the appropriate details, I shall go down to the village myself and send the telegrams. Watson," he turned to me before I could say a word, "perhaps you and Captain Hopkirk could move the body? Mr Watt, if you and Judge Pennington—" He looked about but if the judge had followed us down, he had returned upstairs in the meantime. "In any case, Mr Watt, could you find the maid and ask her to brew up several pots of strong tea and serve them in the dining room? And Mr Reilly, if you could inform the Schells?" He coughed. "At this point, I think it would be best if we were simply to describe Mr Salah's death as a tragic occurrence." He glanced over at Reilly. "That is, after all, the most we can state with absolute certainty."

Each of us nodded our agreement and I turned to Hopkirk to ask him if he would go and fetch a blanket from one of the bedrooms, with which we might transport Salah's body. By the time I turned back, Holmes was already chivvying Buxton up the stairs, keen to be on his way to the village. In a sudden fit of curiosity, I walked across to the door to the catacombs and tried the handle. It swung open easily enough, but I could see nothing inside but darkness. The smell of wet rock and decay was carried on a cold breeze from the depths of the caves and drifted over me. Recalling my thought back in Baker Street that a criminal case was just what Holmes needed, I shivered, and then closed the door again.

* * *

I was unsurprised to find Holmes waiting for me upstairs in the hallway. Everyone else had dispersed to carry out his or her allotted task, and I knew he would wish to speak to me.

"When exactly did you come across Salah last night, Watson?" he asked quietly, pulling me inside the library in order to ensure complete privacy.

"A little after a quarter to midnight," I replied. "I was dozing in the main hall just before, and it was sound of the clock chime that woke me and sent me to bed."

"And he was in good health?"

"Yes, though as I said before, he had been drinking."

"And he was aggressive?"

"Very much so."

"What about time of death? I know you cannot be exact, but any guide you can provide...?"

I had had too little time to perform more than a cursory examination, but he had not been dead long, which made precise timings a little easier. "This is only an estimate, you understand, Holmes. But, allowing for the cold of the cellar, and judging by the lividity of the flesh at the extremities and the degree of movement in the limbs, I would say he was certainly dead by one this morning."

He nodded firmly, as though satisfied in some way by my words, then wordlessly indicated that I should follow him back into the hall.

"What is it, Holmes?" I asked him.

Rather than reply, he crouched down on his haunches and pointed at the floor beside him. "Something I noticed while I was waiting for you. The markings are faint but unmistakable, Watson. Do you see them?"

I squatted beside him, and stared for all I was worth, but in truth, I could see nothing unusual. "Footprints?" I ventured eventually, still uncertain.

In reply, he indicated that I should follow him as he strode behind the main staircase and back into the servants' quarters. He bypassed the stairway to the cellars as I hurried behind him, quickly moved through the kitchens and then stopped suddenly.

"Footprints," he said, tracing the shape of one, clearer on the less frequently swept kitchen floor. "Faint, but fresh. And extremely instructive."

He paused and raised an eyebrow, in the manner he occasionally exhibited when he intended that I should hazard a guess as to an item's significance.

"They are certainly a man's prints, by their size," I suggested after a moment's thought. "So they do not belong to the maid. Salah's killer?"

"That would be a logical inference, Watson. We can go a little further yet in support of my supposition from downstairs though, I think. These footprints lead into the house. Someone came inside last night or early this morning. There is only one set of prints and no sign of dragging, so the killer was already carrying Salah's body. And yet the print itself is relatively faint." He laid a finger across his lips thoughtfully. "I wonder..." he muttered to himself.

Like a hound on a scent, he followed the trail of faint smudges to the back door of the house and pushed it open. Due to the angle and design of the rear of the building, which acted as an inadvertent buttress against the weather, little snow had gathered on the steps directly outside and so no further prints were visible. Holmes gave a small cry of triumph, however, and went immediately to the boot scraper attached to the top step. He prodded at it with his finger, and a long, wet sliver of ice-specked mud fell away, to land atop the small heap of frozen dirt beneath it.

"Whoever it was, he had the sense to thoroughly clean his boots of dirt before he entered." He cast about the surrounding area, his eyes flicking around quickly, never resting on one place for long.

He would have said more, but just then I heard someone calling my name through the open cellar doors. I had completely forgotten that I was supposed to be helping move Salah's body!

"Better that nobody knows any of this yet," Holmes cautioned, already moving back up the stairs. "In retrospect, it was a mistake for me to conjecture at all in the cellar just now. We cannot forget that, though we have no official role here, everyone bar you and I is a suspect. For now, you should go and assist Captain Hopkirk, and I shall take myself to the village. I have something of my own to do at the post office, in any case."

With that, he disappeared into the house. I kicked the snow from my boots and followed him, just in time to hear the front door slam shut. Hopkirk shouted again, so I lit a lantern and trudged down the interior stairs to the cellar, to help with the unsavoury task of transporting Salah's body to his room.

Salah had been a large man, and I suspected that it would be a difficult task to move his body in a decorous fashion. Hopkirk, however – for all his apparent dislike of the Ghuridian while he was alive – was commendably solicitous of his dignity in death. When I arrived back in the cellar, he was busily clearing the more cumbersome obstacles from the path to the stairs. It took some time, but eventually we laid Salah's body on a plank of wood, wrapped in several blankets. Hopkirk took one end of the plank and I the other and, between us, we slowly moved him up first the cellar stairs and then those in the main hall, before laying him on the bed in his room.

We removed the blankets and the plank and, as his coat remained wet and stained, I slid it too from his frame, exposing a canary-yellow jacket underneath. Hopkirk suggested we give the ruined coat to Alice to dispose of, but I knew Holmes would wish to examine it more thoroughly later.

As I opened the cupboard door to hang it up, however, something fell from a pocket and rolled under the bed. I crouched down and reached for it in the darkness.

It was a pocket watch, an expensive one of excellent manufacture, but the front was smashed and the hands stopped at a minute to one. I handed it wordlessly to Hopkirk.

"Cometh the hour, eh?" he said, turning the timepiece over in his hand and running a finger across the gold of the back. "It's got his initials on it, 'A.S.', so it was his, true enough."

"It must have smashed when he fell," I said, holding out a hand to take it back.

"When he was attacked," Hopkirk stated with conviction. "We've both seen service, Doctor. We know the difference between deliberate and accidental death."

On reflection, I was not sure that I did. I had encountered a number of people whom I had assumed to have died due to misadventure only for Holmes to uncover their murder, and assumed a criminal cause for several corpses which had turned out to be nothing but sad accidents. There was no point in saying as much to Hopkirk, though, so I satisfied myself with an equivocal grunt and dropped the watch in my pocket, to show Holmes later.

When I opened the cupboard to hang up Salah's coat, however, we were treated to a second surprise in as many minutes. The cupboard (and, on further investigation, the chest of drawers under the window) was entirely empty, nor was there any sign of suitcase or bags in the room. There was no hairbrush on the dressing table, and no shaving kit in the small sink in the corner. It was as if Salah had never been in the room before we carried him there.

Hopkirk whistled between his teeth. "Well, that's a rum state of affairs!" he declared after I showed him the empty drawers. "Where's all his fancy coats gone, eh?"

I shook my head. I remembered Reilly's claim that Salah might have been looking for the entrance to the catacombs – if nothing else, the fact that his clothing had disappeared ruled that unlikely possibility out. Reilly could hardly claim the dead man had planned to find the long-lost ruby at his first attempt and then to abscond like a thief in the night!

"I think perhaps we should gather the others and go back downstairs to await Holmes's return," I said, as I pulled a sheet over Salah's face.

Hopkirk nodded his agreement. "Capital idea, Doctor," he said cheerfully. "Always best to have the troops in one place in times of peril, eh?"

He was an odd fellow, this Captain Hopkirk. I remembered his earlier attitude and the manner in which he had fought Salah, and then contrasted it with his current bonhomie and his sensible and helpful attitude to recent events. I told myself that a soldier was far less inclined to be troubled by sudden death, but even so, he was surely due credit for the level-headed way he had reacted. I had to admit, I found myself warming to him.

We did not have long to wait for Holmes to return, which was fortunate, for as I entered the main hall, I was buffeted by questions from all sides. Buxton had, it transpired, taken it upon himself to tell everyone that Holmes and I worked for Scotland Yard, and that we would be investigating Salah's untimely demise. I glared at him in annoyance, but if he noticed, he gave no indication, instead giving me a small, happy nod, as though he had done me a great favour.

Mr Schell, whom I had all but forgotten was even resident in the house, was the first to speak, using his age as a weapon by which to push his query to the front of the queue.

"I hope you can assure me that Mrs Schell and I are in no danger, sir!" he barked. "I do not myself read fiction, but Mr Buxton informs me that you are a writer of novels of criminal affairs, and your companion, Mr Holmes, an investigative agent? I cannot deny, I would prefer the involvement of more qualified men, but until they arrive, I place our safety in your hands, sir!"

His speech complete, the old man seemed uninterested in any response from me. He breathed heavily and stumbled backwards, until his wife caught him by the elbow. She led him to one of the fireside chairs, into which he carefully lowered himself. She stood at his shoulder and watched as Judge Pennington stepped forward to fill the gap her husband had vacated.

"The captain says that Salah's clothing is missing?" he began in a hectoring tone more suited to handing down a sentence from the bench than speaking to a fellow guest. "Is this true, Dr Watson? Well, speak up, man!"

I would have preferred to keep that information quiet until I could speak to Holmes but I had not specifically told Hopkirk as much, so I could hardly blame him for discussing it. I should be pleased, I supposed, that he had not mentioned the broken watch. Fortunately, I had no opportunity to reply, for at that moment Holmes walked in.

His face was red with the cold, but he was unmistakably pleased about something. The beginnings of a smile played about his mouth as he pulled off his gloves and hat and placed them on a table. He shrugged off his coat and laid it alongside them, then smoothed back his hair with his hands.

"Gentlemen – and Mrs Schell, of course – if I might have your attention for a moment!" he said loudly, drawing every eye in the room towards him. "I have been to the village and sent telegrams to both Mr Thompson, the Thorpe family solicitor, and to Inspector Fisher in Stainforth, as requested by Mr Buxton. Given the urgent nature of the present situation, I requested an immediate reply from both, and can report that the inspector hopes to be with us tomorrow morning, and that as I have had some experience with the police in the past, Mr Thompson has asked me to carry out whatever preliminary investigations I deem fit in the meantime."

There was a flurry of comments and complaints as everyone in the room spoke at once, but Holmes ignored it and continued in the same tone.

"With that in mind, and for reasons of safety, may I ask that everyone return to their rooms for the moment, and I shall speak to each individual in turn, primarily to ascertain their location at the probable time of Mr Salah's death." He held up a hand to stop a fresh wave of noise. "Of course, I will not be acting in any official capacity, thus anyone is entirely within his rights to refuse to speak to me, should he prefer to await Inspector Fisher's arrival."

I scanned the room as Holmes spoke, eager to spot anyone who reacted suspiciously, but it seemed that everyone was too shocked by events to do anything more than murmur softly to their nearest neighbour, then turn and quietly leave the room.

The only exception to this rule was Judge Pennington, who immediately marched up to Holmes and, from a distance of no more than two feet, declared that he had no intention of being interviewed by anyone other than a professional policeman.

"We have no guarantee that the killer will not strike again," he announced loudly, "and I hardly think Mr Holmes can protect us." He looked about for support, but the only person still left in the room was Amicable Watt, who shrugged and smiled non-committally. Pennington, temporary bereft of an audience, snapped, "I shall be in my room until morning. Please arrange for the girl to bring me sandwiches and tea at six," and stalked from the room, his held high as though he had just won an important point.

I watched him go, then, once the room was empty, handed Holmes the broken watch. He crossed to the window to take advantage of the better light there and twisted it this way and that in his hands, screwing a jeweller's loupe in his eye to examine the watch for telltale marks. After a minute of this, he slipped both loupe and watch into his pocket.

"We must find somewhere private in which to interview everyone," he said. "In a house of this size, there is bound to be a suitable location."

Chapter Ten

Interviews

We set up a table in one of the empty rooms in the deserted east wing and while Holmes sat and considered his questions, I led each guest in to see him. As I remarked to him at one point, it must be very like Lestrade's daily police life at Scotland Yard. He did not smile.

My role in the proceedings was to watch each guest as he answered Holmes's questions and to detect, if I could, any obvious signs of nervousness or prevarication. Thompson's telegram had been very clear: he would be grateful for anything which Holmes could do to bring matters to a conclusion as quickly as possible, but he was to remember that these were guests of Thompson's employer and act accordingly. The unspoken intimation was clear – one of these people would, it was to be hoped, make a successful offer for the manor, and it would be impolitic for Holmes to jeopardise that with any over-aggressive questioning. In London, I have no doubt that Holmes would have washed his hands of the whole affair, rather than work under such strictures, but marooned as we were in the country, he had grudgingly agreed to ask only very general questions.

The first guests to be interviewed were the Schells, who arrived together, Mr Schell having insisted that his wife was not to be spoken to alone by "two young men". I smiled at the description – it was several years since I had been described in such terms – but in the absence of any objection on Holmes's part, invited them to be seated.

As had been the case earlier, Mr Schell wasted no time. "I suppose you want to know where Mrs Schell and I were last night and this morning? We were in our room the whole time. I was feeling unwell, and could not sleep, so when my wife returned from her walk, she read to me briefly, and then I took a sleeping draught. We were asleep by about a quarter past eleven, I should say. We awoke at seven this morning, as is our normal practice, and my wife supervised my morning exercises before breakfast. Afterwards, I sat in the hall and my wife read to me again. We were together the entire time."

He sat back and glared at Holmes, as though daring him to contradict his statement. The change in the man since our initial meeting seemed, at first sight, to be marked. Then he had been quiet, frail and confused, apparently barely aware of his surroundings, but now it was possible to see the shadow of the man who had built a commercial empire. Yet, on closer inspection, it was plain that a shadow was all that it was. His liver-spotted hands lay flat on the table as he spoke but, as I watched him, I saw them twitch very slightly whenever he spoke. His eyes were rheumy, and his lips dry as paper, even though he licked them unconsciously as soon as he stopped speaking. I respected him for the effort, but this new, stronger Frederick Schell was as much a performance as any I had seen on the stage.

Conversely, Mrs. Schell, so vivacious and full of life at dinner on our first evening in the house, was quiet and submissive, saying nothing and deferring to her husband entirely. When Holmes leaned forward and asked her if everything he had said was as she remembered it, she nodded, but not before her husband peevishly snapped in Holmes's direction, 'Will you call me a liar, sir!'

"My apologies, Mr Schell," Holmes said smoothly. "I simply meant whether your wife might recall any small detail that had slipped your mind. We believe that Mr Salah died at some point between midnight and one this morning – if she could pinpoint exactly when you retired to bed, for instance, that would be very helpful."

Schell tapped a bony finger on the table and repeated, "I have told you – we retired at a quarter after eleven!" As he did so, I noticed Mrs Schell give a tiny shiver and cast her eyes in my direction for just a moment.

"As you say," replied Holmes. "Eleven fifteen it is, then." He shifted in his seat and laid his own hands flat on the table. "I have only one more question, you will be pleased to hear. I wonder, did you or Mrs Schell speak to, or even see, Mr Salah after he went to his room on his return from the village yesterday?"

Schell shook his head violently. "We did not! And I can assure you that if I had, I would have taken a whip to the man!" Tiny drops of spittle flecked his mouth as he struggled to his feet. "Do not think I did not hear the filthy slander put about by that man! That he should... That..." His knees seemed to crumple and he swayed forward, resting the top of his thighs against the table. "If someone killed the man then he has my thanks, that is all I have to say. Now if you will excuse us…"

He held out a hand to his wife, and she was instantly on her feet, helping him to turn and leave the room. His short burst of fury had cost him dear, and he shuffled out, the laboured sound of his breathing audible even once he had left.

"He should not exert himself like that," I remarked to Holmes, with a mental note that I should check up on Mr Schell in a medical capacity later on. "He is clearly not a well man."

"But he is a rich man, Watson, and for some young wives the combination of the two is a potent one."

There was little I could say to that, so I said nothing. Instead, I went out to find Mr Buxton, who had agreed to speak to Holmes next.

It quickly became clear that we would learn little more from anyone else than we had from the Schells.

Buxton had at least been awake after eleven, but as he had gone to his room immediately after leaving us, and had neither seen nor heard anything further, he was not in a position to shed light on anything that occurred later.

"I was copying out certain of the more important parts of my history, you see, Mr Holmes," he explained. "The fair copy extends to two hundred and fifty pages and so is too large to copy in the short period of time before the sale of the estate, but I thought if I could save the key sections…" His shoulders slumped and he sighed. "Of course, it is not so pressing now…"

"No, it is not," Holmes agreed. "Did you speak to Mr Salah at all last night or this morning?"

"Not since I passed him in the hallway upstairs, shortly after his argument with Captain Hopkirk. We did not speak, however. I had no desire to speak to him, to be frank, and so pretended to be engrossed in the book I was carrying."

"And you did not see him after that? Not when he returned from the village, for instance?"

"I'm afraid not. I ate a sandwich and went straight to the library. I saw nobody."

As Buxton spoke something clicked in the back of my mind, like a sudden terrible itch which cannot possibly be ignored. There was something that I was forgetting, something that Buxton had said, which had forced itself to the tip of my tongue.

"But did you not speak to him this morning, to ask if he wished to accompany us on our excursion?"

That was it! The question tumbled out of my mouth unbidden and without conscious thought. I expected the little historian to flush and colour in embarrassment, but instead he merely shook his head dejectedly. "As I explained to Mr Holmes when he asked me earlier, I was so vexed with Mr Salah over his unpleasant behaviour that I did not even knock on his door. Had I done so, we would at least have known that he was dead that much sooner."

He seemed utterly crestfallen, and though Holmes assured him that it would have made no difference, it was clear that Salah's death had affected him deeply. I wondered briefly if between the army and my time with Holmes I had become less sensitive to death than other men.

It was a thought for another time, though. Holmes had already risen and thanked Buxton for his frankness. After I had shown him to the door I turned to Holmes. "Why did you believe his story?" I asked. "That he did not attempt to wake Salah, I mean?"

Holmes shrugged. "Had he killed him he would have said that Salah was not in his room at all. After all, what was the purpose of the missing clothing, if not to suggest that he had left the manor of his own free will?"

As ever, it seemed painfully simple when explained by Holmes. I nodded my understanding, and opened the door. Hopkirk was pacing up and down outside and I asked him to come in.

Like the Schells, Hopkirk had been in bed and asleep well before midnight. He too had not laid eyes on Salah after he had stormed upstairs after their fight. Holmes, of course, quizzed him about that altercation.

"I should be more comfortable if we could allow that occasion to fade into the past, Mr Holmes, if you don't mind," he said, with a smile. "Of course, if the police chap who's on his way insists on dredging it up, I'll tell him what I can, but in the circumstances…" He allowed his voice to tail off, implying that any further enquiry by Holmes would be in the poorest taste. "One doesn't wish to speak ill of the dead…"

"Even so, Captain…" Holmes was at his most conciliatory, but it was obvious even to Hopkirk, who did not know him, that he would not be satisfied with anything less than a full answer. He shrugged and lit a cigarette, then leaned across the table towards us, dropping his voice as he did so.

"The suggestion he made was one which related to Mrs Schell

and myself and the... honourable nature... or otherwise of our friendship." He grimaced. "I believe I mentioned to Dr Watson at dinner the other night that I have known the Schells for several years, and have spent each of the past three summers in their company. Obviously, in that time, I have become very close to them both, though Freddie's poor health means that I have spent more time with Mrs Schell than would otherwise have been the case. It seems that Salah saw that closeness and drew entirely the wrong conclusions from it." He gave a tired shrug, as though this little speech had exhausted him. "He mentioned those incorrect and hurtful conclusions to Mr Reilly and, there being no love lost between those two, Reilly passed them on to me. And... well, you saw what happened afterwards."

"Of course, there is no truth to anything Mr Salah said." Holmes framed the sentence as a statement of fact, but Hopkirk treated it as a question nonetheless.

"Of course not. Even were I not an officer and a gentleman, Freddie Schell is a good friend. It was he, in fact, who suggested that I might wish to come here this weekend. I was left a considerable sum by another friend," he explained, "and Freddie knew that I wished to put down roots back home."

"He suggested that you might wish to bid on a property in which he himself had an interest? That is a good friend indeed."

"He is a good friend. But I do not believe he thought my little inheritance great enough to make me a serious contender should he decide that Thorpe Manor suited his purposes. And, in truth, it probably is not. But it would be handy to have me on hand to keep Mrs Schell company.

"Do not be fooled, Mr Holmes. Freddie Schell is a good man,

and a good friend, but he did not become a rich man by being overly generous in business. He is physically not what he was, but in his mind, he is as sharp as ever."

"I had noticed that, Captain Hopkirk," Holmes assured him. "But to return to Mr Salah, I worry that, had I not intervened, you might have done him serious injury during your fight."

Hopkirk nodded, his face colouring. "I might at that, and nobody would be sorrier afterwards. It does me no credit, as an experienced soldier, to lose my temper and become involved in something little better than a street brawl with a civilian." He looked up and held Holmes's gaze steadily. "I am greatly ashamed of my behaviour in that regard. I should have warned the man off, not resorted to fisticuffs. And I should never have lost myself so much that I almost descended into brute savagery."

A silence followed which neither man seemed keen to break.

"Very well, Captain Hopkirk," Holmes said finally. "And you saw no one else before you went to sleep?"

For a second, Hopkirk hesitated, and I wondered if he were about to recall something. But he simply shook his head. "No, nothing. I had a glass of whisky already in my room, and saw nobody until this morning when Buxton knocked on my door."

He allowed his eyes to slide across to me. "I wanted to ask, is it established how Salah died, Dr Watson?" he asked. "Was it the blow to his head after all?"

In all honesty, I was as sure as I could be that that was the cause of death, but I thought it best not to commit myself to a definitive answer yet. "Perhaps," I replied. "It is impossible to say for certain until an autopsy is carried out, however."

"Of course." Hopkirk took a silver cigarette case from his pocket and offered it around. I took one, but found it a rather harsh blend and wished I had not. "I wish I could be of more assistance. Is it certain that Salah's watch was broken at the time he died?" he asked suddenly. "I admit that it seems something better suited to the cheap novels my batman reads than to real life!"

"Such things do happen in real life, Captain, though I agree that it is convenient for us."

"And for the police when they arrive. Will that be in the morning, do you think? I do wonder how their presence will affect the estate auction." He had leaned back in his seat, but now he glanced round then hunched forward again. "I don't mind telling you that I do not intend to bid. I know that Freddie Schell thinks Salah's death will attract adverse reporting, and if that ridiculous outfit of Reilly's is any measure, he's not too keen on our English weather. But even so, the estate's a bit too rich for my blood, now that I see it!"

He grinned and stubbed out his cigarette. "But is there anything further I can help you with, gentlemen?" he asked.

Holmes shook his head. "Not at the moment, Captain Hopkirk. You have been very helpful as it is."

Hopkirk stood and offered his hand, then marched briskly to the door. He stopped for a second with the handle in his hand. "Remember, if there's anything at all I can do, just say the word. I've not read any of your books, Doctor, but I know who you are, and it'd be something to tell the grandchildren to be included in one of them!"

The movement of Holmes's head in reply was not quite a nod, and not quite a shake of the head, but it was enough for Hopkirk. He grinned again, turned smartly on his heel and was gone.

"Do you think he was telling the truth?" I asked Holmes. "He's a likeable chap, but there was something not quite right about him. You saw his hesitation when you asked if he had been downstairs for a nightcap?"

Holmes nodded. "I did. And the way he immediately changed the subject." He stubbed out the cigarette Hopkirk had given him and reached into a pocket for his pipe. "I am not sure if he is exactly likeable, Watson, but he is certainly keen to be liked," he said, as he pressed a plug of shag into the bowl. "But he will bear watching." He picked a shred of tobacco from his tongue and grimaced. "I am never too trusting of man with such appalling taste in cigarettes."

The testimony of Amicable Watt proved disappointing. Though he was obviously keen to become involved in any way he could, he claimed to have switched off his bedroom light at 10 p.m. and to have known nothing further until almost the same hour the following morning.

"I'd tell you different if I could," he declared despondently, "in fact, I wish I could. I like a mystery as much as I like a secret, and I'd no love for the late Mr Salah, so it's no skin off my back if he's dead. But I'm a heavy sleeper, and that's the truth."

He looked crest-fallen at making such an admission, but as there was nothing more he could tell us, Holmes thanked him for his time and sent him on his way.

If the other guests – Pennington excluded – had proven to be a mixed but generally compliant bag in terms of their willingness to co-operate with Holmes's enquiries, Reilly proved utterly obdurate in his refusal to do so.

Hopkirk had mentioned that he had seen the older man in the corridors of the east wing just before his own appointment, and so I had expected him to be waiting outside the door when Hopkirk left, but to my surprise there was no sign of him. I looked in his room, but he was not there, nor was he in the main hall or the dining room. It was only as I made my way back to the east wing, where Holmes still sat, that I literally bumped into him as he came out of one of the empty rooms that made up the abandoned wing.

"I do apologise," I said before I recognised him then, doing so, went on, "but this is a fortuitous meeting, for I am looking for you, as it happens. Mr Holmes is ready to speak to you, if you have a moment."

I turned away and began to walk towards Holmes's room, in every expectation that he would follow, and had taken half a dozen steps before I realised that he had not moved.

"It's my turn to apologise, Doctor, but I have decided that there is nothing to be gained by speaking to Mr Holmes. He said himself that he has no official standing, and I see no reason to repeat myself by relating the same facts to him and then to the police, when they arrive. I think my time would be better spent looking around the house, as I always intended to do today." He laughed. "The climate may not be to my liking, but I have travelled a great distance to visit Thorpe Manor and it would be a shame to return home without seeing it all."

He was correct, of course. Holmes was acting at the request of the Thorpe family solicitor only and, had he not been trapped in the house by the snow, might not have become involved at all.

Even so, I tried to argue that Reilly should speak to him.

"I understand your reasoning," I said, "but Holmes's talents are viewed with the utmost respect by Scotland Yard and any preliminary investigation he carries out is likely to cut down the amount of time the police need before they can release everyone, and we can all go home."

Reilly's hand was on the door of the next room in the corridor, evidently keen to continue his impromptu tour, but at this, he stopped and turned his attention fully on me.

"Release us?" he said. "Do you mean to say that the police will keep us here until they have decided what happened to that blasted man?"

"Until they are satisfied that we each of us had nothing to do with his death, certainly," I clarified.

"Why, that is outrageous!" he snapped. "I have tickets booked on a steamer to take me back home for the day after tomorrow. Mr Buxton told me that the trains should be running again tomorrow, and if they are not, I will hire someone in the village to drive me. It is imperative that I leave by the afternoon at the latest!" He banged a fist against the wall in anger. "This would not happen back home, I can tell you, Dr Watson. The police there would never dream of keeping gentlemen hostage in so high-handed a manner."

I shrugged my shoulders. "Things are done differently in England nowadays, I'm afraid. Perhaps when you left for the Orient, the police were less diligent, but much has changed in the past few decades."

"So it would seem," grumbled Reilly. "Well, I still intend to leave tomorrow. I shall be sure to be the first to speak to any policeman who arrives before I depart. And if one arrives after that, well, they can contact me via the local police at home."

I would have warned him that he would be best served by staying where he was, but there was obviously no point. He gave a small nod of farewell and stalked past me in the direction of the main part of the house. I returned to Holmes, and told him what Reilly intended.

"He will not be allowed to leave the county, far less the country, of course. I informed Inspector Fisher of the names of everyone present at the house, and should the trains be up and running again tomorrow, he will have taken steps to ensure nobody leaves here on one."

"Still, I am surprised he would not speak to you. He must know how it will look that he was the only guest unwilling to give any account of himself."

"An account only to me, Watson, only to me. I doubt that the inspector, when he arrives, will hold it against Reilly that he preferred to wait to speak to him. Police inspectors are a vain lot, in my experience, and it will certainly appeal to his vanity."

I was not so sure, but we would know soon enough. I had just remembered something else that Reilly had said.

"The inspector will be here tomorrow, Holmes. Buxton told Reilly that the trains will be running in the morning."

He nodded, and closed his eyes. "In which case, I have a great deal to consider and not much time in which to do so. I need peace to think for a short while," he murmured. "If you could come back for me just before dinner, that would be splendid."

Thus dismissed, I made my way downstairs and poured myself a drink. There was nobody else around, so I wandered through to the library, and though most of the shelves were empty, I found a beautifully illustrated copy of Dean Swift's Gulliver's Travels and settled down to spend a pleasant hour in the land of the Lilliputians.

As it happened, I nodded off while reading the book, and only awoke when Alice the maid loudly coughed by my ear and said that Buxton had asked her to find out whether anyone wished to eat. In truth, I was not hungry, but Holmes had mentioned dinner, and so I replied on both our behalves that we would appreciate a hot meal.

"But Mr Holmes has gone out," Alice protested mildly. "He said that he wouldn't be wanting anything for dinner. He said he was going to The Silent Man and would get something there."

Instantly, I was wide awake. I looked up at a clock on the library wall. Six fifteen. I had been asleep for two hours, I was shocked to discover.

"When did Mr Holmes leave?" I asked, struggling to my feet and wondering where I had put down my boots.

"About an hour and a half ago, Watson! Time to walk to the village and come back again."

Holmes appeared, silhouetted in the doorway, alternately rubbing his hands together and blowing on his fingers.

"It's lucky that I did not wait for you," he went on with a smile, slipping into the seat opposite me. "I came downstairs ten minutes or so after you left me, and found you already fast asleep."

I ignored Holmes's attempt at humour. "But why did you go back to the village? Surely you had done all you needed to do when you were there just a few hours ago?"

Holmes suddenly looked grave. "Not quite all, Watson. When I was at the post office I sent one or two other telegrams which I did not mention." He held up a hand to forestall my inevitable objection. "Do not think that I was hiding anything from you, old friend, but they might have amounted to nothing. In fact, I do not know that they are of consequence even now, but I have spent the past hour attempting to test the validity of one element, without success."

"What element, Holmes?"

"I would prefer to keep that information to myself for now, Watson. But I will have need of your medical skills in the village tomorrow, if you are willing?"

"Of course. Just give me a little warning, and I will be at your disposal."

"Thank you. It is a trifling matter, but one which it would be best I did not explain in advance." Holmes gave an apologetic smile. "Forgive me for the secrecy, but in this case it is necessary, I think."

I had plenty of experience of Holmes's methods, and so was not excessively concerned that he was unable to take me into his confidence. I had no doubt that he would tell me what he could, when he could.

In the meantime, my nap had left me with an appetite. Holmes had not eaten in The Silent Man after all and was similarly famished after his walk to and from the village, and so we set out for the dining room in search of Alice.

In contrast to our first evening in the manor, the atmosphere in the dining room was subdued. Partly this was due to a paucity of diners. Only Pennington, Watt and Hopkirk joined Holmes and me in a substandard beef stew, with Lawrence Buxton making his apologies part way through the soup, claiming that the day's events had destroyed his appetite. Of the Schells and Reilly we had no word, and I could only assume that they too had been sufficiently moved by Alim Salah's murder to find the idea of food distasteful.

Pennington was as scathing of Buxton's weak stomach as he seemed to be about everything he encountered. "What can you expect of a man like that?" he asked the room in general. "A life spent nose-deep in books with no exposure to the real world leads to a weak constitution and an unwillingness to face realities."

"It's not every day you come across a dead body," Amicable Watt protested mildly, his perennial smile noticeable by its absence. "Buxton's surely entitled to a little consideration, given that he found the poor man's corpse. I can't help thinking that any of us would have reacted the same."

"Not I," Pennington declared. "I have sent more than one man to the gallows and have always held that if one is willing to do so, one should also be willing to pull the lever that hangs the guilty man."

Watt whistled between his teeth. "So you've operated a gallows, your worship!" he said. "In which case, I stand corrected and apologise. You, at least, are made of sterner stuff than I."

Pennington looked momentarily discomfited by Watt's apology and Hopkirk, noticing this, requested some clarification with barely concealed delight. "Have you, Judge? Hanged a man with your own hands, that is? I admit I didn't think that the law allowed for that sort of thing nowadays."

The judge glared at him, but was forced after a second's thought to shake his head. "No, I have not actually done so myself, but I would do so without hesitation, should the opportunity arise. The one great failing of the law of this country is that we are too soft on criminals. Murderers and thieves go free every day who should, by rights, be dangling at the end of the hangman's noose. That would not be the case were it up to me."

"I am sure it would not," Holmes said. "But I have been thinking about what you said earlier, Judge – about the possibility that the killer might strike again – and I have a suggestion to make which may put your mind at rest. Why do we not double up this evening? The Schells already share a room, obviously, and Watson and I have done so on previous occasions. Reilly and Buxton could share, which leaves you three gentlemen to do similarly, if you are willing? Alice informs me that there are unused rooms which already have extra beds in them."

From the frown that immediately creased his face, I thought Pennington would object, but he merely grumbled, "I did not expect to engage in dormitory living again at my age, but I suppose that is a sensible suggestion."

"Oh, I don't know," Watt chipped in, with a smile. "It reminds me of when I was a kid. There was eight of us in the one room, seven nippers and the old man as well. Friendly, it was."

The look that flashed across Pennington's face fell somewhere between shock and revulsion. "I have heard your story, Watt," he said, "and I have no doubt you take pride in your accomplishments, but I cannot believe you would ever wish to return to the filthy conditions in which you were reared."

The change in Watt was immediate, and I was instantly reminded that one does not rise from the depths of London's slums to become one of the capital's richest men simply due to a friendly disposition. The smile was wiped from his face as though it had never been there and he stared, unblinking, across the table.

"I earned my place, your worship," he growled, "unlike some at this table. My old dad didn't have two brass pins to rub together but he worked all his days and taught me to do the same. When I was running with a bad crowd, he grabbed me by the scruff of the neck and tanned my hide, though I thought myself a man. That's how I got where I am today and I'm thankful for it. And I say that makes me a better man than anyone born with a purse of silver in their pocket. Anyone who wants to argue with me over that, well, I've had to use my fists a time or two before now, and no doubt will do again."

"I shouldn't let the inspector hear you say that, old man," Hopkirk laughed, in an attempt to lighten the mood, but nobody joined in.

Watt's words and Holmes's mention of the murder had killed what little appetite for conversation there was and the remainder of the meal passed largely in silence. I was glad, at its conclusion, to bid everyone goodnight.

Holmes and I stayed downstairs for a nightcap, while everyone else went to make their sleeping arrangements.

"Amicable Watt is a surprisingly quick-tempered man," I said as soon as we were settled.

"He felt he had been insulted. He was not incorrect. Any man at the table would have reacted in similar fashion."

"I suppose that's true," I admitted. "But even so…" I shrugged, unsure of what I meant but sure that there was something amiss.

"Even so…" Holmes repeated but did not go on, and a silence fell over us.

"Do you really think there is a chance of a second murder?" I asked after a minute, changing the subject to one likely to have a more definitive answer.

Holmes was non-committal. "Nothing is certain," he said.

"But this way potential panic is avoided and everyone is reassured," I said, with a smile.

Holmes's face was impassive as he replied. "So long as nobody wonders if they are sharing a room with a killer," he murmured, with a small smile of his own.

Chapter Eleven

Inspector Fisher

If a lifetime spent in medicine, in the army and then working with Sherlock Holmes has taught me one thing, it is that plans seldom work out as expected. So it proved the following morning, when our planned trip to the village was postponed before I had even had breakfast.

It was exactly twenty past eight when Holmes re-entered the room we were sharing, and drove all thoughts of food from my mind with the news that the police had arrived twenty minutes before and asked everyone to gather in the main hall.

"The maid has just been up, asking that we all present ourselves at half past eight precisely, so that Inspector Fisher might introduce himself." He shrugged on his jacket and brushed a speck of lint from the collar. "I would rather have spoken to the man privately first, but I suppose we shall have to abide by his wishes."

"It would be polite, Holmes."

Holmes made a non-committal sound, ensured he had his cigarettes with him, and led the way to the main hall.

* * *

The figure with his back to us, busily engaged in giving instructions to the two uniformed constables who flanked him, could only be Inspector Fisher.

Our fellow guests stood arranged in two distinct groups around him, the Schells chatting with Captain Hopkirk and Watt, Reilly standing silently with Buxton and Pennington (the latter of whom glowered with surprising, and unconcealed, displeasure at the inspector), but each group kept their distance both from one another and from the trio of policemen.

Whatever the inspector was saying, it was enough to have both of his subordinates listening intently, but his voice was too quiet for me to make anything out distinctly. As Holmes and I approached, he suddenly stopped and turned quickly round, snapping shut the large notebook he held in his hand and eyeing us curiously. He waved a hand at the constables, evidently an indication that they should now carry out the orders he had just given them, for they split off from him and, with a few quiet words, guided the other guests out of the hall, leaving the inspector alone with me and Holmes. From the corner of my eye, I could see the smallest of smiles flicker about Holmes's mouth at this indication of Fisher's good sense.

The inspector was a fair-haired man of above average height and build. Clean shaven, his face had a lugubrious cast to it, with down-turned mouth and eyes and a sallow tinge to the skin. He held out a hand as he crossed towards us and, when I took it, gave a firm if brief handshake.

"I've seen your pictures in the newspapers, gentlemen," he said, as he shook Holmes's hand. "You've solved some astonishing cases – if the reports are to be believed."

There was a note of doubt in Fisher's voice but Holmes, as ever uninterested in revisiting old cases, was indifferent to either insult or compliment. "How do you do," he said politely. "I hope that the journey from Stainforth was not too unpleasant, Inspector. Any problem with your carriage is no light matter in weather such as this, especially one which forced you to return to your station so soon after you set out."

At this, Fisher gave a grunt of surprise. "Perhaps the reports are to be believed then, Mr Holmes," he exclaimed. "I'd ask how you could know these things, but if the papers are right, I'm sure you'll be happy to tell us!"

"Your waistcoat and shoes," Holmes replied. "An examination of those alone is enough to draw similar conclusions to my own."

"My waistcoat…?" Fisher looked down at himself. I did the same, and could see nothing exceptional. Fisher was smartly dressed, and both his waistcoat and his shoes were spotlessly clean.

"You have lost me, I must admit, Holmes," I said. "Both waistcoat and shoes are entirely ordinary so far as I can see."

"But it is their ordinariness which is most telling, Watson," replied Holmes. He sighed theatrically and turned to Fisher. "You are immaculately turned out, Inspector, and a credit to the police force, but the thread in your waistcoat does not quite match that in your trousers and jacket. Your shoes have recently been cleaned and buffed, but the laces are soaking wet. I deduce, therefore, that there was a problem with your carriage, which necessitated you alighting from the vehicle, at which point you dirtied your shoes and the lower part of your trousers. You had left the town, else the ground would not have been so filthy, but were not so far away that it would be expedient to press on to Thorpe Manor. Therefore, you returned to the station, where you keep a spare suit, but no waistcoat. I happen to know that Lestrade also keeps an extra jacket and trousers handy, for court appearances and the like."

"I could have gone home, and not had the time to change my waistcoat," Fisher protested. "You admit yourself that the pattern is almost a match for my jacket."

"But then you would have changed your shoes, rather than being forced to wash the pair you had on, and your laces would be dry."

Fisher put his hands in his pockets and rocked back on his heels. "Well done, Mr Holmes," he said, less enthusiastically than I expected. In fact, he seemed put out that Holmes had so accurately described his journey.

Holmes again gave no sign that he had noticed. "As I said in my telegram, Inspector Lestrade at Scotland Yard can vouch that I have been of assistance to the police in the past, and I am at your disposal here, though obviously I understand that both Watson and I are currently as much suspects as everyone else."

I had not considered that. Holmes was correct, of course. Unlike our previous cases together, on this occasion we were not interested parties arriving after a murder had taken place, but were instead intimately involved with the crime itself. No matter our previous service to Scotland Yard, Inspector Fisher was obliged to view us as potential suspects.

Clearly, the inspector had already considered the matter. "Perhaps not quite as much as the others, Mr Holmes, but I'm gratified that you realise there can be no special treatment for you and the doctor. As I was forced to remind Mr Pennington, we do not play favourites here in Yorkshire, no matter what reputation folk might have in London. That said, I understand from Mr Thompson that he asked you to carry out preliminary investigations, while memories were fresh, in case I was unable to get through to the house for several days?"

"He did, Inspector. I spoke to most of my fellow guests yesterday."

"Not them all?"

"Unfortunately not. Judge Pennington did not believe it would be useful, and Mr Reilly was of the opinion that it was a waste of his time to speak to me and then repeat himself to you."

"Was he now? That's interesting." Fisher pulled a pencil from his jacket, and began to take notes. "Reilly's the colonial, isn't he? Come back to England after half a lifetime in the tropics? I had one of those a couple of years back, fellow made a fortune in tea in Ceylon, bought some land outside Hatfield, built a big house and proceeded to act like he was still on the plantation." He underlined something in his notebook. "I had to explain to him that Yorkshire is not Ceylon."

Holmes glanced down at the notebook and gestured to his right, towards the rear of the house. "Perhaps we could take a seat, Inspector, and I can pass on what information I was able to glean from my brief discussions?"

"A capital idea." Fisher waved a hand to a constable whom I had not heard returning to the hall. "Halliday, see if you can rustle up a pot of tea from somewhere and bring it here. The kitchen is likely to be through the back, I imagine."

* * *

As we drank our tea, Fisher listened closely while Holmes recounted his conversations with the other guests, interrupting only now and again to ask for clarification on certain points.

"Did Mr Buxton ever actually threaten violence against the dead man?" he asked at one point, after Holmes had replayed the historian's agitation regarding the possible fate of his manuscript. When Holmes replied in the negative, he tapped his pencil against the table and frowned. "Not even when he was angry as you say he was?" Holmes shook his head and when the inspector looked at me, so did I. "Well, fair enough," he conceded grudgingly. "If you're sure."

He made a final note on Buxton and moved on to the Schells.

"An old man and a young girl? Not very likely killers, are they?" he said, but his interest was piqued when he asked Holmes to describe the fight between Captain Hopkirk and Alim Salah.

"Are Mrs Schell and Captain Hopkirk very close friends, would you say?" he asked.

"They are undeniably friendly," Holmes said, "but if you are asking whether there is any truth in the allegation made by Mr Salah, I can only say that I am not aware of any proof one way or the other."

Fisher gave a tut of disappointment and made another mark in his notebook. "But he would have killed the man during their scuffle in the hall?" he went on.

"I would not go that far, Inspector," Holmes corrected him. "All I can say is that he would have struck Mr Salah a considerable blow had I not intervened."

"A dangerous blow though? Would you call it that, Dr Watson?" Fisher pressed, turning to me.

"If it had connected, it might have been, yes," I was forced to agree. "Any blow to the head with a hard object is likely to be potentially dangerous."

"Potentially dangerous," he repeated. "Would you not go further than that, Doctor? I've seen the object in question and it has a wickedly sharp edge to it. Would 'definitely dangerous' not be closer to the mark? Potentially deadly, even?"

"Perhaps." Oddly, I felt as though I were defending Hopkirk, and in some ways I was. I had been shocked by his lapse in judgement during the fight, but I had been impressed with him otherwise, and considered it only that – a temporary lapse, prompted by a rush of blood to the head.

"Perhaps deadly," Fisher said, writing the words down in this notebook. "Well, let's put that to one side for now, shall we? Mr Holmes, you were saying that the maid…" he glanced down at his notebook "… Alice, is it?… told you that she overheard the dead man say that he would not allow himself to be assaulted without retaliation?"

Holmes's eyebrows were raised in surprise. "That is not what she said, Inspector."

"As good as, I'd say. The sense of the statement if you'd rather, then; that it could well have been in reference to the recent fight he'd had with Captain Hopkirk?"

"It might refer to any number of things, Inspector," Holmes insisted. "I could not say what exactly."

Fisher frowned in annoyance. It was plain that he was unimpressed with Holmes's refusal to accommodate his suggestions. "So, Salah could have sought Hopkirk for a reckoning and then come out the worse in the fight which followed? Or

Hopkirk could have decided to finish the job you interrupted?"

Holmes, too, was showing increasing signs of irritation. "I really could not say, Inspector," he snapped. "I try not to engage in idle speculation."

The change in Inspector Fisher was immediate. "In the police force, we call such speculation 'theorising' and do not consider it idle in the least. In fact, I have found it very handy in my police career." As he spoke, his voice became cold and unfriendly. He carefully closed his notebook and laid it on the table at his side. "Another thing I've found, Mr. Holmes, is that the guilty party in any crime is most commonly – indeed, almost exclusively – uncovered due to routine police work. Speaking to the parties involved, checking that their stories agree, digging about in the weeds and the shadows. Dogged and unglamorous, to be sure, but almost always the best path to a swift and successful conclusion." He smiled, but his eyes remained cold and sharp. "The sort of handy deductions with which you solve your cases in The Strand are rare in the real world, Mr Holmes. Cleverness is all very well, but without the embellishment of Dr Watson's pen, I'd bet it's all but useless when faced with actual crime." He retrieved his notebook and tucked it inside his jacket, leaning forward in his chair. "I should tell you now that I decided to speak to you prior to introducing myself formally to the other guests in order that I might judge the type of person you are. I am used to deciding the path my cases will take, and do not appreciate interference from outsiders. Bearing that in mind, you will realise that I did not, therefore, appreciate receiving a telegram from my chief constable this morning, instructing me to make use of your particular talents while investigating this murder. I was rendered even less appreciative on discovering that the reason for this instruction was an earlier telegram from an Inspector Lestrade of Scotland Yard, who somehow knew you were here and took it upon himself to appraise the chief constable of that fact." As he spoke, he rose to his feet, so that he was looking down upon us. "So far as I'm concerned, the fact that you are Sherlock Holmes and John Watson does not make you any the less suspects in the murder of Alim Salah. I have been ordered to make use of you. Very well, you may observe when I deem it appropriate, but nothing more. I am now officially cautioning you that you have no other role to play in this investigation. Furthermore, you may not involve yourselves in questioning the other guests. I would be obliged if you would stay within the house and its grounds, unless you have been given permission from me to leave. That," he concluded grimly, "includes any trip to the village, which is from this moment out of bounds to anyone present in the house at the time of Mr Salah's death. Is that understood?"

A mere half hour had passed since we had met Inspector Fisher, but even on so brief an acquaintance, it was clear that he was a man both quick to take offence and very aware of his own status. I could scarcely help but think that he and Sherlock Holmes were not well suited to working together.

Holmes's reply simply confirmed my theory. "Of course, Inspector," he said coldly. "Now, if you will excuse me, I have some reading to do."

He too rose to his feet and, without another word, stalked from the room. Left alone with Inspector Fisher, I reached for the teapot and poured myself a fresh cup. He looked down at me for a moment then muttered, "Dr Watson," and followed Holmes into the hall. I lit a cigarette and expressed a silent hope that the case would be solved quickly and the two men would in the meantime have no cause to clash. Even then, it seemed a wish that was unlikely to be granted.

Chapter Twelve

Reilly is Suspected

For all my misgivings, the remainder of the morning passed without incident. Fisher spoke to everyone in the house individually, while his two assistants disappeared into the cellar and the grounds, digging about in the weeds and the shadows, as he had put it. Now and again, as I sat in the library, I saw one or other of them scurry past, the bearer, presumably, of new evidence.

Holmes kept himself to his room, emerging only briefly at midday to request a pot of tea and a sandwich from Alice. I was still in the library, discussing some of the more eccentric of the Thorpe ancestors with Buxton over a light lunch, and I only caught a glimpse of my friend as he hurried past the door and again as he hurried back.

I was considering a post-luncheon nap, in fact, when the shorter of Fisher's constables appeared at the library door and asked me to accompany him to the room upstairs, formerly Holmes's interview room, which Fisher had commandeered as his base of operations.

It seemed Inspector Fisher had proven as good as his word. He had promised swift action, and within a few hours, he had fixed upon a suspect and had summoned him for questioning.

We were to collect Holmes on our way, the little policeman explained, but he was already standing outside his room, waiting for us, when we reached him. Even though there was a door, a short flight of stairs and a corridor between us and the interview room, we could clearly hear the sound of raised voices emanating from that direction. One of them was unmistakably the inspector's, but it took me a second to recognise the owner of the other as Stephen Reilly.

"I have never in my life been spoken to in such a manner," he was declaring loudly as we preceded the constable into the room. "Back home, the police force remember that they are employees and act accordingly. They do not harass gentlemen of substance on the say-so of witless subordinates, nor do they make accusations based on nothing more than a... a ragged smudge in the earth!"

I had remarked before on Reilly's bronzed appearance, but even through his tanned skin it was clear that he was furiously angry. He banged a fist hard on the table in front of Inspector Fisher – who sat, his face expressionless, in his chair, a scattering of pages torn from his notebook in front of him – and drew in a huge breath, the better to renew his verbal attack.

"I have not accused you of anything, Mr Reilly," the inspector said quietly, before he could do so. "I merely ask the question. Where were you between half past ten and one a.m. on Sunday night?"

"And I have answered that I was in my room, asleep!"

"Indeed you have, sir, indeed you have. And yet how is it that my constable has just discovered a set of footprints which exactly match those made by your fur boots in the snow outside the rear entrance to the house, and also down the sloping pathway which leads to the door into the cellar? Prints," he went on quickly, observing Reilly about to explode once more, "which could only have been made that night, given that the snow stopped falling at half past twelve on Sunday evening and you spent last night in a room with Mr Buxton?" He looked up at Reilly and waited for a reply.

The elderly planter said nothing. He glared down at Fisher, who returned the stare unblinkingly. Eventually, Reilly looked away, and said, "Perhaps someone else was wearing my boots? They are the best to be had in this house, after all."

"And then replaced them in your room afterwards? The boots supplied by Mr Buxton are still outside your room, but your fur boots were retrieved from the side of your bed by Constable Halliday not ten minutes ago."

"How dare you enter my room!" Reilly's voice rose to a pitch of fury once more, but I had the distinct impression that his outrage was, if not exactly feigned, then prompted more by fear than anger. When the inspector again said nothing, he allowed his expostulation to tail off; in recognition, I suspected, that the manner in which Fisher had obtained the boots was hardly germane at this point. He turned and looked imploringly at Holmes, as though beseeching him to intervene, but my friend remained silent.

"I was in the rear garden late on Sunday night," he said finally. "But I give you my word that I had nothing to do with the death of Mr Salah. And if a gentleman's word is not good enough for you, Inspector, then I shall keep my own counsel until my lawyer is present."

Fisher was no fool. He knew that Reilly was a rich man, and

that once his lawyer became involved there was little chance of him saying anything useful. But what could he do? If Reilly was determined not to speak, then he could not force him. He made one final effort, however. "That's as may be," he said. "But perhaps you would care to comment on a separate, but related, matter? I am informed that Salah accompanied you down to the village after his fight with Captain Hopkirk, and that when you returned there was obvious ill feeling between you?"

If Fisher had hoped to disconcert Reilly by this new line of questioning, he was to be disappointed. Where he had undoubtedly been flustered by the need to explain his presence in the garden, now he was completely sanguine.

"I did not speak to Salah either on the way to the village or on the way back, Inspector," he declared confidently. "In fact, I have no idea why he chose to accompany me at all. I went straight to the post office and left him in the street outside. When I emerged, he was standing in the doorway to the public house, sheltering from the wind. He followed me back up the road, but as I say, we exchanged not a word. And that is all I have to say to you until my lawyer is present!"

Fisher closed his notebook. "Very well," he sighed. "But be aware that juries in this country take a dim view of defendants who will not explain themselves. Halliday, take Mr Reilly to any empty bedroom you can find and lock him in. He is not under arrest at present, but I would like to know where he is. Stand guard outside until I decide what to do with him."

Constable Halliday nodded and politely indicated that Reilly should accompany him from the room. Before he did so, however, the accused man stopped in front of Holmes and me.

"It is nobody's business but my own if I was outside or why. I will explain my behaviour once we are in London and my lawyer is present, but I beg of you in the meantime, do not be like this fool of an inspector. Continue your investigations, Mr Holmes. Discover who murdered Mr Salah – for I promise you that I had no hand in it!"

With that, he left the room, with Halliday in close attendance. Holmes and I found ourselves alone with Inspector Fisher.

"You will have gathered that the police investigation has already borne fruit," he announced. "By means of the sort of assiduous but unglamorous police work I mentioned to you earlier, my men discovered several very distinct footprints in the snow to the rear of the house. Each of these prints was made by an item of footwear the size of a gentleman's boot, but extensively fringed all around." He pushed a piece of paper towards us, on which was drawn the rough shape of a man's shoe, with an array of irregular spikes projecting from it. "As you can see," he went on, "the hairs of the fringe have clumped together in the snow, but tests I made earlier have ascertained that this is exactly the sort of print which would be made by a set of fur-covered boots, such as those worn by Mr Reilly. And as you just heard, he was unwilling – or unable – to explain what he was doing in the freezing cold and pitch dark at the back of the house in the middle of the night."

He lit a cigarette and leaned back in his seat. "We also have the evidence of... well, everyone actually... that Reilly and Salah fought at their first meeting."

"Hardly fought, Inspector," Holmes protested. "A few harsh words were exchanged, no more than that."

"Did you exchange any harsh words with the dead man, Mr

Holmes? You, Dr Watson? No, you did not. I'm sure that you take my point."

"I am not sure that I do, Inspector," Holmes replied. "Mr Reilly's falling out with Salah was by no means the most severe among the guests, and hardly seems likely to provide motive for a murderous attack."

"Even so, he was in the vicinity, for reasons which he will not explain, at the exact time the dead man was murdered. That is an incontrovertible fact."

"Even if that were proof of anything other than the fact that he was standing in the snow in the dark – which it is not – your incontrovertible fact is not one which you will be able readily to demonstrate in court, Inspector."

"Really?" Fisher sneered. "I don't see why not."

"As we speak, your evidence is melting. These clumps of hair are, I presume, reasonably clear at the moment, but they will either melt away if the temperature rises even a tiny amount, or be covered, should it snow again. Either way, you cannot preserve them and will not be able to show any jury the footprints themselves."

The expression on Fisher's face would have been comical had the matter not been so serious. Where he had been triumphant, now he was downcast, as the realisation sank in that his physical evidence had very likely already disappeared.

"A jury will accept the word of a policeman!" he protested after a second's reflection.

"Very probably," said Holmes. "But a good lawyer will have no difficulty in suggesting that the poor overworked policeman, tired after a day's hard work, is not fully to be trusted when it comes to identifying specific items of footwear by the tread they leave in snow.

And Mr Reilly will have a very good lawyer, of that I am certain.

"Besides, you have no reason to suspect Reilly, other than the fact he was outside, near the place where the body was secreted. It is not nearly enough evidence to hold him in a bedroom, far less a prison cell."

Fisher glared at Holmes, but remained silent. Holmes stared steadily back, and it was the inspector who dropped his eyes first. He stalked to the door and threw it open.

"Halliday!" he shouted down the corridor. "Let Mr Reilly go. For now, he's a free man."

He walked back to his desk and sat down, pulling his notebook towards him and picking up his pencil. He began to take notes on a blank page then, without looking up, muttered in our direction, "If you will excuse me, gentlemen."

The almost imperceptible smile that played about the corners of Holmes's mouth was the only thing that betrayed his pleasure at the inspector's discomfiture. As we walked out of the room, I hoped that my own feelings were as well disguised.

With no official role in the investigation, and the inspector's admonition not to leave the grounds still fresh in our ears, we decided to walk down to a structure that Buxton had described as "the finest shell grotto north of Margate".

It was only a five-minute walk from the house, across an area so completely flat that I assumed a lawn must lie underneath the thick blanket of snow. As we walked, we smoked in silence, each of us lost in our own thoughts. My own, I must admit, were largely taken up with the realisation that the appearance of a corpse had, in a way I did not care to interrogate too closely, actually improved the tenor of our trip. Holmes had demonstrated an absolute lack of interest in the question of the Thorpe Ruby and not much more in the missing art collection, but the possibility of a murder had certainly invigorated him. Even walking across the snowy lawn, his stride was brisk and his face flushed with what I was certain was exercise of both a physical and a mental nature.

As if to prove my supposition, he suddenly stopped in his tracks and turned to me. "Now that we are clear of the house and the inspector's prying assistants, I have a confession to make, Watson," he said. "I have not been completely truthful about Mr Reilly."

He reached into his coat pocket, then apparently thought better of it. He pointed to the grotto, a few hundred yards distant. "I think we had better speak inside," he said, and trotted towards it, kicking up sprays of snow behind him as he did so. I manoeuvred to one side of him to avoid being soaked and jogged alongside him through the "cave", which comprised the entrance to the grotto, eager to hear what he had to say.

Once inside, however, I was momentarily distracted from Holmes's secret by the opulent spectacle that confronted me. To call the elaborately decorated interior a cave seemed absurd, for one thing. Directly in front of us was a curving golden wall, illuminated by natural light streaming through vents in the ceiling, on which were picked out a series of stars and planets, each shining whitely, as if made of the finest china. On closer inspection, the stars and planets, indeed the whole surface of the wall, was made up of tens of thousands of shells of varying sizes and colours, carefully affixed to give the impression of the glittering night sky. The wall curved away from us and vanished into the darkness but where we stood, only a few feet inside, the area was as brightly lit as any room in the house and far more beautiful.

Holmes appeared unmoved by the spectacle, however. He moved inside just far enough to place himself directly beneath one of the shafts of light and impatiently beckoned me to join him.

"We do not have a great deal of time, Watson. I would not put it past Inspector Fisher to have us followed, and there is something I must show you."

He opened his jacket and pulled a folded sheet of paper from his pocket. "Here are the contents of the telegram that Reilly sent to London when he visited the village in company with Alim Salah on the evening of his murder."

I took it from him, and unfolded the thin paper. It was printed in block capitals, obviously written down by whoever worked in the village post office, and was short and to the point.

```
SHERLOCK HOLMES IS HERE STOP WILL DO WHAT
I CAME TO DO THEN DEPART BEFORE IDENTIFIED
STOP MAKE ARRANGEMENTS TO LEAVE TUESDAY PM
STOP
```

The meaning was clear enough, but I was confused by one thing. "Where on earth did you get this, Holmes?" I asked.

"From the post office in the village, of course."

"Let me rephrase my question. How did you get this?"

It would be too much to say that Holmes looked embarrassed but there was no doubting he coloured a little as he replied.

"There I must admit to a slight embellishment of the truth, Watson," he said. "I told the young lady on the counter that I was

147

a police inspector and required the contents of both Reilly's and Salah's telegrams as part of my enquiries."

Any hope that our meeting should remain clandestine was destroyed at that moment, as I gave out a belly laugh which must have been audible in the manor house. The idea of Inspector Sherlock Holmes was simply too humorous for any other reaction. I blinked at my friend through tear-filled eyes and, once I had regained my breath, asked him how he had convinced the girl.

"Simplicity itself," he said, regarding my levity with obvious disapproval. "As we heard when we arrived, my name is unknown in these parts and a good speaking voice and an air of authority was sufficient to carry the day."

I shook my head in admiration at Holmes's cheek – and then quickly sobered, as I realised one important fact about the telegram. If Holmes was showing it to me here, then he obviously did not intend to show it to Inspector Fisher. His disregard for Scotland Yard and, on occasion, the strict letter of the law was one thing, but to deliberately withhold evidence of such importance...

I said as much to him as I handed the paper back. "You need to show this to Inspector Fisher, Holmes. Largely on account of your arguments, he has allowed Reilly free rein to go where he pleases. In light of this telegram, that is clearly not the wisest course of action. Who knows what he might do."

Holmes simply slipped the paper back into his jacket. "I showed you this for a reason, Watson, but I hope you will trust me when I tell you that there is no reason to show it to the inspector. Reilly is not a killer, nor will he prove one in the future, I am sure of that. Giving this information to Fisher will only lead him to arrest the wrong man, while the true killer is allowed to escape."

"If you can prove that, Holmes, show Fisher the proof instead, then. Tell him who he should be arresting!"

Holmes was evasive. "Proof sufficient to convince a man as stubborn as Inspector Fisher is a difficult thing to produce. I must admit that, at the moment, I have none to give him." He grabbed my arm and stepped towards me. "I am asking you to trust me for now, Watson. I believe I know what Reilly's words mean, and I do not believe that they have anything to do with murder. Until I can prove that, however, I hope you will assist me in unmasking the real killer."

I hesitated before making any reply. It was true that the telegram did not admit to murder, and might refer to an infinite number of things, but the timing of it was surely more than coincidental, and I knew that Fisher would see it that way too. But Holmes was seldom wrong, and never when he was as certain as he now seemed. Not without reservations, I nodded my head.

I would keep Holmes's secret for now, and help him look for another potential murderer. But I was not happy.

Chapter Thirteen

Hopkirk is Suspected

It seemed that whenever we left the manor house for any length of time, we returned to find the situation had changed. It was quite disorienting.

We had taken a leisurely route back, enjoying the crisp, cold air, and comparing our opinions of the other guests. So it was that an hour had passed between our departure and our return, and in that time it seemed the inhabitants of the house had vanished.

Of neither guests nor police was there any sign, though a faint banging sound could just about be made out towards the rear of the house. The main hall and library were unoccupied, however, and the dining room equally empty. It was only as we entered the servants' area that we encountered another living soul, as Lawrence Buxton appeared from within a large walk-in pantry and greeted us with a soft "hello".

He explained that the other guests were either resting in their rooms or had taken the opportunity, now that the likelihood of further storms had diminished, to view the gardens. An auction was still to take place in a few days, after all.

Inspector Fisher, however, was conspicuous by his absence. It seemed that after his meeting with Holmes he had gone directly to the cellar, where he had set his two assistants to a thorough search and had not emerged since.

Buxton, who had gone down to check on progress and been sent running by the inspector's irascible bark and the threat of arrest, reported that they had set up lanterns where they could and were moving slowly from one end of the still dimly lit cellar to the other, shifting larger items out of the way wherever possible, and painstakingly examining any other areas on their hands and knees. The cellar was large and cluttered and it would take several hours to investigate every inch of its interior. The inspector, Buxton informed me with no small hint of malice, was supervising the operation from a makeshift seat by the outer door.

"Though what they hope to gain from doing so, I have no idea," he continued, chewing thoughtfully on a sandwich.

"It's the way that Inspector Fisher likes to work, I believe," I remarked. "He told us that he is a great believer in meticulous police work of this sort."

"He lacks imagination, you mean," Buxton retorted. Fisher's high-handed behaviour in the cellar had obviously soured his impression of the inspector. "Why are you not investigating, Mr Holmes, that's what I should like to know?"

Holmes explained that he had been ordered not to do so, but this information served merely to irritate Buxton further. He lamented the attitude of the modern police force for a few moments, then announced that he had work to do.

As he left, I turned to Holmes, intending to suggest that we take a look at the cellar. But as I opened my mouth to speak, in perfect time, as though the one action had prompted the other, a loud shout echoed through the house.

"That noise came from the cellar," he said, and smiled. "In the circumstances, I do not think that it could be described as interference if we were to go down to offer what assistance we can, do you?"

"No," I agreed with a matching grin, "I don't think that it could."

The cellar was only marginally more brightly lit than it had been when Hopkirk and I had ferried Salah's body to his room. It had, however, undergone a minor transformation, in that a series of narrow winding walkways had been created among the clutter and junk, allowing access to all but the most impenetrable areas of the room.

Inspector Fisher stood at the end of one such walkway, shining a torch down at a patch of shadowy floor. The smaller of the two constables sat on an upturned crate, cradling his hand to his side.

"Cairns has just trapped his hand between two planks of wood," said the other constable, Halliday, stepping in front of us to block our way. He looked over his shoulder towards his superior officer, who glanced up, hesitated for a moment in thought, then decided we should be allowed access.

"Let them in," he called over. "I've got something to show Mr Holmes."

Halliday stepped aside and we carefully picked our way across the room to the inspector.

"Good afternoon, gentlemen," he said, pulling a watch from his waistcoat pocket. "If it is afternoon yet... ah, so it is, just about. You will be pleased to hear that diligent police work by myself and my two colleagues here has already turned up not one but two important pieces of new evidence. Evidence which, taken with other information already known to me, is of sufficient weight to allow me to build a working hypothesis as to the identity of the killer of Mr Alim Salah."

He tilted his lantern so that it shone at a forty-five-degree angle, illuminating a small space beneath a mass of rotting carpets. Something sparkled in the light. Fisher crouched down and pulled whatever it was towards himself.

"Your timing is impeccable," he sneered. "We only discovered this a matter of moments ago."

With a grunt of effort, he sprang to his feet and turned over his hand, to reveal a long leather wallet, embossed with what appeared to be gold leaf and held shut with a diamond clasp. Embossed on the side were the initials A.S. and a curious emblem, which I recognised after a moment's examination as a large snake, entwined around a precious stone. This had undoubtedly belonged to Salah.

We crowded closer to Fisher as he handed his lantern to the still moaning Cairns and carefully flipped open the catch. From inside, he slid out a thick pile of English banknotes, which he quickly thumbed through.

"Eleven pounds, ten shillings," he whistled softly. "Whoever killed Mr Salah wasn't after his money, anyway."

"Most interesting, Inspector," said Holmes. Then, unknowingly echoing Buxton's earlier comment, he continued, "though I am unclear what exactly has been gained by this discovery. By their very presence here, each of the guests has demonstrated they possess sufficient wealth to purchase the house and all the lands that go with it. I am not clear how it narrows down our field of enquiry to say that the killer was uninterested in adding a little under eleven pounds to his fortune."

I felt sure that Fisher would react furiously to Holmes's deliberately slighting words, but though he stiffened, he allowed no anger to show on his face. Instead, he reached into his pocket and pulled something out.

"You may be right, Mr Holmes," he said. "Which is why the second item my men uncovered is of particular interest. If you will move to the doorway – the light in here is not good enough to see this properly."

We walked across and stood waiting while Fisher handed the wallet over to Halliday. As the constable carried it upstairs, the inspector joined us in the doorway. He opened his hand, exposing a fragment of dull gold metal. In the bright light reflecting from the snow outside, there was no mistaking it.

It depicted an exploding grenade, the cap badge of the Grenadier Guards. The last time I had seen it had been on our first evening in the house, on the lapel of Captain James Hopkirk.

Captain Hopkirk pushed against the heavy table until he was so far back in his chair that its front legs left the floor. He tapped a soft beat against the wood with his fingers and smiled across at Inspector Fisher.

We were seated in Fisher's makeshift office. The inspector sat in Holmes's old seat, with Hopkirk across from him, and we two grudgingly invited observers were perched on two hard chairs across by the window. Constable Halliday stood by the door, where he glowered in a constant rotation between the captain, Holmes and myself.

Hopkirk seemed the most relaxed person in the room. "My dear Inspector," he said, "I am entirely at your disposal. If I can assist you in any way, then I would be delighted to do so. All you need do is ask."

"That is very good of you, sir," said Fisher. "I've only a handful of questions to put to you, so we shouldn't be long." He nodded towards Holmes and me. "I've been asked to allow Mr Holmes and Dr Watson to observe proceedings, but I'm aware that you've already spoken to them, and if you would prefer they leave, I will of course instruct them to do so."

He waited expectantly, but Hopkirk shook his head. "I've no objection," he said. "I'm sure they'll be very useful to you."

A fleeting frown crossed Fisher's face, but otherwise he hid his disappointment. "Very well," he said. "I would remind you, however, gentlemen, that you are here to observe and not to participate. I should be grateful if you were to refrain from interrupting at any point."

I nodded my understanding and Holmes murmured, "Of course, Inspector." Hopkirk glanced between the three of us and made no effort to hide his amusement. Fisher flipped to a page in his notebook and read from it for a moment before he spoke.

"You are Captain James Hopkirk, a former member of Her Majesty's Army?"

"Former? I am no longer active, Inspector, but I remain ready to serve if called upon."

"Really? You surprise me, Captain. My understanding, obviously incorrect, is that you've left the army altogether. Are you telling me that is not the case?"

For the first time since Hopkirk's fight with Salah, I saw the captain's good humour falter.

"What? How…?" he spluttered, momentarily caught off guard. Then, allowing the legs of his chair to thump back to the ground, he recovered his composure sufficiently to give a slightly hollow laugh. "It is not, my dear Inspector, though I can understand how the confusion might arise in a non-military man." He waved his cigarette approximately in my direction. "Dr Watson was an army officer, I believe? He will confirm that, in these times of peace, it can be hard for the War Office to justify all us career soldiers cluttering up the barracks. Some of us, adjudged supernumerary, are asked to drop down to half pay until our country has need of us once again. I, for my sins, am currently one such."

I nodded my agreement, though Fisher had not looked in my direction and clearly had no interest in my opinion. He flipped another page in his ever-present notebook and read it for a moment before looking back up at Hopkirk.

"Yes, sir, I am aware of the half-pay system. I was told, however, that you had in fact been cashiered from your regiment a good four years ago. A matter of honour, I believe?"

"Cashiered from the regiment?" Hopkirk's expression was puzzled. "You have been misinformed, Inspector. A telegram to the War Office will confirm my status." He blew a smoke ring towards the ceiling, all sign of discomfiture gone. "Or I can give you the address of my CO's club and you can send one of your chaps to ask him in person?"

"That won't be necessary, sir. If I can't take the word of an officer and a gentleman, eh?" Fisher was equally composed, ticking something off in his notebook, then tapping his pencil against his teeth in thought. "I should like to speak to you about your fight with the dead man, though. You were defending a lady's honour on that occasion?"

"I was indeed, Inspector, and would do so again. And not just because the lady in question is a personal friend. A woman's good name is all she has. It behoves all men of breeding to defend that name whenever it is besmirched. That is what I was taught at least."

Hopkirk plainly felt more secure with this line of questioning, and I wondered how much truth there was in the allegation that he had been drummed out of his regiment. It would not after all be the first time that a disgraced ex-soldier had held onto his rank, and nobody any the wiser. One did not need to move too far away for past misdemeanours to be left behind and youthful indiscretions forgotten.

Perhaps his hot temper had brought him to blows with the wrong person? Or – the thought occurred suddenly but strongly – perhaps there had been no Holmes to step in and prevent a fatal blow. It would also not be the first time a death in the regiment was dealt with by the regiment, and unpleasant matters handled without police involvement. It was not only women whose good name was everything to them.

And yet, Hopkirk seemed wholly sincere. Inspector Fisher continued to circle around the fight, and the captain continued to wield his righteous fury at Salah's unwarranted slander like a shield.

"Yes," he said, in response to a question about Holmes's intervention, "I was grateful to Mr Holmes for stepping in as he did. I am grateful. I am a soldier, not a pub brawler, and when I kill I do so in the line of duty. Mr Holmes's prompt actions prevented me from disgracing myself and my regiment." He gripped the edges of the table, pulled himself forward so that he leaned halfway across it. "I am ashamed of the way I allowed my anger to get the better of me. It was a momentary aberration which I immediately regretted. I had no wish to see Mr Salah dead, nor do I wish him dead now."

The sincerity in his voice was not faked, of that I was sure. I glanced over at Holmes, who sat, fingers steepled before his face in the familiar pose, eyes closed. As though aware I was looking at him, he suddenly opened his eyes. His attention was not on me, however, but on Inspector Fisher, who had pushed back his chair, causing it to scrape unpleasantly across the wooden floor.

"Very good, Captain Hopkirk," he said, "let us accept that you'd have regretted bashing in Mr Salah's skull in front of your fellow guests. It'd be a hard murder to deny, for one thing. But what about later? What about late at night, when everyone else was asleep? Would you regret killing him then? Did you regret killing him then?"

Now it was Fisher's turn to lean forward, eagerness writ large on his face, his sallow skin reddening with pleasure.

That eagerness caused Hopkirk to hesitate momentarily before he replied. "Did I regret it?" he said at last, attempting to sound indignant at the allegation, but succeeding only in sounding amused. "Well, since I did not kill him, the question is moot, I'd say, wouldn't you?" He picked up his cigarette case from the table and lit another cigarette, his hand completely steady. Once he had it going strongly, he stated plainly, "In fact, I did not see him yesterday evening at all."

"You definitely did not cross paths with Mr Salah after your fight then?"

Now Hopkirk's voice was weary. "No, Inspector. As I said, I did not see the man again until Buxton uncovered his corpse."

"And yet we have reason to believe he was looking for you. 'I won't turn the other cheek to this Englishman's assault,' he said to Dr Watson, you know, and him armed with a club at the time. Did he come looking for you, determined to get his revenge?"

"He did not, Inspector! Or, if he did, he didn't find me. As I said, I did not see him again!"

"So you say. Perhaps you can explain, then, how this item came to be found in the cellar a short distance from Mr Salah's discarded wallet?"

He held out the cap badge we had been shown in the cellar. This was the first I had heard of its location, and I could think of an immediate objection to Fisher's insinuation. Mindful of our instruction not to interfere, I remained silent and hoped that Hopkirk had realised the same thing.

His hand went to his lapel and fingered the small crease in the fabric where the badge had once sat.

"Why, that's my regimental badge!" he exclaimed. "Where did you say you found it exactly?"

"Close by where someone had secreted Mr Salah's wallet," Fisher replied grimly.

"In the cellar, I think you said?"

"Exactly so. In the cellar where the dead man's body was also hidden. A difficult task for the killer, I imagine, and likely to lead to all sorts of things being knocked off or dropped and the owner none the wiser."

"But I helped move Salah's body to his room, Inspector. With Dr Watson, as it happens," Hopkirk protested, pointing at me. "It must have dropped off then. As you said, all sorts of things get knocked off when you're shifting a body in a packed cellar."

"He did," I confirmed, pleased he had raised the objection himself, so that I did not need to.

Fisher was obviously not put out, however. He glanced down at his notebook and, though he was too far away for me to read what he had written there, I could make out the large map he had drawn of the cellar, and the crosses, which presumably indicated the position of Salah's body, his wallet and Hopkirk's cap badge. "I'm aware of that, Captain," he said, "but the badge was not discovered near the body, but to one side, under a rusted grass-cutting machine…"

"A grass-cutting machine with dried blood on it?" I interrupted, unable to stop myself. "That was the machine which Captain Hopkirk brought to our attention just after Salah's body was found, and upon which he spotted a drop of fresh blood."

Fisher glared at me, then turned on Holmes. "This is the first I've heard of such a thing," he declared angrily. "Why was I not informed of it when we spoke earlier?"

Holmes was contrite. "My apologies, Inspector," he said, "but if you will recall, I did mention the spot of fresh blood discovered near the body. However, it was remiss of me not to be more precise about its location and the identity of the man who noticed it. In any case, it hardly seems the action of a man keen to distance himself from a murder."

"Though it might explain when my cap badge fell off," Hopkirk added. "Either then, or when Dr Watson and I actually shifted the poor chap's body." He shrugged. "I wasn't even aware it was missing until you showed me it."

Fisher scribbled furiously in his notebook, underlining several points heavily. Beyond that, he made no comment on this new information. Instead, he asked Hopkirk at what time he had retired on the night of the murder.

"As I told you, and Mr Holmes before you, I was in bed by ten thirty and slept soundly all night."

"You insist that you did not leave your room last night after ten thirty?"

Even if Hopkirk missed it, I could hear danger in Fisher's voice. He appeared oblivious, however.

"Not for a moment," he said.

With cold certainty, Inspector Fisher allowed his trap to close on the captain. "Constable Halliday, please ask the young lady to step inside," he said. His eyes remained fixed on Hopkirk while the constable opened the door and invited Alice Crabtree to enter.

She did so, following Halliday across the room until she stood at the side of the table, shuffling shyly from foot to foot and twisting a rag between her hands, her eyes downcast. Fisher said her name and she looked up quickly, as though concerned she were acting inappropriately. I had never really looked at her before, but now that I did I could see that she was a heavy-set, somewhat plain girl, with a mass of brown hair which she wore wound into a loose bun and crammed beneath an old-fashioned white bonnet, such as servants had worn half a century before. Her eyes were a grey-green colour and there was a long smudge of ash on her left ear of all places. As her eyes flicked nervously towards Hopkirk, he crossed his legs and blew smoke towards the ceiling, with an expression more confused than concerned on his face.

"Miss Crabtree," the inspector repeated irritably.

She gave a start as though jabbed with a pin and turned to him, the rag twisting into a tight rope in her hand. "Yes, sir?" she asked in a small, near whisper.

"Don't be nervous, girl," Fisher went on in a kinder voice. "You've done nothing wrong. All you need to do is tell everyone what you told me earlier."

"About the boots?" she asked. Her knuckles had whitened with the force she was exerting on the rag, I noticed. Holmes emitted a small grunt of recognition at my side, and I suddenly remembered our meeting the previous evening.

"That's right, about the boots," said Fisher. His tone was patient but there was no disguising the excitement on his face. I had seen the same look of anticipation on the face of Lestrade when he believed an arrest was close.

Captain Hopkirk, for his part, evinced no sign of concern. He continued to smoke and to watch the girl with a sort of disinterested puzzlement.

"Well, sir, it was like this." Alice finally began to speak, and as she did so, much of her nervousness fell away. She allowed the rag to loosen in her grip and her voice increased in strength as she went on in a rush of information. "Last night, Mr Buxton asked me to clean enough pairs of boots for all the guests and to put them outside their rooms. He was taking them all for a walk next day, he said, and what with the snow and all, he was worried they'd ruin their good clothes in the dirt and the mud. Well, there ain't pairs of boots for everyone, I says, unless they all brought their own, but they have, he says. So get the ones from the hall that they was wearing today, he says, and give them a clean and put them outside their rooms."

"And did you?" Fisher interrupted, allowing the girl to take a much-needed breath.

"I did, sir. I found most of them boots where they'd been left and gave them a clean and put them outside the rooms."

"All the rooms?" Fisher asked, his pencil poised above his notebook. "Did you leave them all outside the guests' rooms?"

Alice shook her head. "I put them outside every room but his…" she said, and cast a sideways look at Hopkirk. "Begging your pardon, Captain Hopkirk's. His door wasn't shut proper, so I knocked on it, in case he wanted them put inside, and the door swung open but he wasn't there, so I put them outside like the others and left."

"You shut the bedroom door behind you?"

She nodded again, some of her timorousness returning now that she had been brought to specifics.

Fisher scribbled something down as he addressed himself to Hopkirk. His voice was calm but it was all he could do to keep a smile from his face. "What have you to say to that, Captain?"

"The girl's obviously mistaken," Hopkirk replied with, in the circumstances, surprising calm. He swivelled in his seat so that he was facing Alice directly, the first time he had done so since she entered the room. "There are a lot of empty rooms up there, Alice. How can you be sure it was my room you entered?"

At first, I thought Alice would not speak. Seconds passed in silence, and then she replied so quietly that we all had to strain to hear. "It was next door to Mr Reilly's," she whispered. "And I brought you up a jug of water yesterday. That's how I knew it was yours."

Hopkirk had the grace to look embarrassed as he continued to argue with the young maid. "And yet there were no boots outside my room when I rose this morning, my dear girl. I had to take a pair from downstairs to go out with Dr Watson and Mr Holmes."

Fisher shook his head in mock sorrow. "Even though there were – indeed, still are – pairs of boots outside the doors of the Schells and Mr Reilly, who did not accompany Mr Buxton on his little tour. Are you claiming that, inexplicably, yours was the only room outside which no boots were left?"

"No, not exactly that," Hopkirk muttered. A bead of sweat rolled down his face and ran along the line of his chin. "Or rather, yes, I am claiming that. But in any case," he went on more strongly, his manner for the first time visibly agitated, "this won't do, not at all. You drag me up here and all but accuse me of slaughtering Salah, and all because of a dropped badge and the fact that a maid may or may not have put my boots at the wrong door? I've never heard such nonsense, Inspector! Why, I've a good mind to report you! I have friends who could make your life a misery and bring your petty little career to a quick end!"

Secure in the knowledge that his triumph was imminent, Fisher allowed Hopkirk to rant for a moment or two longer. Then he gestured to Constable Halliday, who took a step forward so that he was standing directly behind the captain.

"I'm afraid that I must ask you to keep your voice down, Captain Hopkirk. Both because it's frightening this young lady–" he indicated Alice Crabtree, who did indeed look about to burst into tears "–and because it would not be in your own best interests to lose your temper in such a violent fashion again."

Hopkirk's complaints came to a sudden halt and he sat, red-faced, glaring at the inspector. In the silence that followed, Fisher thanked Alice for her time and informed her she could leave, which she did with considerably more speed than she had entered. Only once she was gone, and the door firmly closed behind her, did he continue.

"Now, sir, if you'll allow me, I'll tell you what I think happened last night. I'd be obliged if you didn't interrupt, but feel free to ask any questions or make any corrections once I'm done." He picked up his notebook and turned back a couple of pages. "What I think happened is this. You were still angry with Mr Salah after he exposed your illicit affair with Mrs Schell, and were fearful that he would repeat his accusations again. You'd already tried to silence him once, but Mr Holmes prevented that, so you waited until everyone was in bed, then followed him on his nightly walk, saying you wanted to have it out with him. You fought and in the struggle you finished off the job you'd started that afternoon. Now," he held up a hand to prevent any interruption from Hopkirk, "I'm sure you didn't mean to kill him, but you've got a bad temper – we've witnesses to that – and it just got the better of you. But now you had a dead body on your hands, didn't you? Even then, you are a soldier – or you were once, at least – and not easily upset by corpses. You only needed it hidden for a day or two, after all, for then you'd be gone, the auction over and the house locked up until the new owner took over. So you dumped Mr Salah in that dirty, unlit cellar. His wallet fell out of his pocket, I suppose, but you didn't need the money, so you threw it away. Salah'd argued with almost everyone after all, and though people might think it odd, they'd be willing to believe he'd done a moonlight flit, if there's nothing to suggest otherwise. It was just your bad luck, though, that

Mr Buxton decided to go and check on the entrance to the caves and happened to spot the corpse."

"That is not what happened at all! How dare you!" Hopkirk's composure had gone now, and he jumped to his feet as he spoke, reaching across the table for Fisher with violence in his eyes. His fingers had merely brushed the fabric of the inspector's coat when Constable Halliday's two substantial hands crashed down on his shoulders and he crumpled back into his seat.

"If you could remain seated, Captain," Fisher said, emphasising Hopkirk's title with a sneer. "I did say that I'd be happy to hear any questions and objections, but I must warn you that, though you are not yet under arrest, that is not a state of affairs which is likely to last beyond tomorrow morning, when we return to town on the first available train."

Hopkirk twice opened his mouth to speak, and twice closed it again without doing so. Instead, he smoothed back his hair and straightened his jacket. He lit a fresh cigarette with a hand that was very slightly trembling, and sat back in his chair.

"Until then, Constable Halliday will escort you to your room, where you will remain for the moment." Fisher nodded to Halliday, who followed Hopkirk from the room. As soon as the door closed behind them, Fisher turned towards us.

"Well then, Mr Holmes, I think that's a very promising start to proceedings. An excellent morning's work, and based entirely on proper, unglamorous police work."

Holmes stretched his long legs out in front of him, then pushed himself to his feet. He lit a cigarette before he spoke.

"I certainly admire the courageous way in which you acted, Inspector," he said finally. "To threaten to arrest a man who claims to have powerful friends on such flimsy evidence is a brave act indeed."

"Flimsy evidence? He attacked and almost killed the dead man, he lied about being in his room when Salah was killed, and a badge he admits is his was found right beside one of the dead man's possessions. I've rarely seen a more cut and dried case."

Holmes sniffed doubtfully. "You may be right, Inspector," he said. "I am merely an observer, when all is said and done."

"I should be grateful if you would remember that, Mr Holmes," said the inspector. He picked up his pencil and resumed writing in his notebook. It was obvious that we had been dismissed.

We emerged from the room just in time to see the top of Constable Halliday's head as he escorted Hopkirk down the short flight of stairs which led back to the main part of the building. By the time we followed him through the door that connected the two sections of the house, the burly policeman was stationed outside the captain's room. There was nobody else about and I wondered if Holmes would want to go downstairs and make further enquiries, but instead he stopped in front of his door and reached for the handle.

"Fisher is correct, of course," he said, in a voice loud enough for Halliday to hear. "The evidence against Hopkirk, while circumstantial, is compelling, on the surface at least. But there is something that does not ring true. The captain is withholding some detail, I am sure of it."

He turned the handle and pushed his door open, then stopped suddenly. On the floor, just inside his room, lay an envelope. It was just far enough inside that Halliday could not see it, and had obviously been pushed under the door. Holmes knelt down as though to tie his shoelace, continuing to talk to me over his shoulder as he did so.

"I think I shall come downstairs for that drink, after all, Watson," he said, as he palmed the letter and rose to his feet, sliding it inside his jacket pocket as he did so. "Listening to a police inspector in full spate is thirsty work."

He nodded to Halliday, who studiously ignored him, and led the way downstairs. There was nobody in the dining room, so we slipped inside and Holmes quickly opened the envelope.

Inside we found a single sheet of paper, headed "Thorpe Manor", of the sort that had been placed by Buxton in every room. Holmes unfolded it, read it, and held it out to me.

I took it and cast my eye over its brief message. "Meet me at the grotto at 2 p.m., I beg of you. A man's life may depend on it."

It was signed Julieanne Schell.

Chapter Fourteen

Julieanne's Confession

Even in distress, Julieanne Schell was a striking woman. She stood at the mouth of the sparkling cave, wrapped in a pale fox-fur coat which stretched down to her tan leather boots, her auburn hair swept up and pinned high on her head. Her eyes were downcast, however, and as she looked up at us, her face was grave.

"Thank you for coming, gentlemen," she began quietly. "I have spent the day unsure what to do for the best, and even now am not certain I am doing the right thing. The consequences…" She stopped and pulled nervously at the fingers of her right glove. We waited for her to speak, as she traced a pattern in the snow with her foot. Twice she began to say something, only to bite off her words unspoken.

"I do not come from a rich family, Mr Holmes, or an influential one," she announced finally, the words coming quickly as if she feared she would be unable to continue, were she to consider them for even a moment. "Quite the reverse, in fact. My father worked on the Boston dockyards until he was crushed beneath a falling cargo container, and I have six siblings, all younger than me. All I had was my pleasing looks, and with them a family of eight to feed."

"Mrs Schell..." Holmes began, but the lady was not ready to stop, now that she had found her voice.

"No, Mr Holmes, do not say anything. Let me speak while my resolution allows. My looks were given to me by God, but I added a sweet voice by my own efforts, through listening to my betters and mimicking them, until I sounded an educated young woman even if, in truth, I was not." She smiled, but it was a weak effort and contained no humour that I could see. "Pretty girls are welcome everywhere, Mr Holmes, in America as much as in England, and I caught the eye of more than one wealthy man. But I rejected all advances until the day I was introduced to Frederick Schell. A bachelor of advanced age, a rich man desiring a young wife to care for him in his declining years. He was exactly what I sought." A strand of hair had escaped the pin that held it in place, and she carefully returned it to its place. "He proposed within a week, and we were married within a month. My family were rescued from poverty, my brothers and sisters given decent starts in life, my mother made comfortable. And all in return for allowing Frederick to believe himself still a vital man, to do as he bade at all times, to tell him the kind lie that he remained the master of his own life. I have simply always done whatever I had to do to survive."

"But then you met Captain Hopkirk?" Holmes's voice was soft.

"Yes, Mr Holmes. Then I met Captain Hopkirk. We were touring Europe, as we had done every year since we married. We were in San Moritz and James asked Frederick for a light for his cigar. They fell to talking and discovered a shared love of racehorses." She hesitated and her face coloured a deep pink. "Do not think me too mercenary, Mr Holmes. I do not love Frederick, but he knew that from the beginning. And I do love James. That is why I asked Frederick to invite him this weekend."

"Do such requests not raise his suspicions?"

"Perhaps they do, Mr Holmes, but I believe that he is aware, on some level, of the attraction between James and myself."

I had to interrupt. "You think he knows about your affair?"

"Not knows, exactly, Dr Watson. But there is something, occasional things he has said, which lead me to believe that he is aware that we are closer than would normally be thought acceptable."

I could see that Holmes was becoming impatient with the turn the conversation had taken. He tutted and drew Mrs Schell's eyes towards him again.

"That is all very well, but I assume that your husband's awareness would not stretch so far as to ignore proven infidelity?"

"No, it would not," the lady replied, and her lip trembled for the first time since we had arrived. "Frederick could not abide public humiliation. It would be the end of our marriage, and the end of the comfortable life I have created for myself. But no matter the consequences, I love James and it would be wrong of me to keep quiet, when all it takes is a word to remove suspicion from him entirely."

"You can vouch for Captain Hopkirk during the period he was absent from his room?"

"Yes," she said simply. The admission seemed to give her new strength, and her voice was stronger as she continued. "You see, he and I were... together... when Mr Salah was killed. That was why he was not in his room."

Holmes did not seem surprised. "I see," he said. "As he was not in his room, I assume you too were not in your own. Were you not concerned that your husband would notice your absence?"

She shook her head. "My husband takes a sleeping draught every night, which I prepare for him. I simply doubled the dose, and there was no chance he would wake before morning."

"You have done this before, then?"

She did not speak, but gave a tiny nod.

"At what time did you leave your room? And where did you arrange to meet Captain Hopkirk?"

"We had agreed to meet at eleven thirty. My husband is a creature of habit and takes his draught at eleven fifteen at the latest. James had identified a room in the east wing, overlooking the rear of the house, which he said he had made comfortable for us. We met there."

"He was punctual?"

"I was early, but he was waiting for me when I arrived. I heard a clock chime a quarter to the hour as I opened the door."

"And how long did you stay in the room together?"

"Over two hours. I returned to my room a little after two in the morning."

"You were never separate during that time?"

"Not for a second." She looked up and ran a finger along the bottom of her eye, catching the unshed tears there without spoiling her make-up.

"Does the captain know you are speaking to us?" asked Holmes.

"Of course not!" she bridled instantly. "James is not the sort of man to shelter behind a woman's skirts!"

"I did not mean to imply that he was, Mrs Schell, merely to

ascertain whether, having kept your assignation secret until now, he too is willing to expose your relationship to public scrutiny."

As though piercing a thin surface with a pin, Holmes's final words seemed to unleash something in Julieanne Schell. Perhaps, for all her brave talk, she only now realised that her world truly was about to be turned upside down. Whatever it was, she reacted as though she had been struck. Her already pale face turned white and she sagged at the knees, only preventing herself from falling completely by reaching out a hand and grasping the side of the cave wall. Even then, such was the force of her collapse that her hand slid down the rough stone, scraping the leather glove and causing it to tear at the seam of one finger. She hung there for the briefest of moments, then let out a single, quiet sob. And that was the only sign of genuine distress that I saw. A moment later, she straightened up, already nearly composed. She examined her glove then removed both it and its partner and dropped them both to the ground at her feet.

"I am willing to swear all of this on oath, Mr Holmes, regardless of the consequences," she stated flatly.

Holmes looked at the house, then back to Mrs Schell. "I hope it will not come to that," he said finally. "But it will be necessary for the inspector to know what you have told us. Would you prefer that I speak to him, or would you rather do that yourself? Or perhaps Captain Hopkirk…"

He left the question unspoken, and Mrs Schell gave no reply.

Instead, she walked past him without a word and began the slow trudge back to the house. I watched her for a moment, and wondered about her nature. She was a complex woman, more complex than I had believed, and one experienced in hiding her true self. I now knew she was not really the timorous wife of a successful, elderly businessman, but was she a hard-faced gold digger, as the Americans phrase it, or simply a woman who had found true love too late, after she had committed herself to a different life altogether? Whatever the truth, I felt nothing but pity for her as she grew smaller and smaller in the distance.

"Captain Hopkirk is an innocent man, it seems, Holmes," I said as she disappeared inside the house.

"Perhaps, Watson, perhaps," my friend replied thoughtfully.

"What... of course he is," I began; then, grasping his meaning, acknowledged the truth of his statement. "Ah, I take your point, Holmes. Innocent in the matter of the death of Salah, then, even if his behaviour otherwise leaves much to be desired."

"No, he did not kill Salah," Holmes agreed. "Of that I am convinced."

"For what it's worth, Holmes, I agree," I said, but he did not react.

"We must tell the inspector what Mrs Schell has told us," he said, and stalked off towards the house without another word. I stooped and retrieved Mrs Schell's gloves and hurried to catch up.

Chapter Fifteen

The Love Nest

There was no sign of Mrs Schell by the time we reached the house. My assumption was that we would immediately seek out Inspector Fisher and appraise him of recent developments. Holmes, however, had other ideas.

"That would be premature, I think," he explained. "At the moment, all we have is the unsupported word of Mrs Schell. The inspector is unlikely to accept that as proof that the captain was not involved in Salah's murder."

"Come now, Holmes," I protested, "you are surely not suggesting that Mrs Schell is lying? Why should she leave herself open to public humiliation if she were not involved, as she claims, in a relationship with Captain Hopkirk?"

"I do not say that she is not the paramour of Captain Hopkirk," Holmes countered calmly, "but I do require more evidence that she was in his company last night when Salah was killed. The inspector has made it clear that he does not welcome our interference in his case; I should be more comfortable approaching him with some material facts, which support Mrs Schell's claim."

I could not argue with Holmes's logic. "Very well, Holmes, but how can we obtain such evidence?"

"Most obviously, by examining the room in which their tryst took place. With luck, there will be something to be found, which argues persuasively that both Mrs Schell and Captain Hopkirk were present there, even though it is unlikely we can pinpoint an exact time."

"The east wing, then?"

"Exactly. One of the rooms must contain some indication of recent residence. Our job is to find it."

The east wing was connected to the main part of the house via a second staircase, which was itself accessed via a large door at the end of the corridor containing all our rooms. The staircase was not long, amounting to only eight steps, and opened out onto another corridor, which ran the length of the building at right angles to the central part of the house. Another staircase led downstairs to the ground floor, from which one could exit through either a side or a rear door, though Buxton had informed us that both had been nailed shut since the late Lord Thorpe had taken to a life of seclusion.

There were not very many rooms, as it turned out, and Mrs Schell had mentioned that the one in which she had met Hopkirk looked out upon the back of the house. It did not take us long to find it.

The contents of the room barely differed from any other in the east wing. It was merely their state that made them stand out.

In each of the other rooms in the abandoned wing, everything was draped in sheets and layers of dust, so that the interior of the house in many ways appeared to echo that of the fields outside: an expanse of rolling white shapes, their precise nature blurred by soft coverings. Only in this single room had any colour intruded. A dust sheet had been pulled back and dropped on the floor, exposing a dull maroon chaise longue and a matching footstool.

Holmes stood in the doorway, taking in the scene, his cigarette burning down unnoticed between his fingers. He ambled across to the footstool and, from the floor behind it, picked up a wine glass by its stem. As he angled it against the light, a single red lipstick print could be seen to stand out starkly at its rim. He crouched down on his haunches and peered beneath the chaise longue.

"The other in the pair has rolled out of reach," he said, carefully replacing the glass in his hand on the footstool. He rose to his feet and slowly walked around it, pointing down at the floor as he did so. "A man's footprints, leading from the seat to the window," he went on, following their path as he spoke. "Perhaps he wished to…" He reached the window and slid it open. "Ah, yes," he said, "this moves smoothly. It has been opened recently, I think." He glanced down at the cigarette in his hand, then flicked it through the open window. "There is no ashtray, so Hopkirk came over here to dispose of his cigarette butt."

I had followed in Holmes's wake, but there was nothing to see in the room other than that which he had described. Even the view from the window was nondescript, comprising merely a small stretch of the rear of the house, with everything beyond occluded by a stand of trees to the right and a high wall to the left. Holmes stood there in thought for a minute or two, breathing in the crisp, cold air, then slid the window down.

"Where to now, Holmes?" I asked. "This confirms that Mrs Schell was telling the truth about her assignation with Captain Hopkirk, but she was hardly likely to tell so damaging a story if it were untrue, was she?" I frowned. "We are rapidly running out of points of enquiry."

"Not at all, Watson," said Holmes grimly. "Far from being the end of our enquiries, this room has revealed to me several points of interest." He glanced out of the window again, and stiffened suddenly. "One of which I think we should investigate without further delay. Come, Watson, we have not a moment to waste!"

With that, he slipped past me and headed into the corridor. I hurried along behind, pulling the door closed after me. Holmes was already ten yards ahead of me, his long stride causing him to pull away, and I was forced to run to catch up with him. I reached him just as he arrived at the top of the small flight of stairs, which led back into the central part of the house, and put my hand on his arm to stop him.

"Wait a moment, Holmes!" I cried, puffing slightly with the unexpected exercise. "Where exactly are we going? What did you see in that room which necessitates such haste?"

"Not in the room, Watson. Outside it!"

He pulled his arm away and bounded down the stairs, taking them two a time and hitting the landing at their base already at a trot. I could make no sense of what he had said, but knew from past experience that when Holmes was energised in this manner, there was always good cause. Not knowing our destination and thus unwilling to allow him out of my sight, I hastened after him.

* * *

I caught up with him as he reached the bottom of the main staircase and swept round its corner, heading towards the servants' area. Frederick Schell stood in the entrance to the main hall with a query on his lips but Holmes bustled past him and pushed open the heavy kitchen doors.

"This way, Watson," he called over his shoulder.

Obviously, he had seen something out of the window, but what it could be eluded me. Somebody in the trees perhaps, who would be gone if given half the chance but whom, if we were quick, we might hope to subdue? In any case, I would know soon enough what Holmes had seen, for as he careered through the back doors, I heard him thunder down the outside steps with a shout of "Get away! You there, get away!" Seconds later, there was a loud smash and an unearthly howl of rage, followed by a series of bangs and crashes.

I had left my army revolver in London, on the assumption that there would be no call for it on a holiday in the country, but not for the first time I reproached myself for my naivety. Whenever I was with Holmes, there was always the possibility of trouble. Even the walking stick I had taken from Salah would have been useful, but there was no time to go back for that now. Instead, I clenched my fists, barged the back door open with my shoulder and readied myself for whatever threat waited outside.

Holmes knelt at the bottom of the stairs, one arm draped loosely around the neck of a thin, curly-haired dog and the other engaged in tickling it behind the ears. To his side lay a metal bucket, tipped on its side, and immediately beyond that several old garden rakes and spades, similarly knocked askew. I grabbed at the stair railing to bring myself to a peremptory stop, for otherwise I would have tumbled down the stairs and landed on top of Holmes and his new friend.

Both parties looked up at me as I did so, the dog with a look of mild disdain, as though I had done something truly foolish of which I should be ashamed, and Holmes with one more quizzical in nature, as though he were not entirely sure why I had been hurrying at all.

"Are you quite all right, Watson?" he enquired solicitously.

I nodded, not trusting myself to speak until I had taken a second to catch my breath. Having done so, I descended the stairs and stood beside Holmes and the dog.

"I'm fine, Holmes," I said as calmly as I could. "But perhaps you could tear yourself away from your pet for long enough to explain why we tore through the house in such a frenzy if, once outside, there seems to be no need for haste whatsoever?"

Holmes kept hold of the dog, but gestured at a patch of snow about ten feet away, at the edge of the stand of trees I had seen from the window of the room. "My apologies, Watson. I realise how peculiar this must look, but I assure you that there is good reason for my actions. If you would step over there carefully and take a close look at the ground, I will be happy to explain."

I did as Holmes asked. Once viewed in closer proximity, the area he had indicated clearly stood out against the remainder of the snowy ground. Where everywhere else was smooth and uniform, here the snow had been churned up and, at its centre, flattened into a winding, elongated tube. More dramatically, however, at one end of the tube was a lengthy slash of scarlet; a thick line of what I was certain was blood, staining the pristine whiteness of the snow. I remembered the chaise longue against the dust sheets upstairs and realised that this was what Holmes must have seen from the window.

At that moment he came up behind me, the dog now in his arms, and confirmed my thought.

"When I looked out of the window, I saw the bloodstain quite clearly against the snow – and also this little fellow nosing about in the area. Dogs have many admirable qualities, but tidiness is not one of them, and I was fearful that he would disturb the snow in his quest for food, hence the necessity of getting down here before he did so. As it happened, I only just succeeded. He was on the verge of tramping right across the bloodied patch when I arrived and I'm afraid I gave him quite a start when I kicked over the bucket to distract him. He ran straight into that set of garden tools and from there directly into me." He ran his hands along the little animal's sides. "I suspect he is a stray. His ribs are quite pronounced and he is obviously in need of a good feed. Hold him for a moment, there's a good fellow," he concluded, thrusting the dog into my arms. "I should prefer it if he were not running around while I make a closer examination of the ground here."

Unmindful of the wet ground, he squatted down and bent low over the snowy indentation, shuffling carefully along one side and then down the other, stopping for several minutes at the bloody mark. Finally, he pushed himself to his feet and stepped into the copse of trees. Thinking I might release the dog, who was now squirming in my arms, I followed him, but there was little to see. The copse amounted to no more than a dozen mixed birch and alder trees and, behind them, a rough path which extended along the side of the house and had presumably been used for deliveries in happier times. Holmes obviously agreed, because he was already on his way back to me as I entered the little wood.

He glanced at the dog with a puzzled look. "Are you intending to keep that animal, Watson?" he asked. "I must say that I do not think Mrs Hudson would be keen on our keeping a dog in Baker Street. It would be better, I think, if you were to give it to the maid, and ask her to look after it."

Any rejoinder I might have made would have to wait, for the little dog's efforts to escape my grasp had become more marked and he had begun to growl deep in his throat. I satisfied myself with an annoyed growl of my own, therefore, and quickly skipped past Holmes and up the stairs, back into the house. From behind me, Holmes called out that now would be an apposite moment to involve Inspector Fisher – could I find him and ask him to join us in the garden?

By the time I had located Alice and deposited the dog with her, then convinced Fisher that he should come with me, ten minutes had passed. Holmes had not been idle in my absence, however.

From some wooden trellis slats he had constructed a fence around the patch of ground, enclosing and concealing both the bloodied snow and the entire flattened area. He stood over it, smoking and staring back at the stand of trees with a thoughtful countenance. Behind me, Fisher gave a low whistle at the sight, though whether in approval or ridicule, I could not say.

"Well, Mr Holmes, what have you to show me?" he asked. "Dr Watson was less than forthcoming in his description, and merely said that you and he had uncovered an important item of evidence."

Pulling on a pair of gloves against the cold, the inspector followed me down the stairs, complaining under his breath about wasting police time. Once he had taken a few steps, however, and could see over Holmes's impromptu fence, he gave a sharp intake of breath and hurried forward.

"That's blood!" he exclaimed. "And fresh too."

He knelt down and levered at the nearest trellis board. Holmes, with an expression of immense annoyance on his face, stepped forward and placed a hand on top of the board, preventing its removal.

"It is not just the blood, Inspector," he explained. "There is also the shape of the snow on the ground. The boards are there to prevent it being erased by accident."

"The shape of the snow?"

"Exactly so. If you would move over here?"

Fisher nodded and the two men stood back and examined the enclosure from a short distance. Holmes pointed to the compacted snow.

"As you know, I initially believed that Alim Salah had been outside the house shortly before he was murdered and had fallen in deep snow, possibly during the violent altercation that led to his death. I further posited that his body was then carried into the house via the back door and the servants' stair, which leads to the cellar."

"I know all this, Mr Holmes," Fisher complained impatiently. "And I told you, my theory is that Captain Hopkirk, enraged by the dead man's slur on the character of Mrs Schell, followed him on his night-time excursions. Having then killed Salah, possibly by accident, he hid the body in the nearest possible location, the cellar, intending that it would not be found until after he had left the house, and possibly the country."

Holmes was not a petty man, but he was certainly capable of enjoying a moment of triumphant drama. "That theory can now be discarded, Inspector. It is, in several respects, demonstrably incorrect."

Fisher coloured, and was immediately belligerent. "In what way?" he barked.

"As I said, observe the shape the indentation makes in the snow, Inspector. It is not a straight line, such as might be made by a thick branch or even a slide of snow from the roof. It begins slightly thinner at the bottom," he indicated the left-hand side, which was indeed decidedly narrower than the middle section, "then curves into a long thicker section, before ending in this distinct, deeper area at the top." He pointed to the far right-hand side, close to the patch of blood. As he had described, this part was deeper, more of a rounded hole than the rest. "It is the form of a man, running from his legs to his head. I would suggest that this is where Salah's body was dropped while the killer checked the back door was unlocked and made sure there was nobody about inside."

"And he could not have been killed here because there is no sign of a struggle in the snow nearby. Thus it is unlikely that the cellar was the nearest useful hiding place to the murder itself." Fisher was a touchy man, and made it no secret that he did not desire Holmes's help, but he was no fool.

"Indeed. There are plenty of footprints, but it is impossible now to differentiate those made by your constables from those made by the killer. We are fortunate that this small section is both sheltered by these trees and sufficiently far from the back entrance that nobody has walked over it."

Inspector Fisher grunted his agreement. "Thank you, Mr

Holmes. My men did make a search of the area, but the significance of this apparently eluded them."

"Easily done, Inspector," Holmes suggested kindly. He looked down at the fenced-off area then back up at the house. "They might also want to take another look at the path which runs along the side of the house. I can think of no other way in which the body can have been brought to this point."

"Naturally," replied Fisher. "But you said that my theory was incorrect in several respects? I can't believe you'd be so imprecise as to say several and mean only one."

"Thank you for the reminder, Inspector. I must tell you that Captain Hopkirk has been provided with an alibi by Mrs Schell for the period during which we believe the murder was carried out."

Holmes delivered this news in the same matter-of-fact tone that one might use when describing a new hall carpet, and Fisher, to his credit, took it in the same calm manner – though close examination of his voice when he spoke suggested that he was controlling his temper with some difficulty.

"Is that so, Mr Holmes? Well, that is rather important, do you not agree? So important that I wonder why Mrs Schell chose to speak to you, rather than a policeman. But in any case, I think we need to put the matter to Captain Hopkirk. He has some explaining to do, wouldn't you say?"

He did not wait for an answer, but turned on his heel, slipping a little on the snow. He had just reached the door when a new thought occurred to him, and he turned to look at us with a grim smile on his face.

"Of course, while this lifts suspicion from Hopkirk, it lays it a little more firmly upon Reilly. He was no more than twenty feet from the body, and at about the same time. Mr Hopkirk is not the only one with whom I shall need to speak."

With that, he went indoors. I heard him shout for Constable Halliday, and give him some indistinct orders, and then he was too far away for his voice to be made out. I turned to Holmes, but he merely looked down for a moment at the compacted snow and the splash of blood, then stalked over to a heap of rotten tarpaulins, which lay piled in the lee of a snow-covered woodpile. He pulled the top canvas away and carried it across, then draped it loosely over the little fence he had created, leaving plenty of space for the cold air to circulate.

"To prevent the rain and wind from disturbing it," he explained, rubbing the dirt from his hands. "I think perhaps we should not follow the inspector," he went on. "I do not think he would thank us for our company at the moment."

He turned on his heel and passed under the trees to the little path that ran along the side of the house. Not for the first time that day, I trailed along in Holmes's wake, keeping as far as I could to the cartwheel tracks which provided the only break in the deep snow, and shaking my head in wonder at his unfailing ability to antagonise police inspectors.

Chapter Sixteen

Hopkirk is Reprieved

"It's not so very complicated, I'm afraid. In fact, it's the oldest story of them all. A fellow falls for his friend's wife and she for him, and... well... and they prove to be weaker than they'd should have been."

In contrast to his earlier appearance before Inspector Fisher, James Hopkirk now sat slumped dejectedly in his chair. I did not doubt his sincerity, nor his contrition. I had known men like Hopkirk before, during my time in the army. Men used exclusively to male company who, once returned to a more civilised world, quickly found themselves overwhelmed and liable to fall into unsuitable romances, seemingly incapable of acting otherwise. It was plain that one such sat before us now. He hung his head low, unable to look any of us in the eye, as he continued his story.

"I met Frederick and Julieanne... Mrs Schell, I should say... just as I said, on the continent. What I did not mention, however, was that I had recently been asked to resign my commission from the regiment. The matter was not a dishonourable one, please believe me, but it involved my striking a senior officer, and resignation or a court martial were my only choices."

"You assaulted a senior officer?" Fisher had been disconsolate since Holmes had relayed Julieanne Schell's account of her affair with Hopkirk, but now he was revitalised. His eyes crinkled with interest and his notebook, left undisturbed in his pocket until now, was taken out and placed on the table before him. He laid a pencil alongside it and lined the two up, then, as though a ritual had been completed, repeated his question. "I said, you assaulted a senior officer, Captain Hopkirk?"

"I did."

"Just as you attacked Alim Salah?"

Hopkirk flushed and half shook his head, but said nothing. Evidently, it had not occurred to him that the two incidents would strike anyone as similar.

Holmes broke the silence. "Perhaps you can tell us what did happen?" he said.

Gratefully, Hopkirk tore his eyes from Fisher's and addressed himself to Holmes. "There's little to tell, in truth, but what there is, I imagine a lawyer might well twist to my disadvantage." He sat up straighter, and took a deep breath. "Still, there's nothing to be gained by silence now, I suppose. The officer I struck was a major in my company by the name of McLaughlin, a dour Dundonian religious sort, who saw the devil in every man he met and thought all women an inducement to sin. He made a disparaging remark about a nurse of our mutual acquaintance and then refused to withdraw it." He looked across at me and a smile flickered over his face. "So I punched him on the jaw and knocked the sanctimonious buzzard out cold. Unlike my bout of fisticuffs with the late lamented Mr Salah, however, I do not regret the action at all, only the consequences. The major's brother was a staff officer with far more influence than I could ever hope to bring to bear, and out the army I went, barely able to hold on to my good name."

Fisher's eyes had not left Hopkirk throughout his speech. In the pause that followed the captain's confession, he growled his own opinion of the affair.

"That all seems very familiar, Captain Hopkirk. A female friend of yours insulted and you losing your temper and assaulting the man you considered to have done the insulting. That's what we in the police force call a pattern of behaviour. It's the kind of thing we look out for, in fact." He scribbled a note and tapped his pencil thoughtfully on the paper. "Was this lady also a romantic conquest of yours? Was she too already married? Do you make a habit of seducing married women, Captain Hopkirk?"

If Fisher hoped to throw Hopkirk off balance by these rapid queries, he was unsuccessful. If anything, the barrage of questions served only to strengthen the captain's resolve. Some of the despondency which had been so evident in his posture and speech seemed to lift as he answered the inspector.

"She was an elderly nurse, Inspector," he said. "Sixty if she was a day and, I believe, happily married to one of the chaplains. So no, old man, I was not romantically involved with the lady. I must say, though, that it says something for your own character that you would apparently only speak up for a wronged lady if she were your lover."

Now it was Fisher's turn to flush as his temper flared. "I said nothing of the sort! Of course, I would defend a lady if called upon!"

"So you admit that you would have acted in the exact same way that I did?"

"I... that is... I am not the one being questioned, Hopkirk, and I'll thank you to remember that!"

Amusing though this exchange had been, it was taking us no further forward. Holmes obviously felt the same way, for he chose that moment to speak for the first time. "Perhaps you could tell us about your relationship with Mrs Schell," he said smoothly. "You say that you met her three years ago, while she and her husband were on holiday in France?"

"I did."

"You were recently out of the army and, presumably, at a loose end?" Holmes glanced across at me. "I recall Watson was much the same when I met him."

"I was."

"You became friends with Mr Schell first? You have a mutual love of horses?"

"That's how we first got to talking, yes. Freddie has a small stable at home in the United States, and I've always ridden. We discussed the relative standard of British and American horses for a while, and then Julieanne joined us, and Freddie invited me to dine with them."

"And you became firm friends. The three of you."

"That's simply how it ended up. There was no intention on my part, I assure you."

Fisher gave an exaggerated grunt of disbelief, but he did not interrupt.

"And how long did it take before the friendship between you and Mrs Schell grew into something more than that?"

Hopkirk, who had entirely regained his equilibrium as he spoke to Holmes, suddenly coloured and looked down at the floor.

"Two and a half years," he said quietly.

"So your affair is quite new? You have been romantically entangled for only six months?"

"Since this summer. September, to be exact."

"Less than six months then?"

Hopkirk nodded, apparently confused by Holmes's concentration on this trivial detail. Inspector Fisher, too, was plainly of the opinion that valuable time was being wasted. He rapped his knuckles on the table, drawing every eye in the room towards him.

"And the affair has continued until the present day? You do not deny, I assume, that you were with Mrs Schell at the time Salah was murdered?"

Hopkirk's face fell, and he shook his head sadly. "I do not deny it, Inspector, now that she has chosen to make our relationship a matter of public record. But I wish she had never done so. It will destroy both a friendship and a marriage." He sighed heavily. "I would happily have remained under suspicion until we returned to London, rather than hurt Freddie Schell as badly as this revelation is bound to."

"You did not fear the noose then?" Fisher's voice was incredulous.

"I did not kill Salah, Inspector. Any policeman worth his salt would soon have realised that."

Again, Fisher only controlled his temper with difficulty. "A damn sight easier when supposedly innocent men tell us the truth," he barked. "So, you agree with Mrs Schell that you and she were together when we believe Mr Salah was killed? You will swear to that?"

"I will. Much as it pains me to do so." He raised an eyebrow and smiled crookedly. "Unless you'd be willing to turn a deaf ear to

Mrs Schell's confession? Play along with the idea that I'm the killer and then let me go later?"

"I don't think so." Fisher's reply was curt. He flipped through his notebook, seeking fresh inspiration.

"Why do you think that Mr Salah's wallet was discarded in the cellar, Captain?" he said finally, tapping a line on the page in front of him. "Why not throw it in the lake, or dump it in one of the many ridiculous buildings which litter the grounds?"

Hopkirk was unperturbed by the question. "A need for haste, I presume, Inspector. The killer had no time to hide it anywhere better, and feared discovery with it in his possession."

"If I might interrupt, Inspector Fisher," Holmes said, doing so. "Surely the important question is not why Salah's wallet was found where it was, but why his clothes have disappeared?"

When Fisher turned and glared at Holmes, I was sure he would remind him of his observational role, but instead he rounded on Hopkirk and muttered "Well?" as though he had posed the question himself. As I had observed before, for all his faults, he was no fool.

Hopkirk, looking between the two men, feigned confusion as he replied. "Is that question aimed at me, Mr Holmes? Inspector Fisher? Because I have to admit to a lack of training in police work..."

"It was largely rhetorical, Captain Hopkirk," Holmes assured him with a thin smile. "I would say that the reason is obvious. Whoever hid Mr Salah's clothing and suitcase wished everyone to believe he had left in the night."

"But that lie would hold only for as long as it took us to get back to London!" protested Fisher. "Even the most basic of enquiries would immediately highlight the fact that he had not returned from the manor house."

"Exactly," Holmes asserted with some force. "The deception only needed to remain in place long enough for this weekend's guests to disperse."

"Meaning the killer is definitely one of those guests!" Fisher concluded.

Holmes was typically cautious. "As I have had cause lamentably often to remind your colleagues in Scotland Yard, Inspector, it is foolhardy to jump to definite conclusions without all the evidence, but certainly that is one reasonable inference to draw."

"Reasonable inference?" Fisher scowled. "Pah. You seem determined to complicate everything, Mr Holmes. Of course, that's how you make your living, isn't it? Muddying the waters so that only you can make sense of the tangle that's left."

I was indignant on Holmes's behalf. The suspicion Inspector Fisher harboured of my friend had been plain from the beginning, but this attack on him overstepped the bounds of reasonable behaviour. I would have said something, but Holmes laid a hand on my arm to silence me.

"Mixed metaphor aside, your description of my methods is almost accurate, Inspector," he said. "The only mistake you make is in supposing that it is I who muddied the waters. Rather, my interest is piqued only by those cases where the waters are already muddied, often to such a degree that it seems there is nothing but wet mud left – if that is not stretching the analogy to breaking point."

As he spoke, Holmes stood up and opened the room door. "I imagine you have finished with Captain Hopkirk," he said. "But even if you have not, you will excuse me, I hope? I have one or two things to attend to and while the captain's reluctance to reveal his whereabouts was foolish, it was understandable – and certainly not criminal."

I knew that Holmes would want me to stay – it is surprising how many people relax their guard once Holmes has left a room – but it seemed that Fisher realised he was wasting his time, for he waved an irritable hand towards Hopkirk.

"Yes, you can go, Captain. I may need to speak to you later, but for the moment, I've no more questions."

Holmes paused in the open doorway. "Presumably the captain is no longer confined to his room?" he enquired.

"No," Fisher conceded. "Halliday," he went on, making a show of dismissing both Holmes and Hopkirk from his mind, "we've got work to do. First thing in the morning, tell Mrs Schell that I want to speak to her. I want to hear what she has to say for myself. Then you and Constable Cairns go over that back area inch by inch. Anything out of the ordinary, mark it off and come and get me. That is, if that's all right with you, Mr. Holmes?" he concluded, turning to the door.

But Holmes had already gone and he was speaking to thin air. Suppressing a smirk, I walked out into the hallway. As I caught up with Holmes, I heard Hopkirk wish Fisher a very good night, then a door closing with a thump, and the sound of Fisher's muffled, angry voice.

Chapter Seventeen

Tuesday Night and Wednesday Morning

So frantic had the last few hours been that I had failed to realise quite how late it was. A glance at my pocket watch confirmed that it was after 10 p.m., and a rumble in my stomach reminded me that I had not eaten since lunchtime. There was no chance that there would be any hot food left, if there ever had been any, so we set off for the kitchens in search of sustenance.

The servants' quarters were in darkness, but there was a full moon outside, which shone through the kitchen windows and provided enough illumination for us to light the gas lamps. In the pantry I found bread, fresh butter and cheese, which Alice had presumably laid in, and Holmes turned up a large bread knife and some plates. There was nobody else about, so we sat at the large kitchen table and chatted while we ate.

"I am glad that we have this moment to pause and reflect," Holmes began as soon as he had eaten his fill and got his pipe going strongly. "The last few days have been altogether too reactive and insufficiently deductive for my liking. Indeed, I must admit that there have been times when I have missed Lestrade, though obviously I would never tell him so. He has entirely too exaggerated a view of his own competence as it is. But there have been moments when relatively speedy access to Scotland Yard would have come in extremely handy."

"I am sure that there are," I sympathised. "But at least Mrs Schell has shortened our list of suspects. Removing one person from the list – two, in fact, since Hopkirk serves as alibi for Mrs Schell as much as she for him – narrows the field a little." I held out my hand and counted off the remaining guests on my fingers. "All that leaves is Pennington, Watt, Reilly, Buxton and Mr Schell. That is not a long list."

"We can rule out Frederick Schell," Holmes replied. "As you remarked earlier, he is physically weak, and an American to boot. He would use a gun, should he feel the need to defend his wife's honour." He frowned. "No, we can strike him from your list, I think. And the serving girl Alice, too, for that matter. Neither has the strength to carry Salah into the cellar and then tip him behind that tumble of machinery." He smiled. "Even if the two of them banded together for some inexplicable reason, they would be unable to lift so large a man from the ground."

"One of the others then?"

Holmes did not reply. Instead, he cut a slice of cheese and slowly raised it to his mouth. As he chewed, he nodded to himself, but said nothing. Only when he had finished eating did he seem to remember that I had asked him a question.

"Mmm? Yes, Watson, one of the others, most definitely."

It was clear that his mind was elsewhere. We sat in companionable silence for five minutes or so, eating our bread and cheese then each lighting a cigarette. Finally, when I was beginning to think of sleep, he said suddenly, "Do you recall what I said to you last night? That I would have need of your medical expertise? Well, be prepared to provide that assistance tomorrow. I cannot say exactly when, as it depends on factors somewhat beyond my control."

"Of course. Will I need my medical bag?"

"I would not think so. But if you were to have your stethoscope to hand, that would be useful."

"Very well." I held his eye for a long moment, waiting for him to say more, but it became clear that he did not intend to do so. I had already trusted him over the matter of Reilly's telegram so there was nothing to be gained by not trusting him now. Besides, I was tired and in no mood to play games, even if I could tease the information out of him, which I doubted.

"It has been a long day, Holmes," I said eventually, and pushed myself to my feet. "I am off to bed."

"I shall stay a little longer, I think," he replied, grinding out one cigarette and immediately lighting another.

I wished him goodnight and walked towards the door. I turned back at the last minute to ask him something but his eyes were already closed as he blew a stream of smoke towards the ceiling. I left him there and headed for the stairs.

Over breakfast the next day, conversation was dominated by the need to place final bids for the estate by noon that day. Lawrence Buxton, it transpired, had knocked on everyone's door late the previous evening to explain that it would not be possible to telegram bids as had originally been planned; a sealed envelope handed to him by midday would suffice.

"Well, I shall not be bidding," Reilly declared as soon as the subject came up. "Even had Salah not met such an unfortunate end, the climate in this country is too harsh for my blood." He paused to take a bite from a slice of toast, then continued, "I have been away too long, I'm afraid. The East is my home now."

Amicable Watt looked across from the sideboard where he was piling sausages on his plate and nodded. "It's not for me, either," he said. "I couldn't risk being up here and getting cut off from London. Who knows what idiocy the fools I left watching things have got up to while I've been stranded by this blasted snow." He slid an egg from its platter. "No, I'll be glad to get home and get back to work. I've seen the countryside now, and I can't say it's taken my fancy."

His plate completely full, he took a seat alongside Frederick Schell, who to my surprise had already been seated at the dining table when we entered. His wife was, however, conspicuous by her absence. "What about you, Mr Schell? Will this place do for one of your health camps?"

"Not health camps, Mr Watt," Schell corrected him fussily. "Sanatoriums. But no, I have decided Thorpe Manor is unsuitable for my needs. Our clients are often sickly. Like Mr Reilly, they would find this climate too harsh." He shook his head and glanced round the room. "The estate is not what I expected."

"That goes for me, too." Captain Hopkirk had barely looked up from his plate as the others spoke, and did so now only for as long as it took to speak these few words. For reasons that were not difficult to guess, he seemed entirely deflated and, for all his inappropriate behaviour with Mrs Schell, I could not help but feel sorry for the man.

The room fell silent for a moment as everyone waited for Hopkirk to continue, but when it became clear that he had said all he intended to, Judge Pennington, who had taken a keen interest in everyone's comments, turned to Holmes and me and enquired as to our intentions.

"I have never been entirely clear what your role here is, Mr Holmes," he said. "Nor yours, Dr Watson. I thought initially you were potential bidders, like myself, but the way you attempted to take control when Salah was killed inclined me to wonder if you had arrived expecting some such occurrence."

He paused, leaving room for a response, but Holmes said nothing and when Pennington looked across at me, I decided that discretion was called for and busied myself with my breakfast.

"Will you be bidding then?" Pennington pressed. "Can you at least tell us that?"

Holmes pushed away his plate and shook his head. "Neither Dr Watson nor I will be bidding on the estate," he said. "Will you? If you do, it seems you will be the only one who does."

Now it was Pennington's turn to avoid the question. "That remains to be seen," he muttered.

"Are you telling us you haven't decided yet?" Watt chided him. "Didn't they teach you to make decisions at that posh school of yours?"

Pennington stared at him through hooded eyelids, which, combined with his hunched posture, again put me in mind of a carrion bird. "They taught me manners, Mr Watt, which is clearly more than you learned in the gutter in which you were educated!"

Watt grunted in anger and, for a second, allowed his constant expression of good-natured amity to slip. He crashed to his feet and leaned forward, intent on coming to grips with Pennington. Then, perhaps remembering that the judge was some years his elder, or recognising their disparity in stature, he stopped and contented himself with standing, staring across the table for a few moments. Pennington attempted to hold his stare, but after a few moments he looked away and Watt, apparently satisfied, picked up his plate and cutlery and strode from the dining room.

In the silence that followed this explosion of fury, Frederick Schell asked Holmes to pass him the salt and conversation recommenced in desultory fashion. One by one, the other diners ate and left, until only Holmes and I remained.

"Do you have a better idea of when you might have need of my stethoscope today?" I asked as soon as we were alone, for the matter of Holmes's need for my medical knowledge had been playing on my mind since he had reminded me of it the previous night. Obviously, I was ready to provide such support whenever required, but the fact that Holmes had forewarned me – that he seemed to know the very item of equipment that would be needed – filled me with concern.

"Early this afternoon," he said. "I have preparations to make, and then I shall be forced to disobey the inspector and spend some time in the village. Can you likewise avoid his scrutiny for long enough to meet me outside the post office at five minutes to two this afternoon?"

"Of course, Holmes, if you say it is necessary. But can you not tell me what this is all about?"

He shook his head. "I would rather not. But I shall do so as soon as I can, I promise you."

He pushed his chair back and rose to his feet, brushing crumbs from his waistcoat. "I had best be away now. I have no idea how long it will take me to obtain... certain items, which I will need later. Should Fisher ask after me, I am sure you will be able to concoct some suitable story from your fertile imagination."

He said no more, but slipped from the room. I heard his footsteps on the stairs as I lit another cigarette and pined for the morning newspapers, which the snow had rendered unavailable since we arrived in Thorpe Manor. As I sat and smoked, I heard footsteps come back down the stairs and then the front door open and close. I crossed to the dining-room window and watched Holmes saunter in the approximate direction of the model Crystal Palace. Whatever he was up to, time was evidently not pressing, for he stopped on several occasions to kick at the snow with his shoe and on another to fill and light his pipe. After a few minutes of this uneventful perambulation, I grew bored of watching, and went in search of Gulliver's Travels and a seat by the fire.

Chapter Eighteen

A Culprit Brought Low

I did not see Holmes again all morning, though that was hardly surprising, as I made an effort to see as few people as possible. For all his talk of my fertile imagination, I was not by nature a good liar and I doubted that I could hide his absence from Inspector Fisher for long. Fortunately, the inspector spent much of the day ensconced in his makeshift office and on the few occasions on which he emerged, I made sure to be elsewhere.

I did seek out Buxton in the early afternoon. He told me that, in the end, nobody had handed him a bid envelope, so the Thorpe estate remained unsold.

"Of course, this terrible death made a sale unlikely. And," his voice fell to a whisper, "between us, I am not disappointed by the delay. A new owner is unlikely to be interested in a history of the Thorpe family. Or sympathetic to the historian writing it!"

"I suppose not," I agreed. "What will happen now, do you think? Will Mr Purser hold on to the estate, or make another attempt to sell it?"

"I really could not say, Dr Watson. Personally, I hope he remains an absentee landlord for many years to come." He laughed and I realised it was the first time I had seen him genuinely happy since the first night we had met him. "But if you will excuse me, I have some notes I made last month on Joshua Thorpe, the so-called Dales Horse Killer, to collate."

He laughed again and headed towards the library with a newfound spring in his step. I heard a door slam upstairs and Fisher's voice calling for Constable Halliday, so I slipped into the kitchens to see if Alice could produce a pot of tea.

Half an hour later, I set out for the village. I could hear Fisher talking to one of his constables in his office, which faced on to the side of the house, and I had not seen the other for some time, so I was confident in walking unobserved down the drive to the path which led to Thorpe-by-the-Marsh. The weather remained cold, but with a definite hint of change in the air. The snow in the overhanging branches was beginning to thaw, causing heavy droplets of water to fall in a constant drip into the stream of water that ran down the gutter of the path. It was a chilly but bracing day for a walk and within a few minutes I felt my mood lighten. I realised that the events of the past few days and the enforced stay in the house had had a suffocating effect on me. It was good finally to be doing something positive, even if, at the moment, I had no idea what that actually involved.

Holmes was standing outside the post office, as he had said he would be. He folded a sheet of paper into his pocket and checked his watch as I walked up, then nodded his approval. "Five minutes to the hour exactly, Watson," he said and pointed towards the entrance to the Silent Man public house. "Would you mind?" he went on. "I have a sudden desire for refreshment."

Given the choice, I should have preferred a hot drink, but Holmes had still not explained why we had sneaked out of the manor house like two schoolboys, and I hoped that he would do so once we were seated in the pub. There was, however, one very good reason why that was not likely to happen.

"It is almost two, Holmes," I pointed out. "The pub is about to close for the afternoon. It will not reopen until six."

"Is that so?" he replied. "Wait here a moment while I speak to our friend the landlord. I am sure he can be convinced to serve us one drink."

He was behaving very oddly, but that was not unusual, so I shrugged in agreement. "Very well," I said. "I have known country pubs to take some liberties with licensing laws, I suppose."

"Excellent," he said, with a grin. "Count to one hundred and then follow me in. With luck I shall have a whisky poured and waiting for you, and then we can talk."

With that, he trotted across the road, and vanished inside The Silent Man. After I had counted a slow century, I followed.

I saw Holmes at the far end of the bar as I entered. He was speaking to Robinson but, hearing the door, he switched his attention to me.

"I was just saying to Mr Robinson that we had once again trudged from the manor house through the snowdrifts, Watson, and would be obliged if he could provide us with two large whiskies before we are forced to make our way home. And take one for yourself, landlord," he continued, turning back to Robinson.

Something had changed in Robinson's mood since last we had seen him. Then he had been full of good humour and a desire to help, but now he seemed sullen and defensive. Indeed, I thought he would refuse the offer, for his face flushed and I fancied I saw a tremble in his hand as he poured the drinks for Holmes and me.

"I thank you for the offer, sir, but as I have explained, we are about to close. In fact, we should have closed two minutes ago."

"A small whisky, then! You just admitted that there is no policeman about to force you to close, and I am sure you can spend a few minutes raising a glass with two customers happy to pay to learn more about the village."

Robinson could hardly disagree. There was nobody else in the bar, nor enough men in the village, I suspected, for the place ever to be particularly profitable, and Holmes had laid a pound note on the bar. He frowned at Holmes, but poured himself a glass and grudgingly muttered, "Your health, gentlemen," in our general direction.

"And yours, landlord," Holmes replied with a bonhomie which was in marked contrast to Robinson's more morose toast. "And that of your dog too. I hope that it recovers soon. I keep no pets of my own, but I am given to understand by those who do that an injury to a beloved animal companion can be very worrying, especially when recovery is slow."

"My dog…?" Robinson laughed, as curiosity overcame some of the initial reticence he had exhibited. "Is conversation so dull at the manor house that news of my Geordie has reached even there? Though I have mentioned it to nobody…" His voice trailed off in puzzlement.

"A simple deduction, landlord," Holmes said with his most friendly smile. "There are several dog hairs on your waistcoat and I noticed numerous scratch marks in front of the fireplace on our last visit. Dogs are social animals but he did not make an appearance then, nor has he investigated us today, despite the loud bang the door made when Watson closed it with too much force a moment ago. Hence he is in some way indisposed. Add to that the bowl of water to the side of the fireplace, in which the water is contaminated with dust, and we can assume that whatever ails the animal occurred several days ago. There is a very faint smell of carbolic acid emanating from your back room – so the dog has not died, but has suffered an injury to which you have applied an antiseptic."

Robinson greeted this speech with a grudging grin.

"You do a good line in parlour tricks, I'll give you that, Mr Holmes."

Normally, Holmes would have taken offence at even his most simple deductions being described in such unflattering terms, but on this occasion, he simply gave a small bow and smiled with apparent pleasure.

"It is a knack I have, a small talent with which I amuse my friends. All it requires is an eye for detail and an ability to extrapolate from observed fact. I am glad to have had a chance to demonstrate it for you before we leave."

I had no idea what Holmes meant by that, but the promise that we would soon be gone was enough to pique Robinson's interest further.

"You're leaving? That is a shame," he said, though the look on his face gave the lie to his words. "Are your investigations over already?"

"You have heard about our little mystery, then?" Holmes asked, almost jovially. "I had thought that Inspector Fisher wished to keep it quiet."

"Someone must have mentioned it," Robinson suggested carelessly. "It's hard to keep a secret in a small place like this."

"I suppose it must be. Perhaps the girl who sends the telegrams has spoken out of turn."

"That's likely it. Like I said, there's no secrets in a village."

"Unlike London." Holmes's voice had turned suddenly hard and cold, as if a cord had been pulled in him. "A great deal of secrets can be kept hidden in a city like London."

Robinson said nothing, but any good humour in his face was gone. He picked up a cloth and polished a beer tap, not looking at either of us.

"I've things to be getting on with through the back," he said. "I'll need to ask you gentlemen to drink up and be on your way."

He turned to go, but Holmes picked up his untouched glass of whisky. "You've not finished your drink, though, landlord," he said.

"But…" I wondered what was happening, for I could see the sweat on Robinson's forehead and it was plain that he had read something disturbing in Holmes's words.

"I do hate to see good whisky go to waste," Holmes pressed, holding the glass out in front of him.

Robinson looked at the glass, then up at Holmes, and appeared to come to a decision. "Right then," he said, "just the one. Then I need to get to my stocking up."

He took the whisky and drained it in a single draught. Holmes did the same with his own glass and as Robinson turned to leave, noisily placed it on the bar.

"If I could just have another, before you go. Watson, will you have another?"

I had barely touched the drink I had. I shook my head.

"Just one whisky then, landlord," Holmes said, placing a coin on the bar.

Robinson hesitated for a moment, then picked up Holmes's glass and reached for a bottle.

"Actually, I think I'd prefer an ale, now that I think on it," Holmes said as Robinson pulled the cork from the bottle. "A half of whatever the local ale is, please."

Robinson's shoulders stiffened and the muscles on his neck became visible. I looked at Holmes, who held a finger to his lips, then silently mouthed, "Be ready," and pointed at Robinson's back.

Before I could ask him what he meant – though how I would manage that without speaking I couldn't have said – Robinson answered my unspoken question for me.

He half turned, stiffly, as though spinning on the sole of his foot, and let the beer schooner in his hand drop and smash on the floor. His mouth opened and closed like a landed fish, but no sound came out. He had gone the grey colour of the dirty cloth he had used to wipe the bar and sweat was running down his face in several distinct places. He tottered towards us, knocking over a jug full of water as he did so, and pressed one fist against the centre of his chest before slumping to the floor.

For a moment, everything was still, and then I was on my feet and pushing past Holmes to reach the hatch, which provided access to the back of the bar. I hauled it open, shouting for Holmes to help me get Robinson out of the cramped area behind the bar.

Between us we manhandled the publican's unresisting body

through the gap in the bar counter and laid him on a long wooden table. His face was pale and clammy and the pulse at his wrist rapid and uneven. It was only as I desperately looked around for a cause for his sudden collapse that my overloaded brain recalled Holmes's mysterious words from just moments before.

"You knew this would happen!"

Holmes nodded. "If you could make use of your stethoscope, Watson, just in case."

"Just in case of what, Holmes? For God's sake, tell me the cause of this collapse!"

"Something of my own creation, Doctor. Do not worry; it is not fatal, nor are its effects permanent, or even particularly long-lasting. I should know," he laughed, "for I have tested it upon myself often enough."

"Tested...!"

"Indeed. A mixture of foxglove, wild ginger and some other more esoteric ingredients. The effects are unpleasant to be sure, but Mr Robinson will be back on his feet in a couple of hours, at most."

"I do not care what is in your concoction, Holmes!" I protested, placing the stethoscope on his shirt above his heart. "What do I need to do to help him right now?"

"Nothing, Watson. As I said, he will be fine in an hour or two. In the meantime, there is something I need to establish, which he was unlikely to allow me to do while he was awake. First though, it's probably best to ensure that no dregs remain in the glass." He crossed to the bar, took Robinson's tumbler and dropped it into the water-filled sink behind the bar. "You noticed his animosity when we arrived?" he asked as he dried his hands on a bar towel. "My deduction about the dog distracted him enough to allow me to slip my concoction, as you put it, into his drink, but it would not have been enough to allow me to do this."

With that, he knelt down by Robinson's recumbent body and pulled the unconscious man's shirt up to his shoulders. Instinctively, I reached out and grabbed him by the wrist.

"What on earth are you doing, Holmes!"

"Identifying Billy Robinson," he replied calmly, pointing with his free hand at the man's exposed sternum.

Tattooed across the breastbone was a curious symbol, comprising, as far as I could tell, a bird in flight enclosed in a black circle.

"What is that?" I asked. "And I thought his name was Walter? Explain yourself, Holmes, for pity's sake. All I see is a man deliberately stricken by you, and no reason for it other than a strange tattoo and a name seemingly plucked from the air."

For once, Holmes looked chagrined. "My apologies, Watson; I have allowed my own enthusiasm to get the better of me. I realise that this must all seem rather strange behaviour to you."

"That is quite an understatement, Holmes. Even by your standards, poisoning a man you barely know is a departure."

"Rest assured, Watson, that though I do not know him personally, I know a great deal about him. Billy Robinson is a very dangerous man who has escaped the noose once already. He is the murderer of Alim Salah."

I gasped. "Are you certain, Holmes? But why? And twice now you have called him Billy Robinson. Am I to assume that Walter Robinson is not his real name?"

"It is not. But rather than answer your questions piecemeal, perhaps it would be better if I explained everything from the beginning, with a little more structure?"

I nodded emphatically. "That would be a very good idea indeed, Holmes."

"I shall, but first allow me to tie him hand and foot. He is not likely to come to any time soon, but I would feel infinitely more comfortable if he were also securely bound."

Had it been any other man making this request, I would have refused. But had it been any other man, I would already have been on my way to the nearest policeman, demanding his arrest for attempted murder. So I did as Holmes asked and helped him tie Robinson – Billy or Walter, it made no difference – with some cord I found on a shelf under the bar. Only once he was secured did we take seats, and Holmes began to explain his recent, incomprehensible behaviour.

"You must understand that, at first, Robinson was no more than a diversion to me, something out of place with which I might distract myself, once I had decided there was no diversion to be had at the manor house.

"Simply put, it was unusual that a Londoner of his sort should choose to retire to quite so out of the way a place as Thorpe-by-the-Marsh, whether his doctor advised country air or not. You have seen for yourself the size of the village. Even if he were well liked, the place would need to be populated entirely by dipsomaniacs before he could make a decent living. And then there are the mirrors."

"The mirrors?" I asked, baffled. I looked around but all I could see was the mirror by the fireplace.

"Of course," Holmes tutted. "Come with me," he said and indicated I should follow him to the door. He snibbed it shut, then bade me turn around.

"Now, Watson, what can you see?" he asked, and pointed straight ahead.

At first, I could make no sense of what he was showing me. Directly in front of us was the same unprepossessing space near the bar that we had seen on our first visit. A mirror hung in one corner, but there was nothing unusual about it.

As I sought in vain for revelation, I could sense Holmes growing impatient, while I grew increasingly irate with his failure simply to explain. Whatever it was he wished me to see, I could not see it.

It was then that I realised that, quite literally, I could see what he meant. The mirror had been so placed that it pointed at the other one in the room, by the fireplace, and as a consequence of their respective angles allowed a view of the far end of the public bar.

More specifically, I could clearly see the water jug, which Robinson had overturned in his agonies. "Anyone standing here could see Robinson!"

"Very good, Watson! But I thought the reverse more interesting – that Robinson could see anyone who came in. It was he who positioned the mirrors, after all. It was a small thing, of course, capable of any number of innocent explanations, but with nothing else to occupy my mind, it managed to whet my appetite enough to have me telegram Lestrade to ask him to look for a Walter Robinson in Scotland Yard's voluminous records."

"And did he find anything?"

"He did not. It was unlikely he would, for a man on the run would be a fool to keep his own name. And that would have been that, had nothing else occurred. We would have spent several dull days in the countryside, completed our business here and returned to London where, with luck, some clever crime or other would have been committed."

"But then Alim Salah was killed?"

"As you say, then Alim Salah was killed. Of course, I had realised from the beginning that a man who wished to remain hidden would scarcely choose to keep his real name, but while the matter was merely an idle fancy of mine, it was not worth even Lestrade's time to make a more widespread search. With Salah's murder, that ceased to be the case."

Just then, Robinson gave a quiet groan. I knelt down to examine him but his pulse was steady, if a little slow, and though his eyes were slightly rolled back in his head, he gave no other sign of distress, and none at all of returning consciousness.

"Go on, Holmes," I urged my friend.

"I now had more information to give Lestrade, with which he might successfully narrow down his search. So when I walked down to the village to send telegrams to Mr Thompson and the police, I sent another to Scotland Yard, asking for a search for a man who had been involved in a race attack in the past ten years, but who had escaped justice."

"My God! You think that the killing of Salah was not the first time he has attacked a foreigner?"

"Not a foreigner, Watson. The same foreigner. Remember what you heard Salah say, the night before he died? 'Must I be expected to turn the other cheek,' he said. The inspector took it to be a reference to the Bible quotation, and potential evidence against Hopkirk, who had so recently fought with him. But Salah was a Hindu, not a Christian. Why on earth would he quote from a holy book not his own? He would not... unless he was speaking literally."

I must have looked blank, for Holmes tutted with irritation. "The disfigurement of his face, Watson! Lestrade replied to my query, in a telegram which I collected shortly before I met you just now. He identified one Billy Robinson, who stabbed and killed a student, Venkata Raju, a little under eleven years ago: a crime for which he was sentenced to hang. However, he escaped from a prison van and has not been sighted since. A witness to the murder, a man wounded on the face while attempting to stop it, gave his name as Alim Salah.

"Now, imagine that, like a bolt from the blue, Salah sees his attacker in an entirely unexpected place, a place where he should never be. The shock would be enormous!"

"But when could Salah have seen Robinson?" I asked.

"Come now, you already know the answer to that question. The mirrors. Reilly said that he found Salah sheltering from the wind in the pub doorway. But we know there is precious little shelter to be found there. I am certain that he had intended to shelter in The Silent Man itself but, opening the door, who should he see but the man who attacked him years before! Of all the places to stumble across Robinson, I doubt Salah could have conceived of a more improbable one. He might have confronted him then, but I suspect that the shock, combined with Reilly's presence, prevented him from doing so." He paused as though finished; then, with an apologetic shake of the head, he went on, "Here I must for the moment descend into conjecture, something I prefer not to do, as you know. I would hazard that Salah was about to set out to confront Robinson when he met you on the stairs. You thought you had calmed his aggression, but he merely waited until you went to bed, and then resumed his interrupted plan. His encounter with Robinson did not end as he hoped, of course."

"Obviously not," I replied. I took a moment to light a cigarette, in order to give myself time to think. "But as you say, this is all conjecture. If Robinson denies all knowledge of Salah, will this be enough to convince Inspector Fisher?"

"There is other evidence, Watson. You forget the tattoo, for one thing! Lestrade's telegram contained the important information that the Robinson sought by the police had a tattoo of a bird inside a circle on his chest." He coughed sheepishly. "I confess I planned to administer my little drug to him in any case, but my original intention was simply to have time to search for incriminating evidence to present to Fisher."

"That was quite a risk to take, Holmes!" I accused. "What if you had found nothing? Robinson would have been within his rights to press charges against you for assault!"

"Hardly likely, Watson. Even if I found nothing, I was certain he was the guilty man, and so would not go to the police for any reason. Indeed, had matters turned out as you suggest, the very fact that he would not have reported me to Fisher would simply have been further proof of his guilt."

"Very well, I will accept that the tattoo means that Robinson attacked Salah in the past, but that does not link him to the man's murder this week."

"No, not conclusively – though it would be rather a coincidence if the two events were not linked. But the wheel tracks we saw yesterday, in the snow on the path running alongside the manor house, certainly do.

"Buxton said at dinner that all provisions had been delivered some days ago – indeed, we saw the very cart which delivered them as we arrived. And as that was before the snow fell, how could there be wheel tracks in the snow to the side of the house? They can only have been left by a cart travelling down the road after that point. I noticed old beer barrels in the cellar, and the path outside slopes down to allow their easy delivery. Clearly, therefore, that is a path Robinson knows. It is not a particularly great leap to link his need to move a heavy body with the cart that he uses to deliver beer or that, with a body to hide, the dark and rarely used cellar would come to mind. Once Fisher compares the wheels of Robinson's cart with the tracks still visible in the snow, he will find they match." He smiled. "I assure you, Watson, I knew he was our man."

As ever, Holmes had left nothing to chance. "In which case, I think it best that we return to the manor house without delay and bring Fisher back here. The sooner Robinson is in custody, the better."

Holmes was already gathering up his things. "First let me ensure the ropes are tight enough. One of us could stay here with Robinson, but given that we have disobeyed Fisher's instructions in coming to the village at all, and considering his already somewhat jaundiced view of me, I believe it will require your corroboration of my tale to convince him to come." He knelt down and pulled at the ropes binding Robinson's wrists and ankles. Apparently satisfied, he rose to his feet. "Besides, he will not come to his senses for some time yet. If we lock the door, that should be more than sufficient."

"You are certain that whatever you gave him will not cause him any further distress?" I asked, kneeling in turn and checking his eyes and his pulse. Both were normal, and he gave the impression of being in a sound, if unusually deep, sleep.

Holmes was waiting impatiently by the door, with the key in his hand. I hurried across and waited in the empty street as he locked up behind us.

The manor house was deserted when we arrived back, slightly out of breath, some twenty minutes later. Though there was no real chance that Robinson would escape, by unspoken consent we were both keen to have him delivered into police custody as soon as possible.

"Hello!" I shouted into the silent house, but there was no reply. We looked in the main hall and the library, then the dining room, but nobody was to be found. Only when we went upstairs and knocked on the bedroom doors did we finally find anyone to whom we could pass on our news.

Lawrence Buxton emerged from his room bleary-eyed and sleepy from an afternoon nap, but immediately perked up when he saw us.

"Dr Watson! Mr Holmes! There you are! I did wonder where you had got to. You've missed all the excitement, you know!"

"Excitement? What sort of excitement?"

"Why, Inspector Fisher arrested Mr Reilly soon after you left, in the main hall, in front of everyone. Apparently new evidence had come to light which confirmed his guilt." He frowned at some aspect of the memory. "So the inspector arrested him where he stood, and had one of his men – the tall one – put him in handcuffs and take him away."

He paused for breath and Holmes quickly broke in to ask, "New evidence? What new evidence?"

"I couldn't say what it was, Mr Holmes," replied the historian. "But the inspector said it proved Mr Reilly's guilt beyond all doubt."

"Then the inspector is a fool. I can guess what his evidence must be, and it no more proves Reilly's guilt than it proves my own!"

"You know?" I said. "How could you possibly know?"

"Later, Watson, later! There is no time for explanations now. We can rescue Reilly from Fisher's incompetence once we have Robinson safely in police custody. But still, that does not explain why there is nobody about."

Buxton was ready with the answer. "That's the thing, Mr Holmes. As soon as he was placed under arrest, Mr Reilly said that his lawyer had advised him that, should he be arrested, he was entitled to legal representation, and that the closest place he would find that was in Stainforth. So that's where they've gone: Stainforth. Inspector Fisher, Mr Reilly and the tall constable. The little one's still around here somewhere. Oh, and I almost forgot. Mr Schell went with them."

"Mr Schell?"

"Yes indeed. He had the most terrible row with Mrs Schell, you know. As soon as he heard that the inspector was heading for Stainforth, he demanded that he be allowed to go too. He didn't even pack a bag, just put on his jacket and scarf and went and sat in the police carriage and wouldn't budge. Fisher had no choice but to take him, in the end."

Holmes appeared a little dumbstruck by these revelations. Here we were, returning in haste with the solution to the murder of Alim Salah and the murderer safely tied up, only awaiting collection by the authorities, and those same authorities had vanished, taking half the manor house guests with them!

"Very well," he said, rallying. "That accounts for a portion of the inhabitants. But where are the others? Of particularly pressing importance, do you know where Constable Cairns and Judge Pennington have secreted themselves?"

Buxton shook his head. "Captain Hopkirk said he was intending to accompany Mrs Schell for a walk in the grounds, hoping to take her mind off her troubles, I assume, and Mr Watt said he was going to his room to pack. The judge mentioned something about freshening himself up, but the constable...? No, I'm afraid I can't help you, Mr Holmes."

"I think perhaps you can, actually. May I impose upon you to go and find Judge Pennington and have him meet us in the main hall? Meanwhile, we will seek out the missing constable." He pointed towards the servants' quarters. "If I know the British working man unexpectedly relieved of the attention of his immediate superior, our missing constable will be either in the kitchen drinking a bottle of ale, or if beer is not available, smoking a cigarette in some out of the way corner."

We found him at the back door, sitting on the step, with a cigarette in one hand and a bottle of beer in the other. He jumped up, throwing away the cigarette, as Holmes coughed beside him, and stood, at an approximation of attention, with the bottle poorly hidden behind his back.

"Just taking a break, sir," he said. "The maid said I could have an ale, seeing as his Lordship won't be needing them no longer."

"I have no interest in what you have been doing, Constable," Holmes said. "What I am interested in is what you intend to do now."

Cairns looked puzzled. "Inspector Fisher said I was to stay here and make sure nobody else slips away before he gets back, or he sends for me."

"A commendably succinct summary, Constable, and an extremely helpful one. I cannot agree strongly enough with your inspector that it is imperative that you stay here, in the manor house. Judge Pennington, however, will soon be leaving for the Silent Man public house in the village. There he will find the proprietor, Walter Robinson, where we left him, tied up on the floor of the bar. The front door is locked, but I shall give him the key. Mr Robinson is the true killer of Alim Salah, and must be taken into custody without delay. Am I correct in assuming that you would prefer not to take that particular burden upon yourself, and would rather await the return of Inspector Fisher?"

Cairns' eyes flicked in animal panic between Holmes and me. The terrified expression on his chalk-white face would have been comical to see in other circumstances. Now, however, time was of the essence and we had none to spare for slow-witted country constables.

"The judge will go down to the village pub and keep an eye on the man lying on the floor there," I said slowly. "When Inspector Fisher returns, he will arrest the man."

Slowly, Cairns nodded his understanding.

"It is of the utmost importance that you tell no one else in the house where the judge has gone or why, and that you keep a close eye on the other guests," Holmes continued. "Nobody must know that Robinson is the killer, and nobody else must leave the house before we return with the inspector."

Cairns seemed to be following this reasonably well, but as Holmes mentioned our departure, his face blanched once more.

"The inspector said nobody was to leave the house," he said uncertainly.

"Nobody who was actually in the house already, surely, Constable."

Cairns scratched his head. "Maybe…" he said.

"And Watson and I have just returned from the village. Thus, we were not in the house when the inspector gave his order and so could not be instructed not to leave it."

This was too much for Cairns. His mouth fell open and he half shook and half nodded his head in hapless uncertainty.

"We have been helping the inspector," I reminded him, before he decided that keeping everybody where they were was the safest decision to make.

"The inspector did call you observers," he agreed hesitantly.

"Exactly!" exclaimed Holmes. "And we can hardly observe without the inspector here to allow it, now can we?" He smiled in what I am certain he thought of as a reassuring manner. "So, Watson and I will take Mr Schell's carriage – which I notice he has conve"niently left behind – and go to the police station at Stainforth. Once there, we will speak to the inspector and then escort him back here to arrest Walter Robinson. Is that clear, Constable?"

Plainly, it was anything but. Cairns' face was a picture of confusion for a short period then, obviously deciding it was best to take the path of least resistance, he nodded decisively. He reached for his helmet, which he had placed on the step, carefully substituting for it the beer bottle. "I'll go and stand at the front then, sir," he said, securing the strap beneath his chin. "I'll keep an eye out for Mr Pennington."

"And don't forget," Holmes reminded him. "Not a word to any of the other guests about Robinson or the judge. So far as they are aware, we have gone to help the inspector in his interrogation of Mr Reilly."

Seeing the panic rising in his eyes, I hurriedly intervened and quickly explained that he was to say nothing to anyone until we returned.

He nodded gratefully and wandered off into the kitchens.

"Remind me of Constable Cairns next time I am overly scathing about Lestrade's men, Watson," Holmes said at my side. "Perhaps I should be thankful that they are not more incapable." He shuddered and shook his head, a wry smile on his face. "But now that he has gone, we must speak to Pennington. He is not the most appealing of characters, but at the moment I should say he is the most trustworthy man in the vicinity."

Until now I had been carried along by Holmes's energy and obvious conviction, but as he turned to follow Cairns into the house, I held out a hand to stop him.

"I admit I am not clear why Robinson's guilt may not be common knowledge, Holmes?"

He frowned and hesitated a second before replying. "It is not so much his guilt as Reilly's innocence which I should prefer to remain between us for now, Watson."

I nodded my understanding. It would not be the first time circumstances had necessitated a degree of subterfuge.

Judge Pennington proved surprisingly easy to convince to carry out his role in Holmes's plan. As soon as he had grasped that Robinson was a convicted felon who had escaped from prison, he was more than willing to watch over him until Inspector Fisher arrived.

"You need say no more, Holmes," he declared. "When it comes to matters of criminality, I can put aside my personal feelings and work with any man. I will leave for this public house at once, and you may assure the inspector that his prisoner will be waiting for him at his convenience."

As Holmes slipped a key from the ring he had taken from Robinson and handed it to the judge, he agreed that we would drive straight from Stainforth to The Silent Man, and Fisher would take Robinson into custody from there.

Pennington bustled off and we hurried out the front door, past Cairns who threw a sketchy salute in our direction. The Schells' carriage was in the driveway and their horses in the stable. It was the work of only a few minutes to hook them up and then, with Holmes in the driving seat and me inside, we set out for Stainforth at good speed.

Chapter Nineteen

Stainforth

The trip to Stainforth was uneventful. We passed Judge Pennington as we sped through the village, and I was reassured to see he was almost at The Silent Man, but otherwise we saw nobody on our journey. Holmes was a more than competent driver and we made excellent time, arriving at the door to the police station a mere forty minutes after setting out.

Even so, Fisher had arrived before us, and was not pleased when Holmes strode past the sergeant on the desk and swept into his private office without so much as a by-your-leave, demanding that Reilly be set free. I trailed behind him, warding off the irate sergeant and trying my best to keep him from being arrested himself.

For a moment it was touch and go whether we would both end up ensconced in the cells, but after a brief hesitation Fisher waved the sergeant away.

"It appears that I may do nothing without your supervision," he grumbled, gesturing that we should take seats against the wall. "You might as well stay now that you're here – though I'll be speaking to Constable Cairns about how exactly that happened – but don't say a word unless requested to do so by me, or so help me, I'll be the first policeman to throw Sherlock Homes and Dr Watson in jail."

I could have answered that he would certainly not be the first policeman to do so, and I might even have reminded him that I myself had spent some time incarcerated, but that would not have been helpful. I glanced over at Holmes, expecting him to speak, but he gave a tiny shake of the head, and so I turned and watched Fisher instead.

He was seated behind a battered and stained but well-made oak desk, with his notebook open before him and, directly opposite, sitting slumped in his chair, Mr Reilly.

I had found both men to be rather quick-tempered, but when Holmes pushed his way in, neither had been speaking; nor did they do so now, preferring instead to sit and wordlessly stare at one another.

"May I speak if nobody else intends to?" Holmes asked, after the silence had stretched on to an uncomfortable degree. When Fisher responded by waving a hand in his direction, he took it to be consent and continued by asking another question. "Lawrence Buxton told us that you had come by important new information, Inspector. Might I ask what that information is?"

Fisher immediately brightened. He flipped open his notebook, which lay on the desk in front of him, and turned to an entry near the back.

"Of course," he said. "You think that you can play the same trick on me that you do on your tame inspector back in London, don't you, Mr Holmes? Keep evidence to yourself, don't share it with anyone and then spring it on them at the last moment, like some kind of conjuror." He grinned, though his lips barely moved and the effect was rather more like an animal baring its teeth. "Well, that won't wash here. I knew you'd sneaked out of the house, you see, in spite of being ordered not to. I had Halliday keeping an eye on you, and when you slipped away, he was right on your heels. He hid round the corner when you went into the post office and after you'd gone in to the pub with Dr Watson, he spoke to the woman who sends the telegrams. He's a clever lad, is Halliday, and he knew what she showed him was more important than watching you swilling brandy." He twisted the notebook round on the desk so that it faced us and jabbed at one section with his pencil. "So it's not just you who knows what Mr Reilly sent to London."

The note of triumph in his voice was so overwhelming that I instinctively leaned forward to read the two capitalised lines he had indicated on the page.

```
SHERLOCK HOLMES IS HERE STOP WILL DO WHAT
I CAME TO DO THEN DEPART BEFORE IDENTIFIED
STOP MAKE ARRANGEMENTS TO LEAVE TUESDAY PM
STOP
```

"Mr Reilly informs me he'll say nothing until his lawyer arrives," Fisher announced. "He says that he can explain everything, but he knows the British legal system of old – whatever that's supposed to mean – and he won't say a word until he's got a witness he can trust."

He glared at Reilly, daring the older man to contradict him. Reilly never raised his eyes from his lap. Holmes, however, reacted as if Fisher's words had freed him from the need for silence.

"Perhaps Mr Reilly would accept that Dr Watson and I are witnesses he can trust?" he said to the room in general. For the first time since our arrival, Reilly looked up, though he still said nothing. "Even better, perhaps he will allow me to explain everything for him. I believe I have the broad strokes of his story, but I'm sure he will correct me should I go astray."

At this, Reilly turned in his chair and examined Holmes minutely. "I doubt you can truly know my story, Mr Holmes, but in our brief acquaintance you have struck me as an intelligent and honourable man, and it will help pass the time more quickly to hear your theory than not. By all means, sir, go ahead."

I thought Fisher would be less keen, but perhaps he too wished to be done with the oppressive silence, for he shrugged his acquiescence and muttered, "Why not?" in a weary tone.

"Thank you," said Holmes, and rose to his feet, the better to address the room. As was his common practice, he paced about as he spoke, illuminating his more salient points by making jabbing motions with his hands and turning first to one person then the next as his narrative encompassed them. So it was that he began by addressing Inspector Fisher directly.

"It will be most efficient, I think, first to lay out the evidence you believe speaks most damningly against Mr Reilly, Inspector. By this I mean the footprints in the snow, indicating his presence in the grounds at the time of the murder, and the telegram he sent, apparently announcing in advance that he would kill Alim Salah." He held up a hand to forestall the beginning of a complaint from Inspector Fisher. "I am aware that there are other factors which you believe indicate the killer – that the location in which the body was left suggests someone who required it to be hidden only for a few days, that Mr Reilly had argued with the dead man recently, and presumably other minor matters, but each of these could as well apply to any of the other guests. Only the peculiar boot prints, left on the night that Salah was killed and near the place his body was dumped, and the telegram you have just showed us uniquely implicate Mr Reilly."

Fisher grunted and smiled thinly at Holmes. "I'll reserve judgement on just how much those points could apply to the other guests, but I'm keen to hear what excuse you've come up with for the boots and the telegram first."

"Not excuses, Inspector," Holmes protested mildly, "reasons. In fact, a single reason explaining both elements. First, the boot prints in the snow. Of course, those were indeed Mr Reilly's boot prints and he was in the back garden when Salah was killed. He denied it, but he was certainly there. What else could possibly have made such distinctive marks? The reason he was there I shall leave to the end of my account, if I may, but the actual events I think I can sketch in now, without too much difficulty.

"For reasons which, as I say, I shall explain in a moment, Mr Reilly had gone into the garden once everyone was – apparently – asleep. Standing in the faint light cast from the back door, he paused, perhaps shivering in the cold. I doubt he was certain exactly where he intended to go. The grounds of the estate are large, after all, and he had had only a day to get his bearings. Thus, he was standing there when he heard an unexpected sound in the otherwise silent night. A crunching sound, I imagine, of the sort cartwheels would make as they turned through deep snow. And then a quieter sound, as this invisible man passed under the trees that stand on the corner of the house, closer to the spot at which Mr Reilly had paused, becoming more nervous with every passing moment. Because he could not be found outside the house at this time of night, not without having to explain himself. And an explanation was the last thing he wished to provide.

"So he hid, slipping down the path which leads to the cellar proper and waiting there in the darkness as first, something heavy was dropped to the snowy ground, then the back door was slowly opened and closed and, finally, everything was quiet again."

Holmes paused and looked down at Reilly. "Nobody could expect you to carry out your task then, could they? Better by far to go round to the front of the house and from there take yourself off to bed, leaving what needed to be done for another night. Is that not how it was, Mr Reilly?"

The planter nodded slowly. "Almost exactly, Mr Holmes. I'm not as young as I used to be, and it was deathly cold that night. I was actually already thinking that I would have to go back inside and try the following night, with more insulation, when I heard whoever it was coming through the snow. I hid just as you said and stayed there until they'd gone indoors. The only thing you got wrong is I didn't hear anything being dropped, just the door opening and then a bit later, closing again." He hesitated and swallowed heavily. "When Buxton discovered Salah's body, I prayed that it had been him I'd heard, and he'd taken a tumble during his night-time explorations. But you put soon paid to that idea, and then I knew it must have been the killer. If only I'd confronted him, perhaps…"

"It is lucky that you were necessarily so discreet, Mr Reilly. Had you challenged him, it is possible that we would have a double murder to investigate. The killer is a large man who has killed before and you, as you said yourself, are no longer in the first flush of youth."

Fisher, who had been listening to this exchange with a look of patient amusement on his face, sat up sharply. "What's that about the killer?" he snapped, but Holmes ignored him.

"I take it you saw nothing at all of the man carrying Salah's body?" he asked Reilly. "There was no peculiarity of his gait or his breathing?"

"Nothing whatsoever. I fear I was too preoccupied with hiding myself to take much notice of the man I was hiding from."

"A shame, but no matter. I doubt we shall need further evidence."

Again, Fisher began to protest and again Holmes continued as though he had never spoken.

"Which brings us to the reason you were outside, and why you could not be found there," he said. "Now here, I know the broad strokes, but not the specifics. I should be grateful if you could fill them in, purely to satisfy my own curiosity. First though, it is about time I started using your real name, is it not, Mr Thorpe?"

The effect of this last sentence was dramatic. Reilly had perhaps expected it, for he simply smiled broadly at Holmes and bobbed his head towards him in acknowledgement. Fisher, however, exploded from his chair, catching his precious notebook with the side of his hand and sending it flying across the room.

"Mr Thorpe! What on earth are you babbling about, Holmes? This is no more Mr Thorpe than it is the prime minister!"

"On the contrary, Inspector. May I introduce Elias Thorpe, son of Edward Thorpe, and nephew to the late Lord Robert Thorpe."

"How do you do?" Reilly – Thorpe – said, with another nod.

"Explain yourself, Holmes, and quickly, or I'll charge you with wasting police time and throw you in the cells myself! Lestrade and the rest of them in Scotland Yard might appreciate this circus act, but I don't!"

"Circus act, Inspector? That is a little harsh. Watson has accused me of a taste for the dramatic before now, though, so perhaps you have a point, if one unkindly expressed. However, I am not entirely sure what it is you wish me to explain first. Would you prefer that I discuss why Elias Thorpe chose to call himself Stephen Reilly while he was in England, or why he was skulking about the grounds of his uncle's estate in the dead of night? Or, indeed, why he sent that particularly damning telegram? Though," he mused, "all three are intimately connected, so perhaps I can satisfy you on every count at the same time." He turned to the newly revealed Elias Thorpe. "With your permission, of course."

Thorpe agreed with a smile of pleasure. "This is the first real enjoyment I've had since I arrived in this dreadful country," he said. "Please do continue."

"Very well. Fifty-three years ago, Edward Thorpe, the younger brother of Lord Robert Thorpe, did what many young men of his class and prospects did at the time, and took ship for the Far East, determined to make his fortune in the colonies. He took with him a reasonable amount of money, given to him by his father, and did quite well for himself, buying a plantation and building it up over several profitable years. Then, sadly, he contracted one of the many unpleasant infectious diseases which are rife in hotter climates than our own and, with none of the inherited resistance of the native population, quickly weakened and died. As was, and is, the practice, his body could not be returned home, but his family were informed, they grieved and, in time, Edward became merely a fading memory.

"A fading memory everywhere, that is, except in the minds of the local woman to whom he had formed a deep attachment, and the son whom he loved. Of course that son was Elias Thorpe, the gentleman who sits before us now."

"Bravo." Thorpe clapped his hands slowly together. "You have uncovered my secret, Mr Holmes, and though I would have preferred that it remain secret until I left these shores, I hope that I can rely on the discretion of everyone in this room to ensure that nobody else finds out."

"Of course," said Holmes, speaking for both of us, though Fisher remained pointedly silent, "but why must it remain a secret?"

"For a number of reasons, some of which may seem foolish to you, but are of paramount importance to me." He sighed, and the smile fell from his face. "Naturally, I was born out of wedlock – no minister would marry an English gentleman to a native woman, even if the gentleman was minded to do so. This is no issue whatever at home, but I know that English morals are… less flexible, and more hypocritical, than ours and I should not wish my father's memory to be tarnished in any way by scandal, no matter how long ago or how remote. Also, I am a wealthy and successful man, used to the respect of my fellows. But if it were known that I was the closest living relative of my father's brother, there would be whispers that I was only in England to seek financial advantage, to make a claim on the family estate. I have no desire to live in England, nor to own the Thorpe lands." He laughed, but there was a bitterness in it. "Oh, I had a half-formed, romantic notion on the ship across that I would fall in love with England, the birthplace of my beloved father, buy Thorpe Manor and set myself up as the new Lord Thorpe. But the reality is that England is cold and miserable and dirty, and I am no Englishman. I could no more make my home here than I could make it among the Eskimos."

I bristled a little at this description, then remembered he had known only the wet heat of the Far East. And he had spent his entire time in England trapped in a freezing snowstorm. I wondered if he would like the country any better in the height of summer, when every tree, every bush and every field was in fecund bloom.

Inspector Fisher, though, had other questions on his mind. He had sat quietly while Thorpe and Holmes conversed, as engrossed in the story as I was myself, but now he spoke up.

"This is all very interesting, but I have yet to hear why Mr... Thorpe was in the grounds at two o'clock in the morning, or the reason for his threatening telegram?"

"Because he loved his father as much as his father loved him, Inspector," Holmes replied.

"Will you stop talking in riddles, Holmes, and give me a straight answer to a straight question. For that matter, how do you come to know all this?"

"I, too, would be interested to know that, Mr Holmes," agreed Thorpe.

"All too simply," replied Holmes. "Almost from the first moment I met the supposed Mr Reilly, there was something tickling at the back of my mind, some sense that I had met him before. It was only when I saw him swinging a walking stick in the hall that I recognised the similarity with the younger of the two Thorpe brothers in the painting in the main hall. The shape of the nose and ears, the spacing of the eyes, there could be no doubt that the two were related. From that assumption, a single telegram to an acquaintance in Malaya confirmed the details, which are common knowledge there."

"I have nothing to be ashamed of back home, it's true," Reilly confirmed. "The opposite, in fact. My workers like to think they work for an Englishman and I am afraid I had grown to think of myself as one. It was only coming here, and living for a day or two among the real thing, that convinced me that I am not." He frowned and allowed his eyes to drop. "I am embarrassed to think of myself only a few days ago, lambasting poor Salah for daring to consider himself a worthy owner of an English estate. My hypocrisy is painful for me to recall!"

Fisher was still staring at Thorpe. "Very well, Holmes, this man's name is Thorpe and not Reilly," has said, "and he's the half-Malayan offspring of a long dead Thorpe brother come to England to look at his father's ancestral home. For the moment, let's say I'm willing to accept all that." He stopped, unable, even hypothetically, to allow his own statement to pass without qualification. "Or at least willing to do so until I get a chance to check the facts for myself. Let's say that – but even if we do, I shall still repeat my earlier questions. If you are entirely innocent, what were you doing in the grounds of the manor in the middle of the night, and what about the telegram you sent?"

Thorpe smiled, then turned to Holmes. "I should not like to steal your thunder, Mr Holmes. I am sure you can enlighten the inspector?"

"Of course," said Holmes. "You recall, Inspector, that I said at the beginning that one answer would cover both of the questions to which you required a response? That answer is, I suspect, contained in Mr Thorpe's suitcase."

"In his suitcase?"

Inspector Fisher and I spoke almost as one, but it was clear from Elias Thorpe's amused reaction that he at least knew exactly what Holmes meant.

Fisher jumped to his feet and threw open the door. "Halliday!" he bellowed down the corridor. "Halliday! Go and find the suitcase the prisoner had with him and bring it here."

He closed the door with enough force to cause the glass to shudder, and immediately confronted Holmes. "I warned you before that I'd arrest you for wasting police time. I assure you that I'll do so, if this suitcase ends up containing nothing but shirts and socks!"

Holmes was sanguine. "I do not think you will be disappointed, Inspector," he said.

"Do not be so sure, Mr Holmes," Thorpe chuckled. "Some men are born to be disappointed."

Before Fisher could react, a heavy hand knocked on the office door and Constable Halliday entered. He placed the suitcase he carried on the desk and, at a sign from Fisher, departed again. With the exception of Thorpe, who remained seated, we all stood round as Fisher turned the suitcase to himself.

The case itself was nondescript, brown leather with brass corners, a little misshapen at one end and with a long but light scratch extending across one side. With a sceptical squint in Holmes's direction, Fisher pressed the locks with his thumbs and flipped the lid open. I leaned forward to see what was revealed inside.

All that was in the case were the usual shirts, ties and the like and, on the side which had appeared misshapen, a metal box, which was slightly too tall for the case but had been crammed inside even so. I realised what it must be a moment before Holmes announced it.

"The ashes of Mr Edward Thorpe," he said quietly. "Brought from Malaya by his son to scatter on the grounds he once played in as a child."

I looked down at Thorpe for confirmation and saw tears rolling down his cheeks, and knew that what Holmes had said was true. Inspector Fisher was also looking at the tearful man and, I was pleased to see, made no attempt to open the tin.

"My mother had promised him, you see," Thorpe said, pulling a handkerchief from his pocket and wiping his face. "His final wish was to be brought home to England, and though she was never able to do it, I thought this was the perfect opportunity."

"The telegram!" I blurted out, suddenly recognising its significance. "You were talking about scattering your father's ashes!"

"Exactly, Dr Watson. The telegram was to my representative in London, apprising him of my intentions. I was keen to do my duty and be gone. I intended to scatter the ashes by the lake. As soon as I had done so, I intended to leave for home."

"Knowing that a police investigation was still active," accused Fisher, but his heart wasn't in it. He seemed to have accepted that Thorpe was who Holmes said he was, and that he had been engaged on a matter of filial duty. He closed the suitcase and placed it on the floor, then opened the door and called Halliday again.

"Take this gentleman to the waiting room along with his case. Keep an eye on him and don't let him leave, but he's no longer under arrest." He turned to Thorpe. "Is that acceptable to you? I can't release you until I've checked a few things, but you are no longer a suspect in the murder of Alim Salah."

As he spoke the dead man's name a change came over him. It was clear that he had remembered Holmes's earlier words about the killer. Suddenly, he was impatient to be done with Elias Thorpe.

"Well, don't just stand there, Halliday!" he snapped. "Get moving!"

Halliday hurriedly grabbed the suitcase and hustled Thorpe out of the door, with barely enough time for Holmes and I to bid him farewell. As soon as he was gone and the door firmly closed behind him, Fisher rounded on Holmes.

"And now, I would be very much obliged if you could explain what you meant earlier by describing Salah's killer as a big man who'd killed before?"

Holmes gestured to Fisher's desk. "I suggest you take a seat, Inspector. I have rather a lot to tell you."

Once Holmes had repeated everything he had told me in the Silent Man pub, and had shown Fisher the telegram he had received from Lestrade describing Billy Robinson, Halliday was called back inside and ordered to prepare a four-seater carriage for the return journey to Thorpe Manor. Fisher suggested we go to the front to wait for it to be brought round.

I had completely forgotten that Frederick Schell had accompanied the inspector and Reilly to Stainforth, but as we passed through the public area of the station, I saw him sitting at the end of a row of hard chairs, his hands resting on a wooden walking stick and his rheumy eyes blinking blearily in our direction. The carriage would be a few minutes, so I wandered over to say goodbye.

"Dr Watson?" he said, looking up and squinting at me uncertainly. "What brings you here?"

"I'm here with Mr Holmes," I explained slowly. "We had one or two things to clear up with the inspector."

"With the inspector?" he asked, but he seemed confused, and those flashes of temper and personality I had occasionally seen at the manor house were conspicuously absent. Clearly, the news about his wife and Captain Hopkirk had crushed the man. Now he appeared to be exactly what I had taken him for, that first night at dinner. A decrepit old man, with only a tenuous grip on his faculties.

"I was betrayed, you know," he went on, without waiting for clarification. "My wife and Hopkirk betrayed me." A single tear rolled down his face. "They were carrying on behind my back, you know. And I wondered why he asked to come here with us." He sighed and wiped at his face with the back of his hand. "Well, I know now."

He shook his head and I looked about for someone to keep an eye on him, but before I could do so, Holmes pulled me out of the way and kneeled by his side.

"What did you just say, Mr Schell?" he barked, his eyes blazing with sudden interest. "Hopkirk asked to accompany you to Thorpe Manor?"

Schell blinked at him but said nothing, and Holmes, realising the condition to which the old man had been reduced by his wife's infidelity, took his hand and went on in a more moderate tone, "Your wife did not make that request? Hopkirk definitely asked himself?"

"Only so that he could betray me," Schell said again. "He

practically begged, you know. I said there was no point in him coming. He'd no money, you know. He couldn't buy the Thorpe place. But he insisted. To be near her…"

His voice trailed off into mumbling and Holmes gently replaced his hand in his lap. "Thank you, Mr Schell," he said. "You have been very helpful."

He straightened up and called over to Fisher. "Is the carriage ready, Inspector? It is vital we return to the manor house as quickly as we can. We should call in at the village on the way, but it is imperative that we reach James Hopkirk before he has a chance to abscond."

"James Hopkirk?" Inspector Fisher was, I think, understandably confused. "I thought you said the publican was our man? Have you changed your mind?"

"Robinson killed Salah, Inspector, of that I am certain. But until now I had been under the impression that Julieanne Schell had invited Hopkirk to visit Thorpe Manor. If that was the case, then it was just as likely that Amicable Watt was Robinson's accomplice as Hopkirk."

"Accomplice, Holmes?" I asked, puzzled.

Rather than reply immediately, Holmes hurried out of the station and climbed into the carriage waiting outside. We followed behind, Fisher complaining loudly that everything must be made clear before we reached Thorpe-by-the-Marsh. We settled into our seats as Halliday swung himself up beside the driver, and as the carriage pulled away, Holmes continued his explanation.

"My apologies, Watson. I confess, I realised that Robinson must have had an accomplice later than I should have. How else would he manage to lift a man as large as Salah over the various items of machinery and place him in such an inaccessible corner of the cellar? It was only when I joked to you that Mr Schell and Alice the maid could not have done so even working together, that it occurred to me that nobody could have done so on their own."

"Meaning one of the other men must have helped him. But why only Watt or Hopkirk? Why none of the others?"

"Buxton is far too timorous to be involved in anything so unsavoury. Frederick Schell, as we just saw, is an old, frail man, of no use in helping heft a heavy body, and Pennington is pathologically obsessed with punishing criminals. He could no more assist a wanted man than commit a crime himself. But Watt admitted to involvement with a bad element in his youth, and is of a similar age and background to Robinson. I admit I thought him the most likely to have assisted Robinson in disposing of the body." He frowned. "Oh, at first, I was unsure about Captain Hopkirk, but when the extent of his infidelity with Mrs Schell was exposed, I put any misgivings I had about the man down to that. After all, I had no definite reason to suspect him, and you appeared to think well of him, Watson.

"He is a clever man, I must admit. I have no doubt that once the inspector discovered he was not in his room at the time of Salah's death, he deliberately allowed the idea of his apparent guilt to gain traction, even to the point of refusing to defend himself against the accusation that he was a murderer. He knew, of course, that he could at any time admit to his dalliance with Mrs Schell and so provide himself with an unimpeachable alibi. As soon as their affair became common knowledge, the police lost interest in him, as he knew they would. As I did myself, to my regret, though I shall allow myself the minor justification that a far stronger suspect presented himself at that same moment."

"Walter Robinson."

"Exactly, Watson. I noticed the very specific alignment of the mirrors in The Silent Man, and recalled what Reilly had said about Salah on their visit to the village. I was certain from that moment that Robinson was the murderer, and so made the elementary mistake of failing to consider the entirety of the crime, including the disposal of the body. Had I done so, Robinson would still be alive to face justice."

Fisher had no time for Holmes's self-reproach. "But now you have decided that Captain Hopkirk better fits the role, is that it, Holmes?" he asked. He had been taking notes the whole time that Holmes spoke, but now he tucked his pencil behind his ear and made a point that had also occurred to me.

"Although, while the fact he insisted that he be invited along to the auction makes a link to Robinson a little more likely, it does not explain why he should be involved in the killing of Salah. You are not suggesting that he also had some role in the assault on the dead man ten years ago?"

"Don't be ridiculous, Inspector!" Holmes snapped. "Salah would hardly have had dinner with Hopkirk if that was the case, and would certainly have mentioned it during their altercation. No," he continued, more thoughtfully, "I think that Hopkirk became involved with the murder purely by chance. I am sure he was exactly where he and Julieanne Schell said he was while the murder was being committed: in the room in the east wing of the house with his lover. But I strongly suspect that when he went to dispose of his cigarette out of the window, he happened to see Robinson bringing Salah's corpse round. Perhaps he even saw

Reilly hiding in the snow, but I cannot be sure of that. Whatever, he raced downstairs to discover what had happened and ended up helping Robinson hide the body in the cellar. He is a clever man, and I have no doubt that he smashed Salah's watch at the same time, to make absolutely certain that, if need be, he could – all too reluctantly, it seems – use his affair with Mrs Schell as an alibi."

Fisher scribbled a last note and closed his book. "That may very well all prove to be true," he said, "but you have not explained what Hopkirk and Robinson were plotting together. Even if they knew each other, and even if Hopkirk helped Robinson cover up Salah's murder, why was Hopkirk so keen to come to the manor house? How did Robinson entice him here in the first place? Because it could have had nothing to do with the presence of Alim Salah."

Holmes nodded, in recognition of a valid question. "I have my suspicions, Inspector, but no more than that. Perhaps Hopkirk and Robinson will provide explanations, given enough encouragement."

He said no more, but instead filled and lit his pipe, and spent the rest of the journey smoking and looking out of the carriage window at the snowy countryside.

Chapter Twenty

Back to the Manor

We arrived in the village little more than half an hour after leaving Stainforth. Fisher was keen to go straight to the manor, but Holmes insisted we stop at the post office and, since we were already doing so, the inspector decided that he might as well take Robinson into custody at once. We waited for Holmes to complete his business, then crossed the road to The Silent Man.

The door was locked and knocking brought no response. Fortunately, Holmes located a spare key on Robinson's keyring and quickly unlocked the door, then held it open for us to enter.

As soon as we crossed the threshold, a terrible sight appeared before us, reflected in the same mirror in which Salah had seen the man who had attacked him a decade before, and so set all these events in motion.

Robinson hung by the neck above the same spot at which I had always seen him, at the end of the bar, facing the fireplace. As we walked towards him, a gust of air entering from the open door behind us caught his body and twisted it a little, so that his face swung in our direction. His dead eyes stared across at us until I stepped on the base of a bar stool and reached up to close them.

Of Judge Pennington there was no sign. I called on Holmes to hold the dead man's legs as I sawed at the rope with my penknife and, as I cut through and the body sagged into his hands, I heard voices behind me raised in further alarm.

"In here, Doctor!" called Inspector Fisher. "Quickly!"

The anxiety in his voice was very different from the irritation and anger he had almost exclusively displayed when roused in the past. It concerned me enough that I left Holmes to grapple Robinson's corpse to the floor, and hurried through the door into the back rooms of the pub.

A short corridor separated the public from the private quarters of the house, at the end of which was a beaded curtain of the type used by gypsy fortune tellers. Beyond was a large kitchen, neatly kept but freezing cold. In the corner, a terrier with one leg wrapped in bandages looked up at me and whined pitifully. It was to the table in the centre of the room that my eyes were drawn, however.

Fisher stood at one side of it, with Halliday on the other, and both men were looking down at the pale-faced, unmoving figure of Judge Pennington. His jacket had been removed and lay on the floor at Fisher's feet, exposing a crumpled white shirt, which someone had opened to the waist. A large circle of dark red blood had soaked through the material of the shirt, staining the breast and right arm.

"He was on the floor here when we came in," Fisher explained quickly. "He's been stabbed in the right side of his chest and struck a blow to the back of his head. The head wound's not too bad, it's barely broken the skin, but the chest wound..." He shook his head. "You can hear it yourself, Doctor..."

I came closer and bent down towards the unconscious man. Even as I did so, I could clearly hear the dreadful wet sucking sound which betokens a punctured lung. "The knife has pierced his lung," I said, "and done a great deal of damage, from the sound of it."

I had no medical equipment with me, but there was a pot of petroleum jelly by the sink which I used to partially close the wound, then bound it tight with a clean shirt Halliday found drying on the back of a chair.

"That may hold him until he gets to the hospital," I said, "so long as the damage is not too extreme. But time is of the essence, Inspector."

Fisher shouted to Holmes and between us we lifted Pennington and laid him carefully in the police carriage outside. Halliday stayed in the back, supporting the injured man and preventing him from moving, while Fisher gave instruction to the driver.

That done, we watched the carriage set off for the hospital, then Fisher grabbed Holmes by the arm and twisted him round so that the two men were toe to toe.

"How did this happen, Holmes?" he snarled. "You assured me that the man was securely tied. How did he break free? At least he had the good sense to top himself after he attacked Pennington. He must have known he wouldn't escape the hangman's noose twice, and preferred to make his own."

He would have said more, I think, had Holmes not spoken first.

"I think not, Inspector. Even had he been able to break free of his bonds, overpower a watchful Pennington and wound him as we saw, even had he been able to do all that in his weakened state, he surely did not pause before he took his own life to clean and put away the knife he had used. Yet I have seen no bloodied knife here, or in the kitchen."

Holmes was correct. Though we searched everywhere, there was no sign of a knife, bloodied or otherwise.

Fisher was the last to quit the search, emerging from the kitchen drying his hands on an old towel. "There's no such knife here, I'd swear to that," he said. "Which means the killer is still on the loose." He threw the towel on the bar. "You realise this brings into question your claim that Robinson killed Salah, Holmes."

Holmes, however, was barely listening. He strode quickly to the door of the pub and pulled it open. Though I could not make out exactly what he was doing from where I stood, it appeared as though he said something, then stepped outside and grabbed at someone in the street. A moment later, he was back, dragging Simeon Forward with him.

"Get your hands off me!" Forward protested as Holmes pulled him towards us. "I'll get the police on to—"

His complaint was instantly bitten off as he was heaved round the corner of the dogleg and saw Fisher standing over the body of Robinson, across which the inspector had just draped his jacket.

"What's going on here?" he asked, crossing himself and swallowing heavily. "Who's done for him?"

Fisher stepped in front of the body, blocking Forward's view. "What makes you think anyone has done for him at all?" he asked, in the familiar tones of the policeman who believes he has spotted an inconsistency. "Why can't he just have slipped and fallen?"

"With his hands tied?" Forward sneered. "I can see the rope marks from here."

Fisher reddened and barked at the villager to sit down. He frowned at Holmes. "What did you bring this old fool inside for?"

"It is more than half an hour past opening time," Holmes replied evenly. "Mr Forward is a regular of this hostelry and one who, if previous experience is any guide, arrives early. Therefore he has been standing outside for at least that long. Is that not correct, Mr Forward?"

The old man nodded glumly. "More'n an hour since I first come over," he grumbled, then glanced across at Robinson's still form and fell silent.

"And in that time did anyone leave the premises?"

"That's why I come across in the first place. I saw the other one coming out and running off, and I reckoned landlord must have opened early. But the door were locked fast, so I went back home. Only come back when I saw you three go inside."

"The other one? What other one?" Fisher asked. "Did you see someone leave the pub? Did you recognise him? What was his name?" His questions rattled out like bullets, just as they had when he had questioned Captain Hopkirk days earlier, but this time the intention was not to unnerve or disorient but simply to extract the information as swiftly as possible.

Forward leaned back, however, and observed the inspector through narrowed eyes. "There's more going on here than just him," he said, pointing at Robinson. "What's happened, though, that's what I'd like to know."

At this, Fisher's hand closed in a fist and I thought he would strike the old man, but he controlled himself with a visible effort. "A man has been stabbed and may die, Mr Forward," he said, his voice flat. "If we are to catch the villain who did it, we need to know who he is. Now, I repeat, did you recognise the man you saw leaving these premises and, if you did, who was it?"

Forward sucked air in through his teeth, considering Fisher's words. "Stabbed, you say? Well, I don't know about that, but it weren't a man I saw at all, anyway. It were a woman, a pretty young thing. Red haired. Not from around here. She come out of the pub like the old Lord's ghost were on her heels, and run up the path to the manor house."

"Julieanne Schell!" I gasped.

"But what has Robinson to do with her?" Fisher asked. "Has the threat of divorce driven her mad?"

He was plainly talking to himself. Distractedly, he dragged his jacket from the corpse at his side, pulled it on and ran to the door.

"No."

Holmes's voice was without emotion or volume but it stopped Fisher in his tracks. He paused in the doorway and looked back at us.

"This is not Mrs Schell's doing," Holmes went on. He picked up Robinson's left arm. "Mr Forward is correct. Observe the marks on Robinson's wrist. They are extensive. The skin has been completely abraded at points and there has been a good deal of bleeding. We left him unconscious and he would have remained so for some time after Judge Pennington arrived unless violently provoked. And here," he walked over to the spot at which Robinson had hung, "there is nothing upon which he might have stood before hanging himself."

"But we know he didn't hang himself, Holmes," I pointed out, unsure what Holmes was driving at. I spied Fisher out of the corner slowly walking back towards us.

"We do," he said, looking across at Holmes. "But I believe Mr Holmes is suggesting that he was hanged by someone else, while he was still bound. Someone dragged Robinson over there with his hands still tied, and winched him up in the air. The deep marks on his wrist were made in his frantic struggles to escape that fate, and the ropes on his wrists only cut after he was dead. And Mrs Schell couldn't have hoisted him. She wouldn't have the strength."

"No, she would not," Holmes agreed. "What was it she said, Watson? That she would do anything to survive? And how will she survive now that her husband has deserted her? To whom must she necessarily now turn for support?"

"Captain Hopkirk."

"Yes, indeed. Captain Hopkirk." He reached into his pocket and pulled out the sheaf of telegrams he had collected from the post office. "Lestrade reports that Hopkirk was drummed out of the army for theft from regimental funds, not for defending the honour of a lady, innocent or otherwise. Furthermore, his batman's name was William Robinson and Hopkirk gave evidence for the defence at his trial."

Seeing the surprised look on Fisher's face, he explained. "I telegrammed Lestrade and asked him to check on Hopkirk's military career. He quickly identified him and was able to turn up rather a lot of other information in a surprisingly short time – one of the strengths of routine police work, I readily admit. He was good enough to send it down by telegram."

Fisher was itching to be after Mrs Schell and Captain Hopkirk, but he was too much the policeman not to ensure he had every scrap of information possible. "What else did Inspector Lestrade say?" he asked, already halfway back to the door.

"There is too little time to go into detail, but I believe that the various facts Lestrade uncovered, once he knew where to look, suggest strongly that it was Hopkirk who helped Robinson escape from prison before the hangman could despatch him."

"The rest will have to wait, Holmes," Fisher shouted from the doorway. "For now, all I need to know is that Hopkirk murdered Robinson and tried to kill Pennington, with Julieanne Schell's assistance. I'm going to the house to arrest the pair of them. You're welcome to come, if you wish."

The last few words were barely audible, for by that point he was in the street, leaving the door swinging in his wake.

I looked across at Holmes, shrugged, and hurried after the inspector. I heard Forward say that he was coming too, and the sound of two sets of boots at my heels as I shoved through the door and headed as quickly as I could to the manor house.

Chapter Twenty-One

An Audience at the Palace

We quickly caught up with Inspector Fisher, and so it was as a group of four that we arrived at Thorpe Manor.

The interior was deserted and the only sound a muffled, irregular thumping coming from upstairs, but there was no doubt that our quarry had been there recently. Lying at the foot of the stairs, his eyes staring glassily at the ceiling, was the untidy form of Constable Cairns. A long kitchen knife protruded from his chest. Beside his outstretched hand lay his truncheon. There was fresh blood on one end of it, but much, much more pooled beneath him.

He was obviously dead.

I looked across at Fisher, and at that moment nothing would have convinced me to swap places with James Hopkirk. I thought I had seen the inspector angry before, but now I realised that those fits of temper I had witnessed had been mere bluster. Now, his sallow skin barely coloured at all, but his eyes were cold and unblinking as he looked down at his murdered constable, and his hands were balled in fists so tight that each blanched completely white. He shrugged off his coat and draped it over Cairns' body, then pointed to the area behind the stairs, where splashes of blood were visible on the wooden floor.

"He went that way," he said and walked purposefully in that direction. We followed him through the kitchen, and from there into the gardens at the rear.

Twenty feet or so from the steps, the crumpled figure of Julieanne Schell was stretched out on the snow. We rushed over to her, fearing the worst, but as I knelt down to take her pulse, she stirred and opened her eyes.

"Dr Watson?" she said groggily, reaching up to touch the back of her head with one ivory-gloved hand. Wincing, she brought her hand back down and gazed curiously at the blood that stained the pale cotton. "I seem to have struck my head," she said.

Her eyelids fluttered and, fearing concussion, I spoke to her loudly, telling her not to go to sleep. Fisher crouched beside me and took her hand carefully, as though she were fragile.

"Mrs Schell," he said quietly, his voice friendly and almost tender. "We're looking for Captain Hopkirk, my dear. I wonder, have you seen him?"

Mrs Schell's eyes widened suddenly and she shook her head, then gasped at the pain of the movement and instead whispered, "He did this! He promised we would be together for ever if I helped him by distracting the judge, and then he did this!" Tears welled up in her eyes and slid in parallel down each cheek. "What am I to do now?" she asked, but nobody answered.

"Where is he now, Mrs Schell?" Fisher asked again. "He should answer for doing this to you, don't you think? Tell me where he is, and I shall make sure that he does."

She looked up at him and smiled, murmuring, "You are a true gentleman, Inspector. He said he had a collection to make, at the palace." She giggled. "At the palace," she repeated, still laughing.

Fisher let her hand drop in the snow, and rose to his feet. Holmes pointed across the gardens to the distant copse of trees that surrounded the model Crystal Palace. "That way, Inspector," he said, and the two men set off towards it, making slow progress through the thick snow in their walking shoes. I inspected the wound on the back of Mrs Schell's head to make sure it was not serious, then told Forward to stay with her. "Do not let her sleep. Keep talking to her until we get back." Though he grumbled to himself, Forward nodded and took my place at her side.

Holmes and Fisher were only a few yards away. As I caught up with them, they shifted position so that we walked one behind the other, somewhat increasing our pace, but even so it was twenty minutes before we were standing beneath the grove of trees, with the stone palace directly in front of us.

The ground was littered with small fragments of stone which turned underfoot, and the few patches of snow were coloured by brick dust. The cause was clear. Hopkirk was nowhere to be seen but evidence of his recent presence was unmistakable.

On the left-hand side of the building, the glass had been smashed and lay strewn about the interior in jagged shards. A chisel and a large hammer of the sort used by labourers stood with its handle upright among the uneven panes, though its primary purpose had clearly not been to smash them. Instead, as we moved cautiously inside, we could see the destruction that Hopkirk had caused to the brickwork, evidently to break into the vault inside. He had not succeeded in gaining entry, as Holmes had predicted earlier, but he had managed to create a small hole, no more than three inches in circumference at one point. I pressed my eye against the hole but it was pitch dark inside and I could make out nothing.

"Use this," a voice said at my side. Simeon Forward stood there, a lantern in his hand. "Alice is with the woman," he said. "I told her to keep her talking, but she'll have no trouble with that. She never shuts up, that one." He did not smile but held the lantern so that it shone some light into the darkness of the palace interior. It was impossible with such poor illumination to see anything clearly, but I fancied I made out the glitter of something golden in the darkness – and then a woman's face and hand stretched towards me!

Forward gasped in horror at my side, and I stifled an oath and turned to Holmes, who had also been staring into the palace. "Only a painting, I suspect," he said, with the smallest of smiles. Forward, ashen-faced, nodded his relieved agreement.

Inspector Fisher had no interest in the contents of the palace vault, however. Whatever lay within would have to wait until later; his only concern was the capture of Hopkirk.

He would not be difficult to track. A red streak on one of the shards of glass indicated that he had cut himself in his abortive attempt to break into the palace, and drops of blood stood out starkly against the white snow behind the building. The presence of more trees and the natural lie of the land meant the snow was not so deep here, and we were able to make good time as we raced along the uneven scarlet trail.

He seemed to be heading back towards the house, but on a

more elliptical line than we had taken, moving across country between a plethora of follies and wooded copses, presumably to provide himself with cover from any pursuers. This, combined with the fading light, meant we could not actually see him as yet. Still, we had the blood trail to follow, and though the further we went from the main paths the slower our pace became, the same was equally the case for Hopkirk.

A few hundred yards from the ruined palace, we stumbled over a deep, bloodstained crevasse in the snow, and I was reminded of the similar indentation in which Alim Salah's body had been dumped.

"We may yet catch him," Holmes commented, barely breaking his stride to examine the area. "He fell here and lay a while. This snow has not only been compacted by his weight, it has been melted by his body heat."

Fisher's face was grim as he barrelled past Holmes and reached a crest in the landscape, which afforded him a longer view of the surrounding countryside.

"There he is!" he called back softly, dropping to his knees as he did so, in order that Hopkirk should not see him. "He's going slowly, and he's walking funny, dragging one leg," he reported.

"How far away?" asked Holmes.

"A few hundred yards, at most."

"He is definitely headed for the manor house?"

"I'd say so."

Holmes closed his eyes and I knew he was picturing the map of the estate that hung in the main hall.

"A quarter mile, as the crow flies," Forward interrupted. "With a bit of luck, we might catch him before he gets there."

"We need to," said Holmes. "Frederick Schell's carriage is still hitched up. If he reaches that and gets away, we will not apprehend him."

Luck did not seem to be on our side, however; as we crested the little hill, Hopkirk chanced to look back and see us, and doubled his pace. The effort cost him – as we closed on him I could hear the laboured sound of his breathing and see how he dragged his feet through the snow – but the distance between us was too great and the distance from Hopkirk to the house too small. He made it to the back entrance while we were still a hundred yards away. It appeared that all was lost. We would never get close enough to prevent him taking off in Schell's carriage.

And then he fell, hard, against the bottom of the steps to the house.

As he slowly dragged himself upright, we put on a burst of driven speed and were only thirty yards away when he seemed to decide that the stairs were beyond him. He looked back at us once more, then half stumbled and half fell down the ramp which led to the cellar, whose doors had remained unlocked following the discovery of Alim Salah's body.

When we reached the rear of the house, there was no sign of Hopkirk. The trail of blood stopped at the open doors of the cellar, though, and there could be no doubt he had gone inside. Fisher quickly ran up the steps and bolted the door which led down to the cellar, then returned to stand beside us as we caught our breath and planned our next move.

We could not know if Hopkirk was armed. He had stabbed

Cairns and struck Julieanne Schell on the head, and he had made no effort to shoot at us, even after he realised how close we were. Even so, the possibility could not be ruled out, which made a frontal assault through the cellar doors inadvisable. One of us would have to go down and check on the captain's whereabouts. Before anyone could object, I pressed myself against the wall and began to edge my way down the slope.

Hopkirk was nowhere to be seen, but the door to the catacombs hung open. I beckoned the others to come down and pointed to it.

"It's possible this is a bluff and Hopkirk is somewhere concealed in the cellar," whispered Fisher.

"Unlikely," Holmes replied. "Even with a weapon, he cannot hope to overcome all four of us, and his only means of escape without doing so is through the cave system." He turned to Simeon Forward. "Where do the caves come out?" he asked.

Forward scratched his head and considered the question. "All over," he said eventually. "There's a dozen places within two miles of this spot where a man can walk out onto solid ground."

"Then we've no time to waste," said Fisher.

He pushed past Holmes and me, but Forward put out a hand to stop him. "Careful, policeman," he said. "Rushing about in the catacombs is a quick way to an early grave."

We followed him into the cellar and approached the open door. The smell of wet rock coming from the darkness was strong, and I felt myself shiver as I stepped over the threshold.

The ground was dry underfoot, but even in the flickering torchlight, I could see a thin sheen of water running down the wall to my right and disappearing into a crack at its base. To the left, the sloping passageway we had entered continued for twenty feet, then was lost in the darkness.

"Wait," Simeon Forward said, directly in front of me, as he fiddled with a bracket bolted to the rock face. A second later, a flame sputtered fitfully into life, then steadied and cast its warm glow in a pool around us. Ten feet further on, another light blinked into being, and beyond that another and, I assumed, so on for some distance.

"Gas lights were the first thing we put in," Forward explained, but I was no longer paying attention. Instead I was staring down at the suitcase at my feet. The lock had obviously been broken, and it lay open, its contents spilled on the wet ground.

Holmes too had noticed the discarded case. He knelt down and tugged a heavy scarlet tunic from the heap of spilled clothing. There was no doubt it had belonged to Alim Salah. An image of a snake coiled round a ruby stamped on the lid of the case merely confirmed that we had found the dead man's missing luggage.

Forward was uninterested in our discovery, however. He moved ahead along the passageway until it opened up into a wider cavern. Gesturing for us to wait where we were, he slowlyc inched along the wall, keeping his back pressed firmly against the stone. As we watched, he lit a match then reached along the wall with his left arm. A second later, a light flared into life, and we had our first real view of the Thorpe catacombs.

We were standing, we discovered, at the entrance to a cave, which stretched into darkness high above us. Forward stood to our left, part way along a narrow pathway, no more than four feet at its widest, which ran round the perimeter of the cavern in both directions. Iron poles, three feet high and with a circular hoop at their top, were spaced every six feet along the edge of the path, suggesting that once a rope barrier had been intended to prevent unwary travellers from stumbling over the edge. Of the rope, if it had ever been put in place, there was no sign. No force on earth would have convinced me to go close enough to the edge to judge the depth of the cavern, but Forward saw me looking and provided an answer to my unspoken question.

"It's as deep as it is high, Doctor, and there's no soft landing," he called over quietly. "So, all of you, follow me, one at a time, and keep close to the wall." He crouched down and examined something we could not see.

"Your man's been this way. There's blood on the ground," he said as he rose to his feet. He took a step towards us – and fell to the ground as a shot rang out.

In an instant, Holmes and Fisher had ducked back down the pathway from which we had come but I, a little further ahead, had no time to do so. Without the option to stay where I was, I threw myself to my right, away from Forward and onto the dark section of perimeter path. In my terror of the drop, however, I misjudged its width. I collided hard with the wall, now on my right-hand side, and bounced away from it, pitching me towards an undoubtedly deadly fall. I landed on the ground with my head and one shoulder hanging over the abyss, and was only saved from plunging to my death by one of the iron poles, which collided with my midriff and round which I gratefully wrapped myself.

I lay there for a second, attempting to quiet my breathing, then pulled myself wholly on to the path and rolled against the relative safety of the rock wall. A large boulder had fallen from the roof at some point in the past half century and I swiftly scuttled behind it. From the security of its shadow I glanced across at Forward, hoping he had not been too badly hurt. But there was nobody in the circle of light cast by the lantern he had most recently lit. I was sure that he had not fallen over the edge, and he could not have crawled back towards Holmes and Fisher. I turned my face from the light and allowed my eyes to become accustomed to the dark, then closed them and slowly moved my head in an arc so that when I reopened them I was staring into the blackness on the other side of the lantern's glow. Sure enough, I could just make out a long, low section of shadow, which was slowly edging along the ground, moving further into the catacombs.

Holmes had evidently seen it too, for rather than make any attempt to outflank Hopkirk (not that I could think of a way in which he could, given the captain's unknown position and possession of a firearm), he shouted out to him.

"Captain Hopkirk!" he called. There was no reply. "Captain Hopkirk!" he repeated, with identical result.

The shadow, which I presumed to be Forward, had disappeared out of sight, and I wondered if Holmes would cease his attempts to engage Hopkirk in conversation. In the silence, however, I heard the sound of a small rock falling somewhere in the dark corners of the cavern. Whether it was Hopkirk or Forward who had dislodged it, it could not be good news, for one indicated that the captain was on the move and we might easily lose him, and the other, if overheard by our quarry, might mean the death of the elderly villager.

Holmes evidently thought the same, for suddenly he stepped into the light and shouted "Hopkirk! We have you trapped!" then dived full length towards me. A bullet slapped into the wall near where he had recently stood and then ricocheted away, followed by another, which clipped the rock behind which I crouched, just as Holmes joined me.

"That was rather too close for comfort," he panted, smoothing back his hair. "The captain, for all his other military failings, is obviously an excellent shot, even when wounded."

"Why didn't you stay where you were, Holmes?" I snapped, irate at his apparent foolhardiness, but I should have known there would be method in his madness.

"Simeon Forward is getting closer to Hopkirk by the minute, and it is essential that we continue to hold the captain's attention until he is in a position to overcome him. We must each keep on the move so he cannot be sure how many people are down here. In that way, Forward may get his opportunity."

"Fisher knows this too?" I asked, and Holmes nodded.

"He does. In a moment, I shall return to my original position while he runs in this direction. As soon as he gets here you must make a dash for that kink in the wall—" He indicated a spot fifteen yards farther along where the wall bent back on itself, creating a small, enclosed section of path. "There is a lantern directly above it. Light that if you can, and then wait there." He laid a hand on my arm. "Be quick though, Watson. We have no idea how much ammunition Hopkirk has and, even at this distance, he will not miss his shot for ever."

There was no need for the reminder. I had been under fire before, but it was not an experience that became more enjoyable with repetition. "And you," I said, as he counted to five and then thrust himself away from our shelter and into the line of fire. Simultaneously, Fisher did the same from the other side. Two quick shots rang out and the inspector was spun round just as he passed

Holmes. Without breaking stride, Holmes grabbed the wounded man under the arms and continued to run, reaching the sanctuary of the sheltered entryway.

There was no time to consider my actions. I rose to my feet and sprinted as well as I could in the direction of the kink in the rock wall. The gradient in this direction was uneven and the ground wet and I slipped almost immediately, half pitching forward and grazing my palms as I used my hands to prevent myself falling entirely. It was fortunate I did, for a bullet smacked into the wall directly above me, exactly where I would have been standing were it not for my stumble. I reached safety just in front of another bullet, which whipped past me and rebounded off the rock surface, to who knew where.

As the echo of the shots died away, a peculiar stillness came over the cavern. I could hear Fisher groaning and Holmes urging him to be quiet and, faintly, water running somewhere far off. The air was cold and there was a slight breeze, and the ever-present smell of wet rock was overpowering in the enclosed nook in which I found myself.

I remembered Holmes's instruction to light the nearest lantern and struck a match..

As though the match scraping along sandpaper was a signal, the cavern exploded into life. Suddenly, the dead air was filled with the sounds of a furious struggle.

What I recognised as Hopkirk's voice gave a cry of alarm, instantly cut off. Small stones skittered and bounced against the rock face opposite and tumbled into the abyss. A bellow of rage echoed around us, and then Forward's voice called out that we should make our way towards him.

I was doing no good where I was, so I darted from my shelter and ran round the pathway, with Holmes following on my heels a moment later. The long curve of the cavern ended in a small chamber with a low stone wall at one end, which looked out over the dark chasm and towards the spot at which we had originally entered the catacombs. The effect was reminiscent of a box at the theatre, where the show, for a few dangerous minutes, had been performed by Holmes, Fisher and myself.

Captain Hopkirk sat with his back against the rock face, both hands pressed to a dark stain on his left trouser leg, just below his waist. A dirty gash on his forehead testified to Constable Cairns' dying truncheon blow. Simeon Forward stood a few feet away from him, a revolver in his hand. As Holmes stepped into the chamber and held up the lantern he had stopped to retrieve, Forward held the gun at arm's length.

"There's no bullets left in it," he declared. "And there's no fight left in this one, either."

I walked towards Hopkirk, but he pulled himself, groaning, to his feet as I did so, and placed one foot on the low wall. "Take another step closer, old man, and I'll be forced to do myself in," he gasped in short breaths. "There's nothing you can do in any case, Doctor. The artery's cut or some such. Even I'm enough of a soldier to know that's me done for."

He pulled the bottom of his bloodstained waistcoat down to straighten its lines, and reached into his jacket. I saw Forward stiffen and begin to move, but Hopkirk pulled out only a silver case and a box of matches. He lit one of his stinking cigarettes, then let the case fall to the ground.

"I'd offer you one," he said, "but that was my last." He laughed, but there was the sound of bubbling blood in it, and it quickly turned into a cough. "No Inspector Fisher, I see," he said once he had recovered. "Did I do for him then? Not bad shooting with a revolver in the dark, you have to admit, eh?"

"The inspector is wounded in the arm, but he will make a full recovery," Holmes informed him quietly. He laid the lantern down on the floor between himself and Hopkirk. "As you rightly say, however, you will not. With that in mind, perhaps we might discuss recent events?"

From his tone of voice, Holmes might as easily have been discussing the price of tobacco or the latest play in the West End, and Hopkirk replied with a similar lack of drama.

"A deathbed confession, eh? How I killed my old batman for messing up our plans and murdered an innocent policeman as I tried to escape?" Hopkirk inhaled deeply on his cigarette, then flicked the glowing butt into the chasm. He watched it spiral down and disappear in the darkness, then turned his attention back to Holmes. "A chance to tell my side of the story for the benefit of the readers of The Strand? Is that what you have in mind, Mr Holmes?" He shook his head. "Sadly, there is no 'my side' to tell. I am exactly what I appear to be – a lazy man and a bad one, probably, with a taste for expensive things and no particular desire to work for them. Could you make much of that, do you think, Dr Watson? Could you make your readers feel sympathy for me? Or would I be one of your black-hearted villains, another Charles Augustus Milverton?" He smiled and cocked an eyebrow in amusement. "I lied about that, too. I have read your stories, old man."

There must have been something in his tone of voice, or some indication in his stance, perhaps. Whatever it was, Holmes sprang forward as Hopkirk ceased speaking – but it was too late. Still smiling, the captain shifted his weight onto the foot resting on the low stone wall and, without a sound, launched himself into the chasm. A second or two later the sound of a heavy, certainly fatal, impact reached us.

We stood in stunned silence, until Holmes bent down and collected the cigarette case from the ground. The catch must have broken on hitting the rocky floor, and it lay open in his hands, exposing two pieces of paper carefully folded into one corner. Fisher held the lantern over him as Holmes extracted each and stretched them smooth in his hands. The first was a crudely drawn map of the manor grounds, with the house sketched in at the bottom of the page and a dotted path drawn over it, running from the side of the house to what I was sure was the model Crystal Palace. The other was part of a letter. It was short and barely literate.

I havent said a word to nobody about this captain. I know what I owe you. But I seen his lordship about that glass building before the sun was up a load of times on my deliverys. And theres all sorts missing from the house they say. Get yourself down here before they sell the place and take a look. BR.

Holmes folded the paper up again and slipped it into his pocket.

"I think it is time we returned to the Crystal Palace," he said. "There are one or two points to be cleared up."

I nodded. "First, we must see to the inspector – and I have just realised that we have no idea of the whereabouts of Watt and Buxton!"

Chapter Twenty-Two

Explanations

The bullet had passed straight through Inspector Fisher's shoulder and, miraculously, had done very little damage in the process. We helped him back into the house where we found Alice sitting with a sobbing Julieanne Schell. There seemed to be no lasting sign of ill effects from Hopkirk's blow to her head, and she was only too keen to blurt out her version of recent events.

"He had me under his spell, Inspector, you have to believe me," she pleaded. "He threatened to cut my throat if I didn't distract poor Judge Pennington, but I never for a second thought he would hurt him."

She began to sob again, but I could have told her that, even at the best of times, any appeal to Fisher's better nature was bound to fail. I could have added that now was not, by any stretch of the imagination, the best of times. As expected, he listened to her in silence, as she by turns claimed to have lived in fear of her life for days and to have been spellbound by Hopkirk's English charms, then formally arrested her and handcuffed her to a table leg. Only then would he allow me to examine his wound.

While I bound it and settled him in one of the armchairs by the fire, Holmes and Forward went off in search of the two missing guests. They returned within a few minutes, Watt and Buxton in tow.

"Locked in their rooms," Holmes announced. I expected the two men to demand explanations, but the sight of Constable Cairns' body, even covered by Fisher's coat, had obviously affected them, and they said nothing, simply stood by mutely as Holmes gave them a task to occupy their minds.

"Constable Halliday should be back with some of his colleagues very soon. If you could move Constable Cairns' body to one of the couches in this room, Watson and I have one final item of business to attend to."

Fisher tried to protest, but he had lost enough blood to make physical effort difficult and was quickly convinced to stay where he was. While Watt and Buxton – the former with fascination, the latter with horror – listened to his account of recent events, Holmes and I, along with Simeon Forward, left the room and made what I hoped would be our final journey back to the Crystal Palace.

We stood once again by the ruin of the palace, and waited for Holmes to explain why he had been so insistent we come with him.

"I saw the look on your face when the painting was revealed in the vault inside the Crystal Palace," Holmes said, turning to Simeon Forward. "You were as shocked as Watson. But, unlike Watson, you did not long mistake it for a living person. You recognised it for a painting because you recognised the person portrayed, and knew she was dead, did you not? Long dead too, for the dress the lady wore has not been the fashion for half a century. A young girl, dead fifty years, whom you knew. Your daughter, perhaps?"

Forward nodded.

"She was linked in some way to Lord Thorpe?" pressed Holmes.

"Linked?" Forward muttered, his voice so soft I had to crane to hear it. "Aye, she was."

Holmes was brisk, as though he wished this conversation to be done with as quickly as possible. "She is the reason that work on the catacombs was broken off?" he asked. "You need not answer. Though I cannot speak as to the details, the timing is too precise for anything else to be the case. You were in charge of the work, if I remember correctly? Am I right in saying, then, that whatever happened, happened due to that particular circumstance?"

Forward nodded again, misery etched on his face. "Margaret used to come up to the digging every day, bringing my dinner. At first she'd just give it me and go; mine workings full of men are no place for young girls, and my Megs was the best girl in the village. Everyone loved her. Pretty as a flower she was, and innocent and sweet natured too." Forward's face darkened. "That was the problem. One day, she was there when Lord Thorpe showed his face, and he was smitten the second he laid eyes on her." Forward's gaze was no longer on us three standing round him, but on a young man and a young woman, decades previously. He stared straight ahead, acknowledging none of us as he continued his story. "Her head was turned, of course. How could it not be, with him a rich man, educated, a man of the world, and her just a simple village girl? I warned her, but she just laughed at me. Fondly enough, but laughter all the same, at her daft fool of a father. Maybe if her mother had still been alive..."

As though suddenly recalling where he was, his head snapped round towards Holmes, and he went on in a stronger, more forceful voice. "For the next month or more he took Megs all over – for dinner in fancy places, on trips to London and to the sea, and long walks through the country. He seemed respectful, I'll say that for him. It'd have been better for us all if he hadn't been. If he'd done something, anything, that I knew about, I'd have warned him off, Lord or no. But he didn't do a thing – or that's what I thought. I was wrong."

Forward's hands were clenched tightly and his voice shook with rage as he continued. "She came to see me, one night. Said she – they – had made a terrible mistake, done a terrible thing. She was in the family way, she said. He wouldn't marry her, she said. Said he couldn't."

There were tears rolling down the old man's face now. "He stopped the diggings at the catacombs the same day. Shut them down and sent everyone home. I spoke to him, of course. Told him I knew what was going on, grabbed him and would have pitched him down one of the shafts, but he'd got some lads in from the city, and they knocked me about a bit, and threw me out on my ear. He shut the estate that day and got them to build his palace for him. It was where they'd gone on their days out, she told me. It was their place."

He choked as he spoke, and Holmes took the chance to ask the question uppermost in all our minds. "What happened to your daughter, Mr Forward?"

"She died having the child," he said flatly. "I sent her to have it at my sister's, who married a Derbyshire man. I wasn't there. She sent her husband to tell me, and she raised the child until she was old enough to go to school. Ellen, we called her." He pulled a handkerchief from his pocket and blew his nose noisily. "Try that, Mr Holmes. I'll bet a penny to a pound Ellen is the name you're looking for."

Holmes looked at the man for a long moment, then turned to the stone wall and carefully pressed five panes. For a second nothing happened, then, with a loud click, a large section of the wall slowly swung open.

With the door open, the interior was reasonably well lit, but still Holmes took the lantern he carried and held it at shoulder height as he stepped inside, the first to enter. I shall never forget the sight that greeted me when I followed a few yards behind.

Whereas the exterior was made of rough stone carved into the shape of glass, the interior walls were smooth plaster, painted a soft off-white. A high-backed leather chair sat in the centre of the room with a small cabinet to its side. Opposite it, on a wooden stand, stood the painting we had spied the day before.

Seen in better light, there was no denying the beauty of Margaret Forward. Long hair the colour of autumn leaves hung down each side of her pale, unblemished face and complemented her large brown eyes, while a playful smile suggested the sweet temper her father had described. Behind me, standing in the doorway without entering, he sniffed loudly and turned away, remaining in the woods while Holmes examined the remainder of the vault. In truth, there was very little to see.

"Lord Thorpe came here often," Holmes said after he had paced the dimensions of the room, examining the walls and floor and investigating the contents of the little cabinet. "The leather of the chair is soft as butter, and on the arms worn away at the points at which his elbows would touch were he to be sitting, staring at the painting."

An ashtray with the remains of a cigar and a dusty glass sat alongside a small collection of what we took to be letters from Margaret Forward, though the ink was so faded as to be illegible, excepting an occasional word. Holmes carefully replaced them in the cabinet.

"Come, Watson," he said. "I have seen all I need to. We have found our ghost, I think."

We closed the door behind us, and heard whatever mechanism it was that controlled the lock click back into place. Forward watched us from the edge of the trees. As we approached, he stooped and picked up a fragment of broken stone from the ground. He examined it for a moment, turning it this way and that in his hands.

"He made sure that her daughter got the best education money could buy, but he never had anything to do with her," he said, before either of us could say a word. "I went up to the manor, the day I got back from her funeral. I marched right up to him, where he was sitting in the big hall, drunk. I told him what had happened and who was to blame for it. He just squinted up at me and said his heart was broken, that he'd had no choice, that it wasn't his fault, lots of tomfoolery like that, feeling sorry for hisself, stinking of wine and beer. He said that he wished he was dead too.

"So I told him straight. You either do right by your daughter or you'll get your wish. I'd a gun with me, an old hunting rifle, you see. Turned out that he'd heard the news already – don't ask me how – but only that she'd gone, not that the baby had lived. That stopped him in his tracks."

"He agreed to pay for the child's upbringing?"

"He did."

"And sold off the Thorpe Collection to pay for it?"

"Why not?" Forward shrugged. "It's not like them paintings were doing anything, sitting in the dark at the manor. I didn't care how he got the money then, and I don't care now. All I cared about was that the money was always in the bank when it was needed. That's where I'd been when I met you on the train. Not a funeral in London, but at the lawyer's in town. Finding out what'd happen now."

"And what did the lawyer tell you?"

"He said that there'd be no more money, now Lord Thorpe was gone."

Holmes's brow furrowed in thought. "I imagined that would be the case. Is that likely to be a problem?"

Forward shook his head. "It will not. There'd been less and less money over the years in any event. And Ellen's a grown woman, married with children of her own now. Thorpe money gained her a good education and a good husband. She wants for nowt, and she'll not suffer for the loss. But I wasn't asking about that."

"You were asking if Ellen might inherit," I said, in a flash of understanding. "I was," Forward confirmed. "But the lawyer said what I knew he would, that she couldn't, not with her being born out of wedlock and no proof she's his daughter." He suddenly noticed that he was still holding the fragment of stone in his hand. With a frown, he tossed it away. "For Margaret's sake, I'd have liked him to have admitted she's a Thorpe, but there it is. What can't be cured…"

I looked back at the Crystal Palace. I wondered at the strangeness of a man who would deny himself happiness with a woman he loved, and then spend the rest of his life in misery, pining for her. And of another who had crossed half the world to find a family, and failed.

"Must be endured," I said, completing the old saw. "But I believe there is a man in Stainforth police station who would be delighted to discover he has a great-niece."

Forward stared at me in confusion, but I simply took him by the elbow and steered him between the trees. "I'll explain on the way back," I said. I saw Holmes smile as he fell into step behind us, and I led the old man back towards the manor house.

Chapter Twenty-Three
❧

One Final Mystery

The remainder of that night and much of the next morning was taken up in dealing with the aftermath of the day's events.

Soon after we reached the manor house, Halliday arrived with police reinforcements in a pair of carriages. Fisher immediately assigned one of them to carry the bodies of Constable Cairns and Walter Robinson to Stainforth, with Simeon Forward, after a brief discussion with the inspector, sitting alongside the driver. The other took Lawrence Buxton back to his cottage, along with Amicable Watt who had swiftly taken advantage of Buxton's offer of a bed for the night.

In normal circumstances, I suspect that Inspector Fisher would have wished to discuss the evening's events, but his wound had left him weak enough that I was able to insist that he get a good night's sleep first. Exhausted as we were, Holmes and I were happy to follow him upstairs soon after.

* * *

Next morning, we came down to find the inspector standing in the doorway of the manor house, looking out at the snowy driveway. To my surprise, Holmes wandered over to stand beside him. He offered Fisher a cigarette and lit one for himself, and for a minute or so, the two men stood smoking in silence.

"Mrs Schell was very chatty while you were away last night," Fisher said after grinding the stub of his cigarette out with his heel. "She claims that Hopkirk inveigled her into securing him an invitation to the auction after he received some news from an old friend. She says she had no idea who this friend was, and I believe her, but there's no doubt it was Robinson. She does admit that she knew from early on what Hopkirk was after – Lord Thorpe had repeatedly been seen by Hopkirk's mysterious friend, entering a building in the grounds in the early hours of the morning. Presumably this was when Robinson was delivering kegs of ale," Fisher explained. "You can just about see the replica of the Crystal Palace from the path at the side of the house."

"And as the letter we found said, Robinson jumped to the conclusion that Thorpe had something valuable hidden inside," I interrupted, as I came up behind the two men.

"The Thorpe Collection, I imagine," Fisher agreed. "The map Robinson drew, though crude, was enough to pinpoint a location, and Hopkirk had been using the excuse of his long walks with Mrs Schell as a cover for his investigation of the palace's workings. Evidently, unlike Mr Holmes, he never figured out how to open it properly, though. Running out of time, and discovering his confederate had been arrested, he must have feared that Robinson was likely to talk, and so decided to kill him and flee. Had he not made one last attempt at the Crystal Palace he might even have escaped." His pallid face crumpled into a frown. "Though not for long. Not after he murdered a policeman."

The thought was enough to silence the inspector. It seemed that he would say no more, for he made to go back in the house, then at the last moment turned back.

"Halliday will be here soon to collect me and Mrs Schell, but one other thing before I go, Mr Holmes," he said. "Simeon Forward admitted that he was the one who sold Lord Thorpe's paintings. He collected them from Thorpe at regular intervals and sold them to 'a fellow he knows'. From the sound of it, he didn't get the best price for any of them, but I got the impression that he didn't care much about that."

"No," said Holmes simply. "He cared only for his daughter and his granddaughter. Who can blame him for that? They are, after all, the only blameless ones in this whole affair."

Fisher nodded and fastened the buttons on his coat. A second later, he was gone and Holmes and I were left standing alone.

"A little breakfast, then we should be going, Holmes," I said. I smiled ruefully. "I'm afraid this has not turned out to be the relaxing few days away that I had hoped. Still, you solved the murder, even if you were unable to put your hands on either the Thorpe Collection or the legendary ruby!"

Holmes cocked an eyebrow in surprise. "On the contrary, Watson," he said. "The location of the jewel, at least, could not be more clear. I am surprised nobody has found it before now, in all honesty. If you will wait a moment, I shall be happy to drop it into your hand."

He strode back into the house, and almost immediately re-emerged, with some bulky object hidden inside his jacket.

Saying nothing, he walked straight past me and into the gardens. As I hurried to catch up with him, he provided a commentary over his shoulder.

"A key consideration in any investigation is to bear in mind that simply because a claim is repeated ad infinitum, that does not of itself make that claim true. No matter if a thousand people say a thing, it is no more factual than if only one had done so. And in this case, as in several in our past, Watson, one claim stood out as so preposterous that its very repetition sent warning bells ringing in my head."

It seemed as though Holmes were heading back to the mausoleum. What business could he possibly have there? Could de Trop somehow have contrived to have the gem hidden on the exact spot upon which his tomb would later be built? Hopefully, I would soon find out, for as Holmes mounted the stairs at its entrance, he halted in order to catch his breath and continue his oration.

"I refer, of course, to the suggestion that de Trop bit through his own tongue rather than tell his Saracen captors where he had hidden the jewel they sought. We were told this by Forward, by Robinson, even by Lawrence Buxton, a historian. And yet, it is plainly the most arrant romance. The brave Englishman preferring pain and death to surrendering to his foreign enemies? Nonsense, I say!

"To begin with, when is he supposed to have done this dread deed? Before he was captured, perhaps? Why on earth would he do such a thing, when for all he knew he might escape? Or after he was taken by the assassins who sought him? When even the most foolish man would have realised that an ability to speak is no defence against betraying oneself, when all one need do is point towards the thing which is sought? No. I will not have it. It is as much a fiction as his ghost."

He pushed open the doorway and skipped down the steps into the crypt itself. Everything was as it had been earlier. Holmes rested a hand on the sarcophagus and faced me, every inch the experienced orator.

"But picture this instead. De Trop, with armed savages at his heels, runs to the catacombs, hoping to escape, but in the darkness he quickly realises that he is far more likely to be killed than earn his freedom – and if he must die, better to do so fighting his savage enemies than running from them, or cowering in fear. But the gem! He examines it in the half light at the entrance to the caves, admires the way in which the ruby catches the light. He can hear the approaching Saracens, knows that he has only moments to contrive a solution.

"He has it! Mere moments before he is taken, he acts and, having acted, swings his sword before him and slays the first man to face him. But there are too many and he is quickly overwhelmed. Blows from fist and boot and steel rain on to him, but he refuses to concede, rising again and again, until his body and face are a bloody mess. He will not speak, not even when he is faced with a terrible death."

"And so he dies, but in doing so, he has won." Holmes's voice had descended to a whisper but now it fell utterly silent. There was only one question to ask.

"But what did he do, Holmes?"

Holmes said nothing, as he reached into his coat and pulled out the crowbar he had presumably picked up somewhere in the house. He inserted it into a crack in a corner of the sarcophagus's carven lid and, with a heave, swung it to one side. He gestured to me to approach and pointed down at the dusty skeleton within. There, nestling in the dust directly below the crusader's rib cage was the jewel, still, after these hundreds of years, a thing of rare beauty.

"He swallowed it," said Holmes. "Egg-shaped, you said, but barbed with golden hooks. It must have torn his throat to ribbons as he forced it down past his larynx, but he was a determined man, and a stubborn one, and he would, I think, have gained a good measure of satisfaction from outwitting his killers, there at the end."

He leaned over and plucked the gem from the coffin, then handed it to me.

"A suitable subject for one of Mr Buxton's monographs of local interest, do you think?" he said, and made his way back up the steps, into the morning sunshine where, here and there, small patches of grass were starting to appear as the snow began finally to melt.

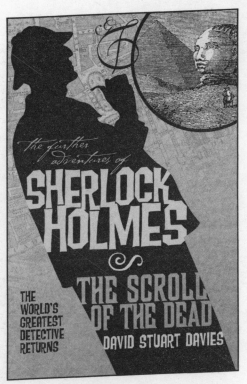

THE FURTHER ADVENTURES
OF SHERLOCK HOLMES

THE SCROLL OF THE DEAD

David Stuart Davies

In this fast-paced adventure, Sherlock Holmes attends a séance to
unmask an impostor posing as a medium. His foe, Sebastian Melmoth, is
a man hell-bent on discovering a mysterious Egyptian papyrus that may
hold the key to immortality. It is up to Holmes and Watson to use their
deductive skills to stop him or face disaster.

ISBN: 9781848564930

AVAILABLE NOW!

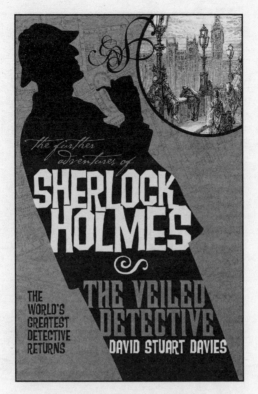

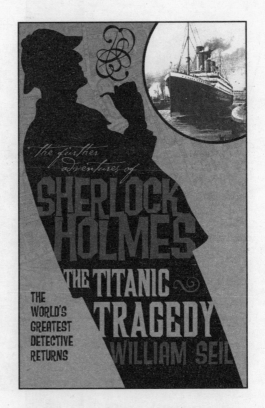

THE FURTHER ADVENTURES
OF SHERLOCK HOLMES
THE TITANIC TRAGEDY

William Seil

Holmes and Watson board the *Titanic* in 1912, where Holmes is to carry out a secret government mission. Soon after departure, highly important submarine plans for the U.S. navy are stolen. Holmes and Watson work through a list of suspects which includes Colonel James Moriarty, brother to the late Professor Moriarty—will they find the culprit before tragedy strikes?

ISBN: 9780857687104

AVAILABLE NOW!